SHADOWS

AND

DARKNESS

Lindsey Blake

SHADOWS
AND
DARKNESS

CHAPTER I

There is a strange comfort that one can find in the darkness. You do not have to pretend to be what others want you to be. You can cry without anyone judging you, whisper your secrets and no one will hear. There is solace to be found within the darkness. It can hide you from what you fear. It will accept you for who you are, no matter what. It will never hurt you, lie to you, or betray you. It is always there ready to embrace you when no one else will. It cares not about status, wealth, or morality. Nothing is so great a burden that the darkness is unable to help. Seek the comfort of the darkness, find safety in the shadows. Nothing will harm you while you exist within.

Like most cities, Selia was a symbol of duality. Always changing and yet ever the same, there was no denying the allure of the beautiful city. Being a port city, Selia was full of activity, and people of many different cultures lined the streets buying and selling their wares. Bright colors, exotic aromas, and more to do than most people could even comprehend, it was a city of adventure. It promised the masses excitement and thrills, it had a way of making even the mundane seem glamorous. It was a place where one could start anew if that was what one wanted, or a place where one could disappear. No one ever asked, so no one ever had to know. It was a port, after all, a place of greeting and leaving. It was a beautiful city but, unlike most cities, Selia's duality was far more apparent than would seem natural. When the sun went down and the city lights cast shadows over the streets the boisterous Selia became a dark, foreboding place, where laughter faded and the only sound to pierce the stillness of the night was a haunting scream.

Selia was a city of order until night fell. When darkness blanketed the city the rest of its denizens stepped forth from the shadows. Selia was a unique city, unlike its neighbors; it had long ago decided to deal with the criminal population in a rather unorthodox fashion. The city was to belong to the night and all who dwelt within. Slavers, smugglers, and thieves wandered the streets looking for entertainment or their next business deal. Of course, these people had rules to obey, just like the rest of the population. Selia was not a city that tolerated chaos. No citizen who remained indoors after sunset was to be harmed, which of course meant that anyone who was out on the streets was fair game. Murder was really the only thing that was frowned upon in the streets and the only crime which was committed after dark that the city guard actually investigated. If a person was stolen off the streets and sold to the highest bidder no one would even bat an eye, yet if that same person ended up dead it was a different story.

Even with all the unsavory characters roaming the city, Selia was still a popular travel destination. Most people liked the way the city was run; after all, what other city dealt with crime in such a forward-thinking manner? It was relatively safe, and you almost always knew where and when something bad would happen. If you were a decent law-abiding citizen or visitor, you simply knew to stay indoors at night. So long as you adhered to this rule you would have no problems, you were safe.

Safety was never the foremost thought in her mind when she ventured out into Selia at night. In fact, it was the farthest thing from her mind. There really was no reason for her to be concerned for her own well-being, since no one ever bothered her. It wasn't because she was not worth the effort, it was due to the fact that no one seemed to be able to see her. Zia Amarra was invisible to all.

This unique situation did not bother her, for she enjoyed the fact that she was able to wander the streets at night unmolested. It gave her freedom, it gave her power. Oddly enough she felt calmer at night, as if nothing could harm her. By no means did she think she was invincible, she was fully aware of the fact that if anyone ever saw her, she was in for a lot of trouble. Still, she had been living in Selia for some time now and nothing had happened. She was quite content living a perfectly predictable life with nothing extraordinary happening to her, ever. She liked anonymity and being able to disappear into a crowd, and there was no better place for that than Selia.

There was only one problem she had with the city of Selia, and it had nothing to do with the criminal element. There was an organization that called this city home, a group that would make her life miserable if they knew about her or, more specifically, Yartu. He was not easy to hide, mainly because he hated to do it, and he was even harder to deny. Yartu was the only being in all of Selia that could see her after dark and he was also the reason she put so much stock in the fact she was basically invisible.

Night was the only time they could be together safely, the only time they had together when she wasn't working. She was terrified that someone would try and take that away from them. It felt like there was always someone who wanted to destroy their Bond, to tear them apart, even if it was only her imagination. It was for that reason alone that they moved from one city to another, never staying in one place for very long. If anyone saw him it would be the end. They were always on their guard and she made certain that she never grew particularly attached to a place or, more importantly, a person. Yartu was all she needed and all she could ever want. He had been with her from the beginning and would be with her until the end. Yartu was her Bonded partner, an important part of her very soul. He also happened to be a miniature dragon who would die for her, if need be.

The Bond that tied a human to a dragon was the strongest bond that existed. It was the physical and spiritual manifestation of two souls becoming one. The Bond gave power and unique abilities to both dragon and human, one of which was a sixth sense of sorts the Bonded partners were able to sense where the other was at all times and if they were in danger. This was how Yartu was able to see Zia at night and how she was able to determine if he was safe during the day while she worked.

Yartu had to remain hidden during the day for all the reasons one could think of, the first and foremost being the fact that he was indeed a miniature dragon. Of course, being miniature he was able to hide fairly well; getting him to do so was a pain but he always gave in. Miniature dragons varied in size but none ever grew larger than the size of an eagle. Yartu was on the smaller side, much smaller, so he could wrap himself around her neck and disappear almost completely, hidden beneath her hair. This did not mean she was able to be with him throughout the day. No matter how well she kept him hidden someone always saw him and that was their cue to move on to a new city where no one knew her or about Yartu.

If their Bond was discovered it would be disastrous for both of them. Miniature dragons were rare and only a select few were able to keep such an exotic pet. They were extremely difficult to find in the wild, next to impossible, which had led mages to start breeding them. Only mages and nobles were allowed to keep miniature dragons, not someone like her. That was why he needed to stay hidden; it was the only way they could be together. If anyone found them, they would try and take Yartu away from her, and that was something neither one of them could handle. Zia would not be able to live without Yartu by her side; he was a part of her that she needed, a piece of her soul that she couldn't lose. He was her best and only friend, and the only being she trusted completely.

"Zia, you have to get some sleep. You can't stay awake forever. I know you don't want to but..." Yartu's persistence was admirable but she was not about to simply give in.

Sleep, the last thing she wanted to do. It was the main reason she liked going out at night—the longer she was gone the less time there was for sleep. She did find it surprising how long she could go without sleep and how well she managed on only an hour or two a night. Still, Yartu was determined to have her sleep more at night. For some reason he felt she didn't get enough sleep and that she always needed more. He always found a way to get her to return to her room but she refused to go without a fight. It was a game neither of them wanted to lose, and yet one of them inevitably had to.

"Zia, I realize not everyone has nightmares every night, but when they do, they try not to let those nightmares keep them from getting some much-needed rest." His tone was gentle but firm, and she wasn't so sure she would win this time. It was nearly impossible when he was like this. It was easier for her to win when he was in one of his combative moods, not a mothering one.

"Well, I do have nightmares every night. I guess that I am not everyone since most people have at least one pleasant dream in their lives and I have never had a single one." She wished he would remember how bad it was for her. Not that she thought her problems were worse than anyone else's; it just so happened that she could barely close her eyes without having a horrible nightmare.

His only reply was a small nod of his reptilian head. Yartu knew all about her dreams but he refused to believe that the answer was no sleep. There was always a chance that her dreams would improve. It was a small hope but one he needed to believe in.

Zia knew that look and she hated it. It was a look she was more than accustomed to, and it was called pity. The last thing she wanted was to be pitied. She was no longer that homeless child wandering the streets lost, alone, and hungry. She had a job now; she was able to take care of herself and Yartu. There was no reason for pity. "Fine, this time you win."

Yartu curled around her neck as she began the walk back to the inn she worked at. Zia was in no great hurry and she did everything she could to waste time regardless of how childish it might seem. Yartu grumbled under his breath the whole time, but refused to say anything knowing it would be a waste, not that such a thing usually stopped him.

The inn came into view much too soon for her and not nearly soon enough for Yartu. The Crystal Dragon was the most prestigious inn in all of Selia, and for good reason. It was large and loomed before her almost menacingly. The inn itself was a product of the people who stayed there; nobles and wealthy merchants from around the world stayed in the masterfully decorated rooms. The Crystal Dragon did everything it could to meet the impossible standards of its wealthy clientele. From the chandeliers in the dining room to the flawless crystal dragon statue that greeted guests as they checked in everything was perfect. The innkeeper, Yalia, would never have it any other way. She took immense pride in the fact that The Crystal Dragon was known as one of the finest inns there was, if not the finest.

The employees of The Crystal Dragon were held to the highest standards and were paid better than most for their efforts. They were given two sets of uniforms and even had separate living quarters in the building so that they were always at hand to serve the customers. Zia was one of the staff who lived there and, while it was useful, she hated being so close to the very people who could take Yartu away from her. The city was where the headquarters of the prestigious Magic Council were located, although they did have branches in other major cities. The Magic Council was responsible for the breeding and distribution of miniature dragons, and they took it very seriously. So seriously they would arrest and detain those caught with unidentified miniature dragons. This is why there was no black market trade involving the creatures. Living here was not her best idea ever. Although there was also the chance that if someone did see Yartu, they would simply assume he belonged to one of the inn's patrons.

The Crystal Dragon was the first place Zia had managed to work for more than two weeks. She knew that it was only a matter of time before someone saw Yartu and actually discovered that he belonged to her. There was always one person who was cleverer than the rest, one person whose eyes did not deceive them, and they were always the one who forced her and Yartu to find a new city. Zia had long ago given up the hope that they would ever find a place where they could live out the rest of their lives in peace and quiet.

They would have to leave The Crystal Dragon eventually, but for the time being it was a decent place. The work was hard but Zia liked it, it kept her mind busy. Yalia was a stern but fair woman who made certain that the male customers and help did not bother the women. She had a room that was all her own, something she had never had before. Yalia treated her kindly and constantly had good things to say about her and her work ethic.

As she silently crept through the back door Zia hoped no one else was awake to catch her sneaking in. Yalia had very strict rules about going out when she did not give express permission to do so. Fortunately for Zia it seemed the hour was so late that even the staff who worked nights were likely dozing at their posts. Finally making it to the safety of her room she slumped onto her bed. There was no chance of her getting more than two or three hours of sleep, and that was perfectly fine with her. She would have preferred it to be less, if any at all, but she knew Yartu's anger at her not taking care of herself was not worth the vast amount of complaining that she would have to put up with.

Yartu curled up next to her neck and softly whispered to her. "Sleep well, Zia, I will guard your dreams." She never truly understood what he meant, yet he said it every night since the nightmares had started, and that was a long time ago. She believed that it was the only way for Yartu to feel like he was of some use to her, for he was fully aware of the fact that nothing could stop her dreams and that no one could guard her from them. It was the miniature dragon's nightly prayer and it had become hers too. While both knew that it could not truly change anything it made them feel as if something might change if they kept saying it would. After some time, she fell asleep and that was when the nightmares began.

It was completely dark. The shadows enveloped her, holding her gently. This was what it was like every night. Nothing existed but her and the stillness of darkness. The swirling shadows started to pull her and Zia would try to wake herself, but it never worked; even though she knew this was a dream there was no escaping it. They continued to pull her. She did not know where they were taking her, only that she was powerless to stop them. It always seemed as if the darkness was trying to tell her something, trying to show her something important. Their urgency was what scared her the most; she so desperately wanted to wake but she could not. It was at that moment when she heard the voice.

"Do not be afraid. The shadows are only doing my bidding at the decree of the darkness, they will not harm you. I only wish to speak with you. It has been so long. I am glad you have finally come to me, my child. You must listen to me, child, and listen well. The need for you is now extremely urgent. You must come to me; the only way you can do this is to trust the darkness and let the shadows guide you to my home. Once you are safe within my home, I will be able to teach you the skills you require. On your journey remember to trust no one but the shadows, they will lead you to me and the darkness. Our time runs short; you must hasten to my side. Hurry, my child, hurry."

Zia was shaken violently awake. "Get up, girl. You have work to do and I have lots of customers to tend to. The longer you sleep the more work you'll have to do later and, trust me, I will find plenty for you."

Her eyes snapped open to find Yalia standing next to her bed. The woman was pursing her lips and had her hands on her hips. Blonde hair was pulled up into a neat bun and her dress was feminine yet reserved, much like the woman herself. Zia liked Yalia, which was more than she could say about her former employers, and she did not like disappointing the woman.

She wondered how long she had slept. It was unusual for Yalia to come into her room. There had to be something wrong. Yalia did look disturbed, now that she thought about it. What worried Zia was the reason the generally composed woman had lost her cool. The girl really hoped it had nothing to do with Yartu, who had disappeared. He could have been anywhere; she just hoped it was somewhere secluded and out of sight.

"Get out of bed right now. There is no time to waste, girl. We have to prepare. If things are not perfect there will be hell to pay. The others and I can't do everything by ourselves, you know." Yalia was growing angrier with each passing second. No one of sound mind ever tried to purposely incur the woman's wrath and, while Zia might not have been entirely sane, she was most definitely not stupid. There would be no talking her way out of this one. It was time to start the day. Hopefully Yalia would calm down once the work was done for whatever event it was she had planned.

As she got out of bed Zia noticed that Yalia was holding a hand to her forehead, shaking it ever so slightly. "What?" She almost cringed at the harshness in her own voice.

Yalia sighed as she pointed a finger at Zia, "Do you always sleep in your uniform?" There was a tiniest hint of amusement in her tone and Zia found it more than a little irritating, not that she would have ever mentioned it to the woman.

"No, I sat on the bed to rest for a moment. I guess I fell asleep without realizing it." There was no way she was going to tell Yalia about her nightly excursions. The safe thing to do was lie and the best lies always held an element of truth. Zia hated lying, but it wasn't entirely a lie, she had fallen asleep without realizing it.

Yalia left the room shaking her head and muttering something about insanity under her breath. Zia sighed in relief the moment the door was closed. Calling softly for Yartu, she grew worried when he did not appear. Still, it wasn't as though he couldn't take care of himself. He was so used to, and good at, hiding at this point the only way she could find him was to track him through their Bond.

As she stepped into the hallway, the door closing softly behind her, she suddenly began to feel very alone. Regardless of how many times she walked this corridor one thought always surpassed the others. How much longer will this place be a safe haven, how much longer will I walk this corridor, how much longer? Of course, there was no way for Zia to know the answer, but she knew with utmost certainty that it was going to be soon, real soon.

Part of her morning routine was to stop and watch everyone milling about the main hall of the inn for a few moments. This large room was connected to the dining room which was home to one of Selia's finest restaurants. The doorway leading to this room was always open unless there was a special function taking place there; reserving the restaurant was difficult and required a good deal of advanced notice. It was rather surprising that the doors were closed this morning. The staff was usually informed of such events, given that it required much more work on their part. Zia wondered if this was what had put Yalia in a tizzy. If that was the case than it was cause for concern, since she could not think of anyone who had the power to just come in and take over The Crystal Dragon unless it was a king or someone similar to one in status.

It really was disturbing how the wealthy seemed to think they could just do whatever they wanted and never have to apologize for the inconvenience it caused others. Zia knew that there was no helping it and decided to start her chores before Yalia caught onto the fact that she was just standing there. The last thing she needed was another reason for the woman to think she wasn't doing her share of the work. As she turned to go a hand grabbed her wrist.

The second she felt the touch of another human, instinct kicked in. She spun about, pulling her wrist out of confinement and twisting it so that she was the one with the hold on the other person. Zia barely even noticed that she held the small dagger that was normally concealed safely in her uniform pocket against the man's neck.

"Zia, it's me, Ren." The man held out his hands in an attempt to prove that he meant no harm.

It took her a moment to recognize the young man and to realize that the only real danger she was in would be when Yalia found out about this. Ren was amicable and almost everyone who knew him liked him. His warm smile, easy laugh and handsome features made him quite popular at the inn, especially with the female staff. He had tried many times to befriend Zia but she had never been receptive to his offer. She felt sure that he would not be so willing or ready to offer his friendship after this, considering that she was still holding a dagger to his neck.

He seemed very uneasy when she didn't remove the dagger the moment she recognized him. Zia slowly pulled the dagger away, noticing Ren's obvious relief when the metal was no longer touching his skin. She didn't know why she had drawn her blade, she wasn't even aware of what she doing. Her rationalization for such an act was that she must have been on edge from the night before; the voice speaking to her from the darkness was not a normal part of her nightmares and had made her anxious. Zia was extremely confused, but she was not about to let it show. "I am sorry, but you startled me."

"Startled? I believe that is an understatement," Ren laughed. "Oh, and don't worry, I won't tell Yalia that you tried to kill me."

Zia stared at him in amazement. Did anything ever bother him? Was he always in such a good mood? What did he want in return for not telling Yalia? Whatever the price she was not willing to pay it. Maybe it was time for her to leave before something forced her to go, something like this. If Ren told Yalia, Zia knew she would be thrown out. Yalia would not tolerate some girl threatening her precious younger brother's life. She most definitely would not let the girl continue to work for her. "Why are you always so nice to me?" Zia really did wonder about his motives, but then again maybe she had just grown too suspicious of people. "What do you want from me?"

"I just came to find you because Yalia is getting a little impatient. She wants you to get to work right now. She really is on edge this morning, she already made one of the other girls cry." He didn't seem upset by her questions. Zia's hesitation made him smile and make a shooing motion. "You better go. I don't want you getting into trouble because of me. Yalia might make me cry."

His attempt at humor was lost on her as she rushed past him to start her day formally. She never looked back at Ren. The concern on his face was evident only to him.

It wasn't until later that afternoon that Zia discovered that there were very important guests at the inn. The Magic Council had reserved a large portion of the inn and every single staff member was tasked with making their stay pleasant and enjoyable. Zia did everything she could to avoid contact with any of them. Her mind was reeling with thoughts about Yartu and whether or not he was safely concealed. Every free second she had she spent trying to locate him, with no luck whatsoever. Normally she would have been able to trace his location through the Bond, but for some strange reason that was not working the way it should have been. Was it due to her current level of stress and anxiety? She did not know if she should have been glad that she at least knew Yartu was alright or worried about this as it had never happened before. She just hoped he wasn't anywhere the Magic Council could find him.

When night fell Zia felt relief wash over her. The daytime was strenuous for her, she always felt safer at night. In the darkness she could hide. She wondered if anything was going to get better for her and Yartu. Probably not.

CHAPTER 2

Morning came far too quickly for Zia. The previous night she hadn't gotten any sleep and for some strange reason Yartu hadn't pressured her to do so. He had arrived back at the inn after her shift had ended without a single explanation of where he had been. This wasn't all that unusual for him but it didn't help make the strange insecurity she had been feeling since yesterday go away. She was feeling fairly good about herself for having won last night's round of their game, yet that was the only good feeling she had. She felt as if something was wrong, horribly wrong. The feeling would not go away and Zia was beginning to think it was time to leave Selia.

"Why do you let these things bother you, Zia? Not everything that goes on in this world affects you personally. The Magic Council has come to The Crystal Dragon to relax before they have their annual gathering. It has nothing to do with you. It's not like they are here hunting you down." Yartu couldn't believe that she was taking the whole thing so personally. It wasn't like her and he knew that something was wrong. Zia was truly worried, and she was never this nervous about anything without a reason.

"I couldn't find you," she snapped, "I had no idea where you were. What if one of them had seen you? They would have taken you away from me and what would I have done then? Tell me, Yartu, why don't I have to worry? One person is all it takes. If just one person sees you the Magic Council will take you from me and give you to someone else. I would not be able to live if they took you from me."

Zia had intended to say more but she was interrupted suddenly when the door opened. Yalia stepped into the room with Ren following closely behind. Zia was a bit surprised by Yalia's presence but the fact that Ren was with her made that awful feeling Zia had even worse than it was before. She looked at both of them for a quick second to see if she could determine what they were there for. Zia only needed that short glance to know that something dreadful was transpiring. For the first time since Zia had started working at The Crystal Dragon, Yalia looked extremely nervous and Ren appeared quite disturbed.

"Who were you talking to?" Yalia asked, looking around the room distractedly. Zia also cast a hasty glance around the room and found that Yartu was nowhere to be seen.

"I was just talking to myself. I'm sorry if my doing so bothered you."

"Oh no, it didn't," Yalia shook her head. "I am here for a different reason. I'm not quite sure how to say this but..." She stopped talking and turned to Ren with a pleading look.

Zia couldn't take it anymore. She wanted them to tell her what was wrong. She had to know what Yalia couldn't say, she needed to know. "What is wrong?" Zia begged, "Please tell me. I haven't done anything wrong, have I?"

Ren put a comforting hand on her arm, which of course she pulled away from. When he spoke she clearly heard the apprehension in his voice which mirrored the concern that showed plainly on his face. "Zia, I don't believe that you have done anything wrong, but you have attracted the interest of a certain group of people."

"What group?" She whispered, terrified of what the answer might be. Ren's reply was simple and contained only three words, "The Magic Council."

Zia swayed as a wave of dizziness washed of her. Ren steadied her, and for the first time since she had come to the inn she did not shy away. She couldn't, she was barely able to stand.

Yalia came over to her and gently placed a soothing hand over hers. "Girl, I don't know why it is you they are wanting to meet but whatever it is they say you have done I'm sure they are mistaken."

The room seemed as if it finally had decided to stop spinning, but Zia's head was whirling faster than the room with a million different thoughts. She wasn't able to fully focus on any single thought except that she felt sick.

"The Magic Council is waiting for you in the dining room. They said it is most urgent that they speak with you. If you are feeling better, you should probably go see what it is they want. Yalia and I will be there as well to make sure that you are not treated unfairly." Ren gave her a small reassuring smile. Zia appreciated the fact he was trying to comfort her, but she doubted that anything could make her feel better at that moment.

She pulled away from Ren and started for the door. Zia wanted nothing more than to run away and hide but she knew it was a futile dream. The Magic Council probably had all the exits being watched. The short walk to the dining room seemed to be double the length it normally was. Though she was distraught, Zia maintained a calm exterior, for she did not want to give the council any reason to believe that she had something to hide from them, which of course she did. When Zia walked through the door to the dining room she stopped, stunned by what she saw.

The Magic Council had rearranged the dining room into a makeshift courtroom. At the far end of the room there was long table at which sat six people on one side. In front of the table, a few feet away, sat a solitary chair. Zia knew it was meant for her. The rest of the tables had been shifted to the back of the room out of the way. She noticed that two of the doorways that led out of the room were being blocked by the Magic Council's very own guard. There was to be no escape for her. One of the guards motioned for her to take the unoccupied chair. As she took her seat, she examined the fearsome Magic Council.

There were six of them, six extremely powerful mages who could mean a lot of trouble for Zia. The council was made up of three men and three women, each one the head of a different division of magic. They wore different colored robes to differentiate the multiple divisions. The woman in the blue robe, she was a master healer. The second, a mousy looking woman, wore a simple yellow robe to mark her status as the administrator of the arcane school of magic. The big man on the far end of the table wore a sturdy brown robe that indicated his position as overseer of the welfare of all the magical beasts in the material plane. Seated next to him was an exceptionally intimidating man in a red robe. He was head of the battle mages, a particularly malicious lot who took pleasure in using their exceptional repertoire of powerful spells for destructive and horrible purposes on the field of battle. They were known to be even more volatile in times of peace, for their talents were not needed and they lived for the fight. The last two, a man in a white robe and a woman in a green one, were seated in the center of the table. Zia had absolutely no idea as to what they were masters of but she could tell that they were important, possibly holding the most vital positions on the Magic Council. The air about them was vastly different from that of the other members.

"You are the girl Zia Amarra, are you not?" The woman in the green spoke first. This was it, it had started; Zia couldn't help but wonder what was in store for her. She did not bother to ask how the woman knew her name. The Magic Council had many sources of information. Learning her name would have been of no great difficulty, but that did not mean that she had to talk to them. Fortunately, she didn't have to, Yalia did.

"This is Zia, Lady Yena. Please tell us, what has she done wrong?" Yalia spoke mildly. It was almost as if she was afraid of the other woman. Zia didn't think Yalia was intimidated by anyone. Who was this woman?

The woman in the green robe, Lady Yena, was visibly irritated by the fact that Yalia had spoken, but she answered her question regardless. "The girl has committed no crime in the way you would describe the word. We are here simply because of the special circumstances that have arisen. Zia Amarra is a unique individual and we are here to ascertain what is truly going on."

"That's not an answer," Ren said moving forward to stand at Zia's side. "You claim that she has done nothing wrong, nothing we would consider wrong, yet your reception of her is the same as if she were a criminal. You say there are special circumstances and you claim that Zia is unique, but you don't say why. Why don't you tell us what is really going on?"

The man in the white robe stood up angrily. "How dare you speak to the council in such an impertinent manner? You are to show the council and Lady Yena the proper respect. What this council's business is with the girl is none of your concern. You would do well to learn your place. I suggest that you remember your station and address this council with the respect due to us."

Ren took a step closer to the older man, almost as if he was going to start a fight with him. Zia knew that Ren would get himself into trouble to keep her out of it, although she really didn't know why. The one thing she did know for sure was that the situation was getting out of hand. She had to do something before Ren got himself into the type of trouble that was difficult to get out of. So she did the only thing she could think of.

"I wish to know why I have been brought before you. It is not every day that someone like me is granted a private audience with the esteemed Magic Council. Pray tell, what has made me so fortunate to be graced by the presence of a group of such highly respected individuals as you." She stood up when she spoke to draw the attention away from Ren. It worked too, all eyes were on her as Yalia came forward silently to pull her brother out of the room.

If Zia's attention had been on the Magic Council instead of Ren she would have noticed that they were quite surprised. They were a bit taken aback by the fact that she had finally spoken but what truly shocked the council was the way she spoke. They did not expect the servant girl they had come to see to speak so well or sound so well-educated. She wasn't, at least not in the traditional sense, it was a habit she had developed for self-defense. People with status spoke differently and they were paid attention to, people listened to them. She wasn't someone who was normally taken seriously, and she was frequently ignored, so she mimicked the way they spoke and had developed a rather bizarre habit of speaking that way when she was mad. Zia had accomplished what she had wanted; the Magic Council had completely forgotten about Ren and all their attention was focused upon this unusual girl.

"You do not seem to trust us very much," Lady Yena stated.

Zia shook her head, "Is there any reason for me or anyone else to trust the Magic Council? You are renowned for your clandestine operations and unorthodox methods, and if a group such as yours is interested in me than I have even less reason to trust you."

The Magic Council was silent for a few minutes, stunned by the fact that this girl had spoken to them in such a manner. They were not accustomed to obstinacy. Lady Yena was the one to break the silence, "You presume much for one who is in no position to make any kind of assumptions. We are here only because of certain information that has been passed on to us. The Magic Council has no interest in arresting you."

"No," Zia interjected, "You are here to study me. To treat me like some kind of rare creature that has just been discovered. Like some kind of oddity, a rare find, something no one has ever seen before. I do not wish to be treated as such. The least you could do is tell me what sort of information was passed on to you, so I may know what I have done to deserve this kind of attention."

Lady Yena was not quite sure how to respond to the girl's request. The Magic Council had not expected to divulge any information about why they were there; rarely did the Magic Council ever tell anyone anything. They had not expected this girl to be as perceptive and intelligent as they were quickly discovering. What Lady Yena found most disturbing was that Zia, a mere servant girl, had manipulated the Magic Council into a position where they would have to tell her what they wanted in order to get her to talk to them. Of course, the council could try to force the truth out of the girl, but they were not that kind of organization, at least not publicly. No one had ever before tried to manipulate the Magic Council, for everyone knew that to try and use the Magic Council for their own gain would put that ill-fated person in the most dreadful of situations. Lady Yena had to wonder if Zia knew what she had just done. When she met the girl's defiant gaze she found that Zia understood exactly what position she had put the Magic Council in and she was not the least bit afraid. Lady Yena was a trifle concerned, for if this girl was not afraid of the wrath of the Magic Council how were they to get the information they needed from her?

"This council is not here to mistreat you, Zia Amarra. I admit that we did come here to discern whether or not you are a hazard to Selia and her people." That was all Lady Yena was about to reveal to Zia. She wanted to see if the girl would lose the calm and controlled attitude she seemed to have perfected in light of the new developments.

The councilwoman was disappointed, though, for Zia's expression did not change, nor was there any sign of fear in her eyes. Zia was not about to let the Magic Council guess what was going on inside of her mind unless they read it. She met Lady Yena's gaze and noticed that was exactly what the woman wanted, to unnerve her, to show that she was scared. Zia wasn't about to give them the satisfaction.

"A hazard? Pray tell, why would I be a hazard to Selia? This city and her people have only ever been kind to me, why would I want to bring them harm?" Zia was lying, but only just a little bit. She knew that the council would not necessarily believe what she had said, and she didn't care. Zia was not going to let them think she was scared of them.

Lady Yena's eyes narrowed. The councilwoman was slightly more than annoyed by the fact she had to reveal the truth as to why the Magic Council was there, the whole truth and not bits and pieces of it as the council normally did. The servant girl would soon learn what a grave mistake she had made in trying to alter this meeting to benefit herself and make the Magic Council look like they were insignificant fools who had been easily manipulated by a mere girl. No longer was this the time for secrets; Lady Yena was going to tell her exactly why they were there, and maybe then Zia's aloof exterior would fade to fear. "This council believes that you could be dangerous to this city that has been so kind to you. For it appears that the Magic Council has made a slight miscalculation in how many miniature dragons have been given away and which people have been deemed acceptable to receive such a wondrous gift."

Zia closed her eyes for a moment as she tried to calm her rapidly beating heart. They knew, somehow the Magic Council had uncovered the secret of her and Yartu. She didn't know how she was supposed to respond; should she deny everything the council was saying or was she to admit that Yartu was indeed Bonded to her? Zia did the only thing that seemed right without causing any more harm to herself or Yartu, she remained quiet.

Lady Yena knew she had hit a nerve. So, the icy Zia Amarra did have a weak spot, a crack in her impenetrable armor; apparently the information they had been given was correct. This posed a problem. The Magic Council had to handle this situation with great care, for they could not let this girl go. They had to ensure that she stayed in Selia for them to study her so the Magic Council could discover how such a thing had happened.

"It would seem that you might be able to help this council find the missing miniature dragon. Perhaps you will tell us where it is. This is quite a serious matter; we would greatly appreciate your assistance." The lady's tone was one of smugness, as if she had just won a major battle, and to all appearances she had.

Zia was trapped, there was nowhere left for her to run, they had finally found her. She accepted it; it was hopeless to fight anymore, what was the point? It was all hopeless. Zia closed her eyes and silently called for Yartu.

All of the Magic Council, except for Lady Yena, were surprised when a stunning miniature dragon suddenly flew into the room, landed upon Zia's shoulder and glared at them with amazingly brilliant red eyes. Lady Yena was impressed by Yartu—she had never seen a miniature dragon with his coloring. Of course, they did not all look the same, but Yartu was different. His scales were the color of the night sky, a shade of black that was exactly one and the same as Zia's hair color. He would have blended perfectly into her hair if not for the delicate streak of silver that ran along the outside of each scale.

Nothing could have possibly prepared the Magic Council for what happened next.

Lady Yena cast a glance in the direction of the brown-robed man. "Sevi, I take it that you do not recognize this miniature dragon."

The man in the brown robe, Sevi, shook his head. "This particular miniature dragon is not one that I have overseen the hatching of. I do not recognize the coloring of this one and what I find most disturbing is the fact that this one does not have any distinctive traits of the miniature dragons that this council has raised. It is far too small and never have I encountered a black miniature dragon. Since miniature dragons are next to impossible to find in the wild, there is no proof that this particular coloration is normal there. The eyes are not normally red either, at least not that particular shade of ruby. The secondary markings on the scales are also most unusual. I don't think I have ever seen a miniature dragon with scales that aren't a single solid color."

"You are saying that it is,—" Lady Yena started to say, but was interrupted by Sevi.

"Feral, wild, not of the same lines, in short this dragon is unlike any I have ever seen. I am ever more certain that we must study this one. There could be—"

"No!"

The Magic Council had momentarily forgotten about Zia in the confusion about Yartu, but her outburst drew their attention back to her. Lady Yena knew that this was it. The girl would try to resist the Magic Council and fail. They would then take her with them as they had intended to all along.

"You have something to say, Zia Amarra." It was not a question. Her tone was one of lofty superiority and Zia hated it, much like she was beginning to hate the Magic Council and all of Selia.

"I will not let you take Yartu from me." Zia tried to remain calm, but even she heard her anger coming through.

"Take Yartu from you?" Lady Yena smiled and shook her head, "Girl, we are not here exclusively for your dragon, this council has great interest in you as well. You see, Zia, this is the only time this council has ever seen someone in possession of a miniature dragon that we did not give to them. We don't wish to study Yartu alone; we desire to observe the both of you."

She motioned the guards to take Zia. They started moving towards her when Lady Yena noticed that Zia had stood up and seemed to be in immense distress.

There was nothing but anger, rage. It was as if there were no other emotions in her entire body. It was consuming her; she vainly tried to suppress her anger, to control her rage, but the feat proved impossible and failed horribly. Her anger was trying to find a way out, to break free of its small confines. Unfortunately it did.

Lady Yena was about to call the guards off for a moment so Zia could regain control of herself when she realized that something was horribly wrong. All of the Magic Council noticed it a moment later. Someone was working magic and it was none of them.

The room began to grow very dark as the sunlight shining through each window in the room seemed to become black. The room was full of shadows. The light was fading faster with each passing second as shadowy tendrils coiled around and snuffed out every source of daylight. Lady Yena tried a simple spell of illumination, but the shadows consumed that as well.

"Impossible," the woman in the yellow robe said, "The spell should have worked, that should not have happened."

"What does it matter?" the mage in the white robe shouted. "The shadows are coming from the girl. We must stop her." He spoke the truth, the shadows were coming from Zia, although it was almost impossible to see her in the practically pitch black room. The only thing they could see was a pair of red eyes gleaming in the darkness—Yartu's eyes.

"I'll get her," The battle mage muttered under his breath, thrilled with the chance to do battle.

Lady Yena knew it was futile, how could they stop her? Her power was unlike anything the Magic Council had ever seen. How could they possibly stop her? She was dangerous, a threat to the Magic Council and all of Selia.

Lady Yena's worst dreams had come to be, all in the form of this girl.

The battle mage started to cast a powerful spell that was normally impossible to deflect. His words were taken from his mouth before he even began to utter them. He even started to forget most of the spells he knew, which was an unfeasible concept; he was a master, how could he possibly forget his spells?

It was not just him; all of the Magic Council were starting to feel the same way. None of them knew what was going on. For the first time in centuries the Magic Council were helpless, unable to use their magic, they were defenseless. All but Lady Yena started to panic.

Then it was over. The darkness disappeared. The sunlight returned to the room, the momentary amnesia the Magic Council had experienced was gone. Gone too was something else. The reason the Magic Council had come to the Crystal Dragon in the first place. Zia Amarra had vanished.

CHAPTER 3

The Magic Council were in shock. They had no idea where Zia had gone. True, not many of them were still interested in the girl and they would have preferred to forget that she existed. It was easier to ignore a problem than address it, especially when it dealt with the unknown, and the darkness was most definitely unknown. Little was actually known about those who had a connection to the darkness, and none of it was good. The others didn't know, since they didn't have access to the same documents she did; only Lady Yena knew about the darkness. In her possession were incomplete records with insufficient knowledge that spoke of a strange few, barely a handful, who had a connection to the darkness. All of them ended up becoming an incredible force of destruction, an instrument of death. Lady Yena was not about to forget what had happened; she was not about to let the girl go. She knew they had to find her, and fast.

✱✱✱✱✱

Lady Yena was in her office at the Magic Council's headquarters waiting for the man she had summoned. The other council members did not know she had called upon him and she didn't want them to. They would not understand the urgency of the situation which forced her to meet with this man. Even she didn't fully approve of what she was doing but she had to do this no matter how much she disliked dealing with a particular person.

"Lady Yena, as always it is a great pleasure to see you." The voice was masculine and had a smug tone.

She knew her guest had arrived. She would have cringed but she would not give him the satisfaction. Lady Yena turned to regard her guest. He looked just the way she remembered him. He was of average height but the rest was hardly average. He was young and quite handsome, with dark brown hair and hazel eyes. Lady Yena remembered those the most, the kind of eyes that held no light, the kind of eyes you just wanted to turn away from. He was dressed in traveler's clothes but anyone could see they were of good quality. He was trouble, and she hated what she had to do.

"The things I do for Selia," she muttered to herself.

"Everything for Selia, isn't that right?" There was that smug, sarcastic tone again.

"You really should mind your manners, young Nicolai. It would not do well for you to upset me." Her voice was stern and would have scared most people. Nicolai was not most people.

He smirked and shook his head, "My lady, you of all people should know that I never try to anger you."

"You say that but you do not mean it. Enough of this, Nicolai, I have asked you here because of a very serious matter."

"So you sent for me. How desperate are you?" He sounded a little stunned that she had come to him. It was all an act. He was more surprised that she needed him that badly. How much blood was she trying to keep off her perfectly manicured hands?

Lady Yena gave a small smile. "I know that this seems a bit incredible but it is true. There is a certain matter the Magic Council has to deal with. It is crucial that no one knows that the Magic Council is involved."

Nicolai did another one of his trademark smirks, "You mean the Magic Council wants nothing to do with this, which is the reason you sent for me. The other council members know nothing about this, do they?" He laughed. "I am proud of you, doing the same exact thing for which you despise me."

"This is serious, Nicolai, how dare you mock me? I didn't even want to do this, but I have to. It is a sensitive matter. There is someone I need you to find."

Nicolai looked a bit confused. "Why me? Why don't you just use your magic to find this person?"

"I hate to admit this but my magic is useless when it comes to this one. Her name is Zia Amarra; she is around your age, maybe a little younger. I need you to find her. She is extremely dangerous, Nicolai, I know that you will be able to find her. You are good at that sort of thing."

"A girl? What is so important about her?" He stopped for a moment and then his eyes went wide when he finally realized what she had said. "Your magic is useless? How is that possible? You are the strongest mage in all of Selia; your magic can't possibly be useless."

Lady Yena told him what had happened the other day, much to her embarrassment. Nicolai listened to her story in amazement.

"You see why she must be found. The others don't understand the importance of this; they just want to forget yesterday even happened. That is why I need you, Nicolai. I don't have the time to find Zia, and the others can't even know I am searching for her. I really do need your help in this matter, Nicolai." The last thing Lady Yena had intended was to sound like she was pleading but that was exactly how her words came out. She had put herself in a position where Nicolai knew just how much she needed him, giving him the position of power.

"This Zia, you have no idea where she is? She just disappeared?" He smiled, "This is not what I had expected, then again what is? I'll help you find her."

"You will?" Lady Yena was astonished. Nicolai had agreed so readily. It was very much unlike him, normally he required far more persuasion, things she was never comfortable giving. This whole thing was starting to get a little strange.

Nicolai shrugged, "Of course. You really need me, you hardly ever do. Still, it is a start. I need to know where to begin, though. I can't find someone without knowing where to start."

"Try the Crystal Dragon. That is where she worked. Perhaps you can find something there."

He nodded, "Got it. I'll go do that then."

As he turned to go Lady Yena stopped him, "Nicolai," she hesitated for a moment when he looked back at her, "Thank you for doing this. I appreciate it more than you could imagine."

"I know. Everything you do is for Selia, I understand that." He gave her a smile and left.

Lady Yena let out a small sigh. Everything she did was for Selia, Nicolai was right, but at least he understood. She wished he had understood before this, though; things might have turned out differently for him. What was important was that he was helping her, which was all that really mattered. If anyone could find Zia Amarra it would be Nicolai.

The Crystal Dragon was closed. Yalia had decided it would be for the best for a day or so and then resume business as usual. Fortunately, since the Magic Council had practically reserved the entire inn the other day she was able to do so. She was still a little frazzled from the day before; all she wanted to do was relax for a few minutes. Unfortunately, she was not going to get her few moments of peace. Ren was worried about what happened to Zia. He was going to ask Yalia if she thought the Magic Council had taken her when a knock on the door interrupted him.

"We're closed for the day, come back tomorrow," Yalia shouted.

"I am afraid that tomorrow is not an option for me. I must be on my way and I require your assistance."

The voice belonged to a man, but not one that Yalia or Ren knew. That was not what bothered them, they were used to strangers, it was the way he said it. He spoke as if they had no choice in the matter and it would be futile to try and keep him out.

Yalia went to the door and opened it slightly to get a glimpse of their visitor. What she saw surprised and scared her. There was no denying the fact he was quite handsome, but there was a dark intense look in his eyes, and it terrified her. It made her wonder whether he could read her mind. The small smirk that appeared on his face made her convinced that he could.

"How may I help you, sir?" she asked tentatively. He smiled and she began to feel a little better, until he said what he wanted. "Zia? I don't ..."

"You do know who I'm talking about, don't you? Zia Amarra, she worked here for a while until she left yesterday. I want to know where she is." The comment seemed innocent enough but Yalia heard a slightly threatening undertone.

She didn't know what she was supposed to do. Yalia felt she should tell him something, anything to get him to leave. The only thing was she had no idea where Zia had gone.

CHAPTER 4

A few minutes later an annoyed Nicolai left the Crystal Dragon. Where could the girl have gone? How does someone just disappear? Why did he agree to help Lady Yena? This was getting more complicated than he had thought it was going to be. Why couldn't this have been a simple assignment, something easy that Lady Yena had just blown way out of proportion? Nicolai had no idea where to go now, since his search at the Crystal Dragon had proven to be useless. Zia really didn't do much other than work. Before he had gone to the inn, he had spoken to several people who lived and worked in the area, and no one had even seen someone who matched Zia's description outside the inn. Did she ever leave the place? Unless... Nicolai smiled to himself; yes, that was exactly what he was going to do.

An hour later Nicolai stood before a very depressing looking house; it appeared to be falling apart, but Nicolai knew better. This house belonged to an extremely eccentric witch who was not overly fond of visitors, so she tried to make her house seem uninviting. He walked up to the door, stepping over fallen pieces of wood and stone, and when he reached the door it opened. Standing in the doorway was a very confused-looking woman. Her hair was steel gray, but her eyes were bright and inquisitive. She shook her head when she saw him.

"Nicolai, tell me what brings you here to visit little old me." Surprisingly the witch's voice was quite youthful. Nicolai knew the witch was only thirty-four years old, at least that was what she had told him, although there were rumors that witches could live much longer than the average person. It just didn't seem like she was young because all the experiments she had done in her life had changed her hair color as well as given her a more haggard appearance. Nicolai knew better than to underestimate her; many had been lost in this house having thought they were superior to the witch or angering her.

"I need your help, Crystal. May I come in?" He was very polite and sincere. She appeared to be in a good mood and he had no intention of changing that.

The witch motioned him to follow her. The inside of her house was completely different than the outside. It was clean and orderly, barely a speck of dust in sight. She led him to a large room that appeared to function as both a library and sitting room. Bookshelves covered the walls and windows, letting only a little light into the room, just enough to see and read by. There was a desk with an array of papers on it in neat stacks, as well as a couple of chairs and a sofa currently occupied by a cat. Crystal sat next to the cat on the sofa and gestured for him to take a seat. Only when he was seated did she speak.

"What exactly do you need, Nicolai? It is a rare thing indeed for *you* to ask for help." Crystal was a bit perplexed by this whole situation. She had known Nicolai for some time now and knew that this was unusual for him. She had learned early on in their friendship that Nicolai never asked for anyone's help for anything. He did everything on his own, he thought it was better that way. Crystal had no idea why, he had never told her the reason, and this wasn't the time to find out, either.

Nicolai told her everything Lady Yena had told him. When he was done Crystal just sat there petting her cat, she didn't say a word. This was quite intriguing, the Magic Council afraid of some girl. A small part of her was amused, but she was mainly worried. What the Magic Council was afraid of, she should be more afraid of. This time she thought Nicolai just might have gotten into more than he could handle. She didn't know if that worried her more than the fact that Lady Yena was scared.

"This still doesn't explain why you need my help."

Nicolai sighed. "I thought that you might be able to find her for me. I know that Lady Yena tried to find her using magic and it failed..."

"You thought I could succeed where she failed. Nicolai, Lady Yena is the strongest mage in Selia, maybe even the world. She wouldn't be the leader of the Magic Council if she wasn't exceedingly powerful. If she can't find her, how am I supposed to?" She shook her head. "I am sorry, but I don't think I can help."

The smile came back, "That is where you are wrong, Crystal. You can help. Like you said Lady Yena used *her* magic and failed, not *your* magic. A mage's magic is completely different than a witch's; true, it is all magic, but you use it differently. I believe that where she failed you will succeed. All we have to do is find out how." He sounded a bit unsure at the end.

Crystal was a bit surprised. Nicolai had this whole thing planned out, except for the how. Now that she thought about it she realized that he was right, Lady Yena was a mage, she was a witch, and there was a difference, a bigger difference than most knew. Crystal could do things that Lady Yena could not; one of those things could possibly be finding this Zia Amarra. "Alright, Nicolai, how do you suppose we do this?"

After many hours of hard work, various failed attempts at divination and scrying, some weird explosions from whatever potions she had mixed, and some interference from Crystal's cats, they were able to locate Zia Amarra. A strange potion poured on a reflective surface was what had done the trick. Well, they hadn't found her exactly, but her dragon Yartu.

"You sure this is what you needed? Unless my eyesight has gotten really bad, I don't think that is a human girl." Crystal was a bit confused; they had done just about everything to find this girl and all that they had to show for it was an image of a miniature dragon.

Nicolai was completely immersed in his study of the image. He knew the miniature dragon was Yartu based on Lady Yena's description of him; which meant that Zia was close by. He hadn't really expected to find Zia herself. If they had he would have been quite shocked. Something protected Zia from magical sight; maybe it was the strange magic she seemed to control, he had no idea and did not care. All he needed to do was find Yartu and bring Zia back to Lady Yena. Nicolai wanted this over with as soon as possible.

"It's Yartu, her dragon."

Crystal shook her head in confusion, "You wanted to find the dragon? I thought that you wanted the girl. I can try again if you want and maybe we will see the girl."

Nicolai gave Crystal a reassuring smile, "I did not think that we would actually find Zia, something is protecting her. This power of hers is different from anything else that I have ever heard of. In truth you did not fail, you found the dragon. Where Yartu is Zia can't be far behind. You have been more helpful than you realize. You have succeeded where others have failed, including the Lady Yena."

The witch wondered what exactly Nicolai had planned for the girl. He would obviously take her to Lady Yena, but how would he deal with her in the meantime? "Now that you have a basic idea of where the girl is what are you going to do?"

"What I have to do." Something in the tone of his voice worried Crystal. She knew Nicolai better than most and yet he still found ways to unnerve the usually stoic witch.

"You do understand that she is going to be wary of everyone she meets, including you? She is probably aware of the fact that the Magic Council will search for her. She is going to assume that you are involved with this search."

"She will be assuming correctly, then; what is your point, Crystal?"

He had no idea what she was trying to tell him. Truth be told he really didn't care. All that mattered was finding Zia Amarra and getting her back to Lady Yena. It was of no importance to Nicolai how he would get the girl just as long as he got her to Lady Yena. The less he had to deal with her the happier he'd be.

"My point is simple. How in the name of all the gods are you going to deal with a scared girl who will probably run at the mere sight of you? If she doesn't run the dragon will most likely attack you—either way it will make the task of retrieving her much more difficult."

Nicolai paused to consider her words. Crystal was relieved that he seemed to understand what she was trying to tell him. She wasn't sure how good a thing it actually was, though. Nicolai had a habit of never listening to anyone. This characteristic of his was not the problem, she was more than used to it. The real issue was that when he did take someone's advice, he did it so rarely that Crystal was not sure what to expect. Whatever he was going to do originally, Crystal had a feeling she had just made things worse.

That smirk of his returned and Crystal began to feel nervous. "Perhaps I have been going about this the wrong way. Crystal, you are absolutely right. It did not occur to me how the girl would react. As you know I have not had much experience dealing with scared teenage girls, and I will probably just make matters worse than they need to be."

The feeling of unease was even worse than it had been a few minutes ago. Crystal knew that she had done something that was irrevocable. The witch knew that she could not let Nicolai know this, that is, if he did not know already. His smirk revealed nothing. It simply made Crystal more frustrated. She believed that was the true purpose of the smirk, to further infuriate the person he was speaking to. She wasn't sure if she should speak or not, considering the fact that she could make matters even worse then she already had.

Crystal did not have to wonder for too long, "I cannot be trusted to treat the girl fairly or properly. That is why I believe you should come with me. You and your magic will prove quite useful to me."

The witch stood silently in disbelief. She was stunned. Of every possible plan he could have thought of he had to include her in this whole mess. Crystal wondered if he had planned this all along or if he had just come up with it on the spot. It didn't matter, either way it was just like him to ignore someone else's feelings and do whatever he wanted, he enjoyed toying with people. Her disbelief soon turned to anger. "Me, go with you! Are you truly insane? I have no intention of going anywhere, especially if it is to benefit the Magic Council and Lady Yena. How could you have possibly come up with such an absurd idea?"

Her anger did not seem to bother him at all. "I believe that this little quest will be more successful with you coming along. As for helping Lady Yena, think of how grateful she will be when we return the girl to her. She will be indebted to you. Imagine it, the head of the Magic Council indebted to you, a witch, who was able to do that which she and all of her mages could not."

Crystal liked where he was going with that thought. Imagine having that arrogant, self-righteous mage indebted to her. No, she told herself, he is just manipulating you, and doing a very good job of it too. The witch paused a moment before responding. "Fine, I'll go. Just don't expect me to be congenial."

"Good. We leave early tomorrow morning. I assume that will give you enough time to get everything you need."

Crystal nodded in agreement. A few minutes later Nicolai left her home, but the feeling that she had done something horribly wrong lingered.

# CHAPTER 5

The moon was partially concealed by a dark cloud and the stars shone faintly in the night sky. A silvery mist covered the ground. It was a strange night, almost otherworldly. Most of the people who inhabited the area stayed indoors on nights such as this one. The stories were many of souls that had been lost forever. The villagers were a superstitious lot who did not welcome strangers into their isolated area of the world. Few travelers would go there to begin with, it was a dangerous area often plagued by storms, and various forms of monsters were hidden in the surrounding hills. Monsters were not what were to be feared that night, however.

The shadowy figure moved silently through the mist. There was no one else around for miles—or so he had thought. He had sensed another not too far away. A part of him was curious as to why someone else was out this late at night; he assumed it wasn't a villager. That alone made him curious about this other person. A few moments later he found her.

He could tell she was unconscious, not asleep, as he knelt down beside her. When he reached out to touch her a dark shape flew at him, knocking him to the ground. It took him a moment to find where the creature had gone. Gleaming red eyes were all he could see glaring at him in the darkness, and they were right above the girl. He wasn't sure but he got the feeling that the creature was trying to protect the girl.

"I am not going to hurt her. I just wanted to make sure she was alright. I mean her no harm."

The eyes blinked for moment then a voice came from the darkness, "If you truly mean no harm then I shall ask you for your assistance."

The darkness enveloped her in its shadowy embrace. She was alone, all alone. It was different this time. She still felt the pull of the shadows, and their urgency. Yet she did not feel frightened, the darkness felt more comforting than it had before. She felt safe. The shadows would protect her, watch over her, never let anyone hurt her. This was whispered to her as they gently held her, this and more.

"We can keep you safe. I will give you power beyond your belief. All you have to do is give in. Stop fighting the darkness; I will not be able to help you if you do not give in to the shadows. You have no reason to fear them or me. You must let them guide you to me; only then will I be able to help you. The shadows are a part of the darkness and are only trying to help you. The shadows and I both serve the darkness. All the darkness wants is to protect you. Come to me, my child, and remember as long as you remain separate from the darkness, the longer you take to return to it, to me, the worse things will be for you. Trust no one but the shadows."

Zia was not sure what had woken her. When she opened her eyes the sunlight blinded her momentarily. She let her eyes adjust to the light as she stood up. She had no idea where she was. She was also alone. "Yartu," she called, but there was no answer. He had to be around somewhere.

The room she was in was old and dusty. It appeared as if no one had been there in a very long time. The only piece of furniture was a tattered old chair. As she left the room Zia discovered the rest of the house was in much of the same condition. It was very old, and cobwebs covered every corner. Much of the house was dark even though the sun shone brightly outside. It reminded Zia of what most people would consider a haunted house. Zia wasn't scared as others would have been; to her the house was just an empty shell of what had once probably been a beautiful home.

She had been through the entire house and still there was no sign of Yartu. She could sense he was close by but she had no idea where. She thought of searching outside of the house but she could not find the exit. Zia went through the house again in case she had missed anything the first time. Once again her search for a way out was futile. Zia was about to give up when she noticed a shadow moving behind her.

Zia's first thought was one of panic; the moving shadow brought to mind her dreams. The thought quickly passed, though, for the shadowy figure seemed to have realized that she had seen it. Zia turned towards it; she could barely see what it was. She did not know what to do. She had nowhere to run, she was trapped.

Zia was determined not to panic. Whatever the thing was it obviously meant her no harm or it would have acted already. She decided to try to talk to it, show that she didn't want any trouble. Hopefully it would understand her.

"I'll be going as soon as I find the way out. I did not mean to disturb you." She spoke calmly and clearly so as not to upset the creature. She hesitated a moment before resuming her search, she glanced at the creature and asked, "Do you know where the exit is?"

Zia knew that whatever the thing was it probably wouldn't show her the way out anyway. So she went back to her search. A few moments later she was surprised to find a great deal of light coming in from outside, light that had not been there before. Zia had been in this particular room several times before and had found nothing that could possibly be an exit. This time, though, she found a large broken window. The drop from the window was not that bad, so Zia climbed out and landed easily on the ground.

As she started to wander around outside Zia sensed Yartu was very close. She called his name again and a few moments later he flew right into her arms.

"I was so worried, where have you been? I looked all over for you, and there was this creature in the house..."

"Creature? What creature?" Yartu interrupted Zia mid-sentence.

She shrugged and shook her head. "I don't know what it was. I did not get a very good look; it was very adept at concealing itself in the shadows. I didn't get the impression that it meant to harm me; it just wanted me to leave."

"I don't understand, he said he would watch you while I was gone. Why would he leave?" Yartu seemed confused, though not as confused as Zia.

"He? What are you talking about, Yartu? There was no one in that house except me and that thing, whatever it was." Zia had no idea what he was going on about and on top of everything else she had no idea where they were or how they had gotten there. She was about to ask him about everything when he flew out of her arms.

"You! Why did you leave her? You said that you would watch her, and did you? No!" Yartu was angry and he was obviously speaking to someone behind her.

Zia turned around to see who Yartu was yelling at and came face to face with a young man. She was a bit shocked at first by his appearance; he was dressed all in black, shirt, pants, and boots. He was unlike other men she had seen, for he had very fine features and a flawless complexion. The only word that could be used to describe him was beautiful. His black hair fell to his shoulders with the exception of a few strands that fell in front of his right eye. His eyes, they were what was most captivating about him. They were dark and intense, they drew her in, made her feel as though he could see into her soul, read her very thoughts, all just by looking at her. The young man fascinated and frightened her.

He looked past her and spoke to Yartu, "I did not leave, you did. It is your responsibility to stay with her, not mine."

The dragon flew right in front of his face; the young man did not flinch. If Yartu had been human his face would have been flushed with irritation. As it was the miniature dragon was barely able to contain his agitation and when he spoke, he sounded as if he was about to have a fit. "You are accusing me of leaving Zia. I am not the one who refused to leave that house simply because it was daylight. What a lie, I never should have believed such a stupid excuse. It is daylight now, isn't it? I had to leave Zia because of *you*. If you had agreed to get help then I would not have had to leave her. It turns out that I shouldn't have left to begin with, since you left her all alone in that dismal house with some strange creature wandering around. You said that she would be safe there—you were obviously wrong."

The young man shook his head. "I don't need this. She's awake, just go." He started to walk back towards the house.

Zia watched him for a moment then ran after him, she was not quite sure why. "Wait. Forgive Yartu. He is just overly protective of me."

The young man did not answer her, although he did stop walking and turned towards her, waiting for her to continue. "I do not exactly know what has happened the past day or so. I am a bit confused by all of this, and I'm sure Yartu is as well. We have no idea where we are or how we got here. You seem to be from around here and must know the area really well. We would greatly appreciate your help."

"Fine, I will help you, but on one condition."

Zia nodded, "Anything."

"You will not ask questions about me. I do not like to talk about myself."

"That makes two of us," Zia said. It was an odd request but one that she could fully sympathize with.

He did not ask her what she meant and she was glad. She wouldn't have to tell him about her dreams or the Magic Council, especially how she escaped them.

Zia might have been relieved, but Yartu was not pleased with the situation. "If we do not know anything about you then how are we supposed to know if we are to trust you? You already have a mark against you for leaving Zia alone in that house."

"For the last time, I did not leave her." The young man was becoming slightly agitated.

The miniature dragon was about to lose his temper. "Then explain why Zia was alone in there. Let's not forget the creature that was in there with her. You left her alone with that thing in there."

Yartu was about to say more when the young man interrupted him, "That creature was me, not some vicious monster about to kill your precious girl. I did not leave her, although I am considering leaving the both of you now."

The dragon was silent, not knowing what to say. Zia did: "That was you?" She shook her head in disbelief, "Why didn't you reveal yourself to me? How did you manage to hide so well in the shadows?" She would have said more except that she couldn't. He had hidden his true form from her; she was always able to see what hid in the shadows. She did not know what to say. He was unlike anything or anyone she had ever encountered.

The young man did not answer her questions, he simply said, "I will show you to the nearest town. You're on your own from there."

Zia was still a little confused about what he had been able to do, and she wanted to ask him about it again, but she didn't. It was Yartu who spoke. "As much as I don't like this situation you are the only one around who can help us. I suppose I will just have to tolerate you for the time being. I presume you have a name, of course I really could care less what it is."

"Yartu!" Zia exclaimed, "Don't be so rude. He has offered to help us; the least you could do is be civil."

The young man shrugged and shook his head, "Don't worry about it, I have heard far worse. I'm used to it at this point. My name is Shadow."

Zia froze, unable to speak or move; it was just like her nightmares, they were slowly becoming reality, this is what the voice had told her. Shadow; his name was Shadow, and she was going to follow him.

CHAPTER 6

A couple of days had passed since Zia had disappeared from Selia. A few days since, the Magic Council had chosen to ignore the girl's existence out of fear; they did not want to acknowledge that the darkness might be waking, or that Zia Amarra had anything to do with it. It had also been a few days since Nicolai and Crystal left Selia in search of the strange girl; a few days too many in both Crystal's and Nicolai's minds. Crystal just wanted to go home and Nicolai wanted to find the girl and give her to Lady Yena and just be done with everything. The longer it took to find her the longer he had to work for Lady Yena, a thought that was unbearable. The thought of being in her service was quite agonizing. In the beginning this task Lady Yena had given him seemed simple enough; find a girl, how hard could that be? It was a great deal more difficult than he had originally thought.

His intention had been to find the girl in a day or so—even though Lady Yena had told him of her disappearance, he did not believe that she could have possibly gotten so far from Selia. That assumption had been entirely false. Zia had teleported farther away from the city than was possible. Teleportation was an advanced form of magic very few mages were able to master. The farther the distance the harder it was to control the spell; only a handful of mages were able to teleport themselves outside the city and a mere girl had teleported herself so far from Selia it had taken almost a week to reach the spot in which he and Crystal had originally seen Yartu. Nicolai was beginning to understand why Lady Yena was worried about the girl and why she wanted her back in Selia. This also upset him, because one of the few things he hated more than working for Lady Yena was agreeing with her. With each passing day his deepening resentment towards Zia Amarra and his desire to find her grew more and more.

Crystal, on the other hand, was not entirely thrilled with the prospect of finding the girl. She still believed that she should be concerned about the whole situation. If the Magic Council were unable to use their magic around Zia, would she face the same predicament? True, she had been able to find the miniature dragon when the Magic Council, more specifically Lady Yena, couldn't. The witch was still able to find the dragon—though a lot of good that did. The dragon seemed to be in a different location every time she searched for him. They had not been making very good progress in their search and Crystal was getting tired of the journey. She was also tiring of Nicolai and his attitude.

The witch knew Nicolai better than most, but she had never seen him this way before. He had become slightly obsessed with finding Zia. To be honest, slightly was an understatement. The man was becoming more and more agitated as time went on. He was also becoming intolerable.

"We should see if we can find the dragon again," Nicolai said again for what seemed like the thousandth time.

Crystal shook her head in dismissal, "I just did. We will not find anything new if I search again. It will be pointless and a wasted use of my magic. We can only continue on as we have been, nothing is going to change anytime soon. The only way we'll determine the girl's exact location is if she stops for longer than a single night in a town or such. So far she has not, so stop asking."

The witch was tiring of Nicolai's incessant interrogation regarding the whereabouts of Zia Amarra's miniature dragon. He continually asked her if she should look for him again, and she did in the beginning. She had given up listening to him, there was never any new information. Informing Nicolai of this had proven to be quite disastrous. The man would become rather sullen and Crystal would have to deal with his moodiness until he asked her once again to search for the blasted miniature dragon.

She had been waiting for a chance to find the dragon while he was not moving. It was proving to be more difficult than she thought, for the dragon was in constant motion even when night had fallen. Crystal was beginning to wonder if the blasted creature ever slept. So far the answer to that question was no. All of this was just making the witch more miserable, and made her yearn even more for her home and the company of her cats. They were at least pleasant company. In fact, Crystal would have preferred to spend the day with Lady Yena and the entire Magic Council if it got her away from Nicolai.

This was all about to come to an end, or so the witch thought, for that night Crystal was able to discover the exact location of the miniature dragon Yartu.

"Where are we?" They had been traveling four days and there was not a single sign of civilization. "You said you were going to show us to the nearest town and so far all we have seen is trees, more trees, and the occasional field of grass."

Zia shook her head and hoped that Yartu had not angered the young man again. *Shadow,* she reminded herself, his name is Shadow. Zia was still having a bit of difficulty adjusting to this odd young man and an even more difficult time learning to use his extremely unusual name. How was she supposed to call him by his name when hearing it made her skin crawl? Anything that had to do with darkness or shadows made her anxious, it was like she was being forced to live her nightmares. Whether or not this was from fear she had yet to discover.

Yartu, on the other hand, was not the least bit intimidated by Shadow's presence, it actually seemed to vex him. Every opportunity Yartu could find to bait Shadow he used to the fullest. Generally, it led to a rather one-sided argument that the miniature dragon refused to give up. Shadow mostly ignored the dragon. On the few occasions Yartu had actually managed to anger him Zia had been a little scared.

They knew nothing about him and Zia thought that this might make Yartu slightly more wary of Shadow; she was, of course, wrong. Yartu had already decided that he did not like the young man regardless of the fact that he did not know him. The miniature dragon was not likely to change his mind either, once Yartu made up his mind about certain things it was almost impossible to change it.

It was a part of his nature, stubbornness came easily to the diminutive creature.

Zia was not as judgmental as her dragon, she was intrigued by Shadow and yet afraid. Every time she looked at him she was reminded of her dream. Follow the shadows, the voice had said. Zia could not get that dream or the sound of the voice out of her head. What if Shadow was what the voice had meant? What if... there were so many what ifs. Her entire world had been turned upside down and she could do nothing about it. She did not even know how or why either. Zia might have said it was like a dream, not a good one though, if she had ever had normal dreams like other people. Truth be told, Zia had never lived a *normal* life. She had always known her life was different from others, or what others considered to be normal. One moment everything was normal, well as normal as things got for her, the next it had all changed.

It was not as if Zia was unused to change, her life since meeting Yartu had involved a great deal of moving from place to place. Yet, while she had to keep uprooting herself, her life had always maintained a predictable pattern. She would move to a new place, get a job, someone would see Yartu, and she would have to move again; this just kept repeating in a seemingly endless cycle. Now what? Zia had no idea what to do anymore, she was lost. Lost and following a shadow.

"Once again, where is this town you told us about?" Yartu was truly losing his patience. Zia could not really blame him. Four days had passed and they had not seen a house, much less a town. It was rather odd.

Shadow did not seem bothered by Yartu's growing impatience. "The nearest town is not much farther, only an hour or two."

"An *hour* or two," Yartu had lost his temper, "Not much considering that we have already spent four days searching for a town that is only an hour or two away."

Zia noticed that Shadow was ignoring Yartu and probably intended to continue doing so, which would only aggravate the miniature dragon more. She decided to intervene before Yartu got completely out of control. "The town was probably farther away before, most likely four days away from where we started. Yartu, he did not have to help us, you should be more appreciative of what he has done. I'm sure that he probably had better things to do than guide us to some town."

Yartu snorted, "Better things to do. Ha. If he had better things to do then I'm..."

"A real dragon;" quipped Shadow. Zia cringed, there was nothing Yartu hated more than someone saying he was not a real dragon.

This comment pushed Yartu too far. The miniature dragon was literally trembling with fury. Yartu flew at Shadow in a rage, intent on harming the young man. Zia managed to grab the dragon as he darted past her. It was all she could do to hold onto him as he was fighting to break free of her grasp. The miniature dragon's fury could not be contained, though, and he screamed insults and various curses at Shadow, all the while struggling against Zia's hold.

She was shocked at Yartu's behavior; she had never seen him so enraged. Shadow, on the other hand, did not seem the least bit concerned with the dragon's extremely violent outburst. He cast a glance in Yartu's direction and looked away as if he was a mere inconvenience, not an extremely furious miniature dragon.

Poor Zia did not know how much longer she could keep Yartu at bay. The snarled threats and the constant flapping of his wings as he tried to escape the cage that

Zia's arms had become were proving to be too much. Her strength was starting to fade.

When he lunged for what seem to be the thousandth time, Zia decided that she was not going to deal with this anymore. "Apologize!" she practically had to shout at Shadow to be heard over Yartu.

Arched eyebrows were the only response Zia received. "Apologize now!" Her patience was running out, as was her strength.

"Why?" Shadow asked calmly, "Why must I apologize to him? I have had to put up with all his snide comments. I did not have to help you, but I did, and all I have received in return is insults and threats. If anyone should apologize it should be him."

"Fine! Yartu, apologize to him now," an exasperated Zia told her furious dragon, which made him all the more hostile. His struggle with Zia increased dramatically, causing her to lose her hold. The sudden forward motion of the miniature dragon knocked Zia to the ground.

Zia tried to catch him and failed, all she could do was watch as Yartu flew at Shadow. The young man did not move as Yartu came charging towards him.

CHAPTER 7

She waited for the cry of pain as sharp dragon talons tore into soft human flesh, but it never came. Yartu's mad rush for Shadow ended with the miniature dragon slamming into the air just before he reached the young man. It was as though he ran into a wall, yet there was nothing there, just air. An extremely dazed Yartu fell to the ground. Shadow made no move to help the dragon, he just stood there silent and unmoving, he didn't even blink. Zia thought for a moment she saw a stunned look on his face and confusion clouding his eyes, but only for a moment. His face became unreadable and showed no sign of what he might be feeling.

Zia knew what she was feeling. Her Bond with Yartu also meant she was able to feel his pain and he was able to feel her pain. She felt his pain almost as if it were her own.

She went to Yartu to make sure he was alright, but the pain she felt was not acute, so she wasn't too worried. Still, he had fallen and she was a bit concerned, this had never happened before. When she reached his side she pulled him into her arms, not to restrain him but to examine him. She found nothing seriously wrong with him.

"I... I'm fine," Yartu stammered. "What happened?"

Zia shook her head, "I don't know. You were going to attack him and you just fell. I do not understand it." She didn't either, none of it. Zia wondered if Shadow did. When she looked up towards him, he said nothing and did nothing, he just stood there.

Yartu noticed this as well. "What, are you not going to ask how I am? This is all your fault, you know. I'm not sure what you did, but whatever it was, you did it. You owe us a very good explanation."

Shadow did not explain. He remained as quiet as he had been before. The only difference was that he was no longer looking at them, or anything else for that matter. His eyes were unfocused and seemed to have glazed over. Zia found she was worrying about him now.

"What's wrong with him now?" Yartu demanded. The miniature dragon didn't really care. He just wanted Shadow to apologize for whatever it was he had done to him.

Zia was quite distressed. She had no idea what to do. Yartu seemed to be fine, but Shadow? She did not know what was wrong with him, what she did know was that she had to find out.

She set Yartu back on the ground and went over to where Shadow was standing. He did not move, he did not seem to notice her at all. It was almost as if he had gone blind, but something made Zia uncomfortable. It was obvious that he was not blind, and no one could become blind just like that, it was more like he was looking at something that was far away, or something no one else could see. His eyes were unfocused but they still seemed to be gazing at some sight that was not visible to Zia and Yartu.

"Shadow?" It was hard for Zia to say his name but she was more worried about his well-being at the moment than his name. He still didn't respond.

Yartu flew towards her and tried pulling her back from Shadow's side. "Don't, Zia. Something isn't right. We should leave." There was a hint of concern and the tiniest bit of fear in his voice, which concerned Zia. Yartu was afraid of nothing.

"Yartu, we have to help him. You are right. Something is wrong. I know you don't like him but we cannot leave him like this."

The dragon shook his head vehemently, "No, Zia. We are leaving now. He has led us far enough. I don't care about what has happened to him. It is not safe for us to stay here anymore."

Zia could not believe what she was hearing; she knew Yartu didn't like Shadow but what he was saying was completely wrong. She was so confused, she knew that it would be wrong to leave Shadow, but Yartu always had her best interests at heart, they were Bonded. She wanted Shadow to look at her and tell her she was the one seeing things, she wanted him to say that he was alright.

"Zia, we need to leave. I don't like this; something is just not right with him. It is dangerous to stay here." Yartu, as always interrupted her thoughts. She waved him away, focusing on Shadow, trying to make some sense of everything that was going on. "Zia!" He was pleading with her now. She ignored him.

Shadow was her main concern at the moment. She was unable to figure him out, from the first time they had met until now. For every second she spent in his company the less she seemed to know about him; this did not make the situation better.

Now most people would have been scared and done what Yartu wanted. Zia was a bit nervous about Shadow, but her nervousness was being overpowered by anger. She was annoyed by just about everything involving him. He had been able to hide from her in the shadows, his name was Shadow, he was a constant reminder of her dreams, he insulted her dragon and he confused her almost every waking moment just by being himself. Zia had had it. She was fed up.

Zia knew that whatever was going on with him she had to snap him out of it. She did the first thing that came to mind. She hit him.

The exact moment her hand came in contact with his cheek the strangest thing happened.

The world around her seemed to disappear. What she saw she did not believe. Instead of a serene meadow she was in the midst of a battle on a treacherous mountain path. The stench of blood and the screams of the dying surrounded her. She watched as a man was cut down before her, and she almost cried out, she had to bite her lip in order not to. The man's killer turned towards her, an awful look on his face. Zia watched in horror as the man raised his sword; she stared with morbid fascination at the blood slowly dripping along the edge of the blade and knew death was only moments away. She tried to close her eyes but found she could not. All she could do was watch. Zia waited for the fatal strike.

It was over as quickly as it had begun. Bright sunlight and blue sky met her eyes instead of the eerie light of a village in flames filling the sky. Cool, clean air entered her lungs instead of smoke. She was alive, although her throbbing headache made her wish differently.

Zia must have fallen on the ground at some point, although she did not remember doing so. She figured that it must have happened when she had come out of that dream. Was that what it was, she wondered, or was it something else? What else could it have been?

"Zia? Zia!" the persistent calling of her name brought her back to her senses. Yartu, as always, was there; he looked as if he was going to die from sheer panic. "Are you feeling alright? I was so worried, I didn't know if something terrible had happened or not."

Yartu would have gone on and on but Zia interrupted him, "What did happen?" she asked.

"You hit him and then... then, I don't know. You were in such distress but there was nothing going on, you were in no physical danger. I want an explanation as to what happened if you don't mind. Now that you have scared me to no end." The anger in his voiced masked his fear. His fear of what had just happened, fear of the unknown, and the worst, fear of the thought that he could have lost Zia. The only way the miniature dragon could handle this fear and retain some semblance of control was to be angry.

Zia shook her head, "I have no idea what happened, Yartu. Honestly, I am just as confused by what occurred as you."

"There is no explanation. I don't even know what happened, and it happened to me." The voice belonged to Shadow.

Zia turned towards him. He was sitting on the ground as well, except he appeared as if he had just sat down for a moment's reprieve. He seemed fine, as he did only minutes before all the strange things occurred.

"*You* have no explanation. It happened to *you*. Are you insane? Whatever happened to you also happened to Zia. How dare you endanger her and act as if nothing had happened?" Yartu was yelling quite loudly, causing Zia to wince in pain. Yartu noticed this and started to berate Shadow for once again being the cause of Zia's pain.

Shadow, as always, ignored him. Zia noticed he was looking at her. Feeling quite uncomfortable with his eyes on her she closed her eyes. She sensed movement near her but she did not open them.

A slight touch on her arm startled her. When she opened her eyes she found herself face to face with Shadow. "It hurts a lot, doesn't it?" It was not a question. Zia wondered how he knew, and she was about to ask him when Yartu interrupted.

"Get away from her! I will not let you cause her any more pain."

Shadow turned towards Yartu, an angry expression on his face. "Shut up, for once in your life. I am not the one causing Zia pain at the moment; you are."

Yartu was taken aback by Shadow's comments. So shocked, in fact, he actually was at a loss for words.

This did not seem to bother Shadow at all. Once again, his attention was on Zia. "I know the pain is excruciating but it will go away."

"Really? I would love to know when." Her head still hurt and the pain did not seem to be going away. She was not in the most pleasant of moods.

Shadow must have found her remark amusing, because he was smiling. Zia felt as if her heart had skipped a beat. She barely felt the pain anymore; instead she felt as if... she did not know what it was she felt. His smile was so beautiful. She could not turn away, it was hypnotizing. Her headache had all but disappeared. It surprised her that just seeing him smile could affect her so. This had never happened to her before.

"Sarcasm will not make the pain go away faster." Shadow informed her.

"Maybe not, but it helps." Zia muttered. He had not stopped smiling, and her retort seemed to make him smile even more. This of course put Zia in an even worse mood than before. She did not like what his smile was doing to her. She could not decide whether she wanted him to continue smiling or to stop. What she did want was to know what had happened and why she was feeling so strange. "Would you please stop that!" she snapped.

"Stop what?" The smile was still there.

His smile distracted her from the pain. Although the worst of the pain had passed, it was still there. Zia was really getting tired of it, "I am so pleased you find my pain amusing, but maybe, just maybe, you could stop finding me so amusing and start explaining why I am in so much pain."

This time he shook his head. "Regardless of what you may think I don't find your pain amusing." The smile suddenly disappeared. "I know how you feel. Every sound, every word spoken makes it worse. The headache does go away after a while."

"How do you know?" There was no sarcasm in her voice this time. She wanted to know how he knew about the headache, the pain, and if he felt it too.

Shadow's gaze fell to the ground. "It used to hurt a lot in the beginning. I was barely able to open my eyes, let alone stand up. I would just sit on the ground for hours wishing the pain would go away. I've gotten used to it now; it still hurts but I deal with it."

Zia wanted to ask him what he meant, what caused the headaches, and more than anything else she wanted to ask him how long he had dealt with this. She didn't ask him anything. Zia remembered what he had said when they first met. He did not want to talk about himself. Although she did want to know more about him, she understood why he would want to keep his life private. She knew what it was like keeping secrets from everyone you met, never really being able to trust anyone, hiding who you really were from the rest of the world. Zia remained silent.

She did not notice his eyes return to her, for she had lowered her head and her long black hair fell around her, obscuring her view of him. If she had known it would have made her more uncomfortable than she already was.

"You're not going to ask anything else?" Shadow sounded surprised that she had not questioned him further.

That soon ended, for Yartu, having gotten over his shock, demanded to know what was going on. He flew over to Zia and sat in her lap, staring angrily at Shadow. "Well. Are you going to explain yourself? If not, I have quite a few things I would like to say to you about your unseemly behavior."

"Yartu, he does not have to explain. I'm not sure if I really want to know what happened." She paused for a moment, closed her eyes and spoke softly, "Or what I saw."

Yartu looked up at her, "What do you mean by *saw*?" There was a bit of worry in his voice.

She shook her head, not wanting to explain. Her head still hurt, and she did not want to relive that horrible moment.

Her silence seemed to fuel Yartu's anger and concern over her safety. "What did you do to her? I know this all happened because of you." The miniature dragon was shouting at this point, which did not help Zia's headache. "I want an explanation now."

Shadow glared at him; the intensity was almost too much to bear, and Zia wondered how it was possible for Yartu not to look away. She knew why Shadow was angry, his privacy was being invaded. She did not blame him for wanting to keep whatever it was he was hiding a secret. She had told Yartu that she wasn't sure she wanted to know, but she knew she did not want to know. She didn't want to know what could possibly cause such an intense visual experience or how often Shadow experienced this.

Zia pulled Yartu into her arms, "Leave him alone, Yartu. He does not have to explain right now. We should just focus on getting to the town and finding out where we are."

Yartu started to shake his head in protest; he stopped for a moment and thought about it. He wanted to know what was going on with Shadow, but Zia was obviously uncomfortable discussing what had happened. Yartu did not like it when Zia was upset and he would do just about anything to make her happy. Yartu considered this his main duty as her miniature dragon. Many of his kind were used by mages to assist with spells and such, while others were just status symbols for the aristocracy—not him, though, he was different, and he always had been. He was supposed to take care of Zia. That was his purpose in life; truthfully, his entire life revolved around her.

He did not care about any other human in the whole world unless they were somehow connected to Zia; even then his concern was extremely minimal. He had always believed humans were a waste of time but, of all the humans he had met, Shadow was the worst. The young man was nothing but trouble and a constant source of distress for Zia. Yartu despised him and wanted nothing more than to be rid of him. Unfortunately, they needed him to get out of the wretched area they were in. Yartu knew Zia was right, they had to get to that town and finally be rid of Shadow once and for all. Then they could finally go back to their lives.

"Fine." Yartu turned his gleaming red eyes towards Shadow. "Lead on."

Shadow said nothing. He stood up and shook his head in disbelief. Zia placed Yartu on the ground and started to rise as well. She was barely able to get off the ground and the second she tried to stand she lost her balance and fell. That is, she would have fallen if Shadow had not caught her.

64

CHAPTER 8

Zia found herself in a rather awkward position. She was leaning against Shadow and his arms were around her. She could feel the warmth of his body close to hers. It was strange, Zia had never been so close to another person before; she normally never let anyone touch her. It made her uncomfortable being so close to him, having his body so close to hers. She tried to pull away but started to sway, which caused her to once again lean on him for support, the only difference was this time her head was resting on his chest.

She could hear his heartbeat. She found it strangely soothing. Closing her eyes, she began to feel her heart beat in time with his. It only lasted a moment, but that one moment seemed to last forever, until the shadows started to surround her mind.

Darkness enveloped her. She was in the shadows' embrace. They held her gently, whispering ever so softly. She knew not what they whispered, but for some reason it did not matter. Words had no meaning here; they hurt whomever they were spoken to. She was safe. No harm could come to her here in the shadows. The darkness would protect her from anything that might cause her pain.

The whispers slowly began to make sense. Follow, they wanted her to follow them; they needed her, wanted her close to them. If she came to them, they would keep her safe and protect her always. She did not need anyone else, they were all she needed and she was all they wanted.

Fear started to replace the belief that the darkness would not harm her. The urgency had returned. They wanted to show her something, but they could not as long she fought them. The darkness wanted and needed her to give in. A very small part of her wanted to do what they asked. Zia dreaded what might happen if she did, though. She tried to escape, to wake from this unbearable nightmare. Her efforts were in vain; she was losing. They would overpower her, take control. There was nothing she could do. The shadows' whispers began to consume her; nothing else existed in this otherworld of darkness. There was no way out, she was trapped.

Something began to break through the all-consuming darkness. A soft steady beat could be heard through the barrier that the constant whispers of the shadows had built around her. She could not figure out what the beat was or where it had come from, but she did notice that the darkness did not seem to like it. The whispers grew louder, deafening, but the steady rhythmic beat surrounded her. Zia suddenly knew what it was that had come to her aid and was making the shadows so infuriated. It was the soft, steady rhythmic beat of a heart.

Zia's eyes opened as she was violently shaken, and she heard her name being called over and over again. The moment her eyes opened the shaking stopped. Yartu flew over to her; he seemed to be saying something but she was unable to make out the words. Her mind was in a fog. She tried to remember where she was and what had happened. It was a great deal harder than she thought it would be.

She looked around trying to get her bearings. The first thing she saw was Shadow watching her with a carefully guarded face. Why was he there? And why was he looking at her that way? She could not figure it out, although he seemed to be holding on to her arms. Was he the one shaking her? Why did nothing seem to make any sense?

Yartu looked as if he was trying to speak to her again, his words were still inaudible. He looked at Shadow and said something to him. Zia could not hear the words he had spoken. The whole thing was starting to frighten her.

Shadow did not respond to whatever it was that Yartu had said to him. He just continued to watch her. She did not like it, she felt as if he was studying her and it made her uncomfortable. This of course made it even more difficult for Zia to figure out what was going on. Her mind still had that foggy quality about it and the fact that she could not hear anything was starting to truly worry her.

Zia decided she should try to talk to them; maybe they were affected by whatever it was too. The moment she started to try and speak Shadow shook his head and let go of her.

"Stop it. You're making things worse." His words broke through the silence that had been plaguing her. Zia did not understand what he meant or why she was able to hear him and not Yartu.

"What?" She was surprised to hear the shakiness in her voice. It sounded as if she had not spoken in some time.

Yartu flew to her side. "Zia, you're alright. Thank goodness; I was so worried." He looked at her accusingly. "Why didn't you answer me before?"

"I... I don't know. I could not seem to hear what you were saying. I am sorry I worried you."

"You couldn't hear me. Zia..." She heard the concern in his voice. She could not blame him for being troubled by the situation, she was.

Her gaze fell to the ground, "Yartu, I don't know what happened; I don't understand what is going on. I had... I had the dream again, Yartu. I was *not* asleep. I don't know what to do. You have to help me, I feel like I'm starting to lose my mind." The moment she said all she did, she remembered the dream.

How could she have forgotten? Why had it affected her the way it did this time? It had never made her feel any different before. Why did it now? She could not make any sense of what was happening. First, the whole problem with Shadow, and now this. She had not had the dream since she woke up in that ruined old house. Now she was having it while she was awake, it made absolutely no sense whatsoever. Maybe she was losing her mind.

"Who knows about you? I know I feel like I'm losing my mind." Shadow's sarcastic comment interrupted her thoughts.

Zia looked at him in amazement. She did not know why but all of a sudden she started to laugh. "It has been a really interesting day, hasn't it?"

Shadow's brilliant smile returned to his face. "Interesting is not the word I would use. It does not even begin to describe today. Between the two of us it has definitely been a weird day."

"Yes, weird is the word for it. Bizarre might work too." Zia still found herself laughing. She did not know why she was laughing, maybe because it kept her from crying.

Shadow started to laugh too. His laugh was like his smile and the rest of him, perfect. "Bizarre is good. What other words do you think might work? Strange, maybe?"

"No. It is too simple. Odd?" She thought about it for a moment and shook her head, "No, peculiar is a good word for it."

"Crazy is definitely the word I would use."

The two continued to laugh and come up with new words to describe the unusual day. Yartu just stared at them. He could not believe what he was seeing. Normally Zia was terrified after the dream, and here she was laughing. It was completely unbelievable, she did not seem to care that this time the dream had come when she was awake. She just stood there laughing with *him*. "In my opinion you are both crazy."

The two looked at each other as if they shared some sort of secret. Then they looked at him and began to laugh as if he was not in on their little secret. Whatever the secret was it did not matter to Yartu. He only cared that Zia seemed to be having a wonderful time with Shadow. It angered him that she was becoming more comfortable around Shadow. It was not right, they knew nothing about him, and after the day's events they truly had no reason at all to trust him. There was just something wrong with the young man. Yartu could see it; he just didn't know why Zia was unable to.

Yartu did not like any of this. What angered him the most, though, was the effect the strange young man seemed to have on her. It appeared as if she actually was becoming fond of him. It was almost as though they were becoming friends. This Yartu would not allow. Every time Zia started to trust someone, they proved to her that no one could be trusted. He was not about to let her become friends with Shadow only to have him break her heart. It was his responsibility to protect her from those who would only cause her pain. She needed to know that he was the only one she could trust, humans would only bring trouble. He did not understand why she did not seem to realize this after everything that had happened to her, all the lies, betrayal and pain that humans had inflicted on her in her eighteen years of life. He knew about the evil of humans and he was determined to never let them cause her any more grief, on top of the damage they had already done. He would protect her regardless of what the cost might be. Yartu was not going to let this human hurt his Zia, even if she started to befriend him. Shadow would get them to a town and they would be rid of him for good.

CHAPTER 9

Town was an overstatement; it was more of a village. A collection of houses and a few stores were the only visible signs of civilization. The town was rather rundown, and the people who could be seen walking its streets appeared much the same. It was a town that looked as if it were caught in the middle of a nightmare. A thick fog blanketed the ground and dark clouds covered the sky. The people of the town showed the signs of what living in this hostile and harsh land did. They were a cold, hard people, who did not take kindly to strangers in their midst. Strangers only brought trouble and they had enough of that living in this untamable area of the world.

Most of the people who came to this remote region were adventurers and treasure hunters; people who heard of the dangers and the whispers of a treasure that was lost centuries ago. There were various rumors of those to whom the treasure had belonged. One story said it belonged to a long dead king who had managed to build a prosperous kingdom in this wild land. The story explains that the land itself grew angry at the king who dared to try and tame it. A massive storm the likes of which had never before been seen darkened the sky above the kingdom. The cities, towns, people, everything that was not a part of the land itself, disappeared in the violent storm's rage. Ruins could be seen the further one ventured into the land. The townspeople believed these ruins and the forest that surrounded them were haunted. Whether or not they were haunted by the spirits of those who had died in the storm, the townspeople did not know.

A lesser-known rumor involved a dragon and its hoard. There were whispers of a dragon that lived in the forest, not a miniature dragon but one of their larger cousins, hidden from the rest of the world. Full-sized dragons were rarer than their smaller counterparts. They generally lived in remote areas of the world, preferring to stay hidden from humans who would dare to steal their treasure. The rumor stated that this dragon hid itself and its riches somewhere within the forest, maybe even in one of the ruins. A dragon's hoard was worth even more than the riches of a king, and guarded by things far worse than the spirits of the dead. Dragons were an ancient and mysterious race that were magical in nature, very little was known about them, and much of which was known was merely speculation. The one thing that was known to be definite was that dragons were extremely antisocial. Dragons were supposedly capable of summoning powerful creatures from demons to ghosts, anything that would guard their hoard from treasure hunters. If one was lucky enough to get past a dragon's initial defenses, they would more than likely find themselves face-to-face with the dragon itself. This of course signified the end of the unfortunate and rather foolish soul who dared to enter the dragon's lair in the first place.

A few people had speculated on the kind of dragon that might dwell in the forest. Some said it was the oldest and most powerful dragon there was and it chose to live in their forest because it knew that the people in the nearby towns and villages would leave it alone if it did not bother them. So far it had not, that is if the rumors were true about a dragon. If they were, whoever saw the dragon did not live to tell anyone, and no one in the town had ever seen signs of a dragon living nearby. So the dragon remained a story that was whispered to unsuspecting travelers and adventurers in the tavern along with the story of a long dead king and his haunted treasure. Some were foolish enough to go in search of the treasure. It did not matter if it belonged to a king or a dragon, the thought of all the riches that were hidden deep in the forest called to them like a siren's song. Few who left in search of glory and riches were ever seen again, lost to the ominous forest and whatever lurked in its shadowy depths.

Zia did not like the look of this small town; it was cold and dark and the people seemed even less welcoming than the weather. It amazed her that the sky had been completely clear, there was not a single cloud to be seen, only a few hours ago. Now the sky was a depressing shade of dark gray and appeared as if rain was going to fall soon and ruin everyone's day, but not her day.

Soon after she and Shadow had broken into hysterics, Yartu had somehow managed to calm them down and get them to start towards the town. Zia did not mind so much, although she was a bit apprehensive about what might happen once they got to town. A small part of her was disappointed that Yartu had interrupted her and Shadow and their momentary uncontrollable laughter. That was the first time that she had been at ease around Shadow since she had met him. The situation that had caused their hysterical behavior had not been pleasant, but for the short time in which she had been laughing and joking with him she felt like nothing had ever happened. She had felt as if she was normal, as though she was just a normal girl and he was just a boy, perfect looking, but normal. It had been a nice moment, and she had been sorry to see it end.

Things had returned to *her* normal. Shadow had become quiet and appeared to be deep in thought as he led them to town and Yartu, perching on her shoulders hidden beneath her long hair, had become quite sullen, refusing to talk to either of them. Zia did not mind his behavior, Yartu had always been rather moody; she did wonder about Shadow, though. On their almost silent journey to get to the miserable-looking town he had barely said anything at all. She wondered what it was that had him in such deep thought. Every so often Zia thought that he was looking at her, she could feel his eyes on her, but when she glanced his way, he was scanning the road ahead. She was unable to figure out why he would be watching her, and a part of her wondered if she was what he was thinking so deeply about.

That made her wonder why, or even if, she would want him to be thinking about her. She had no idea why he made her feel so strange. She did know that she did not want to feel whatever it was she was feeling. Zia did not understand the feelings she was experiencing, she had never felt this way before. She didn't want to feel that way at all. It scared her almost as much as her dreams and she knew even less about it.

She closed her eyes for a moment. She tried to clear her mind and focus on the task at hand, finding out the exact location of where they were. She did not know what she and Yartu would do afterward. Zia knew he probably would have some sort of plan. A plan that included where they would go and what they would do. Yartu was always prepared for everything. She had always been able to depend on him to make the best decisions concerning their well-being. This made her wonder how much longer they would be traveling in Shadow's company. The agreement they had made was for him to lead them to the nearest town and he had done as promised. They now stood on the edge of the town's boundaries.

Zia was not sure what she was supposed to do. She knew that Yartu would want her to just leave Shadow where he was standing and move on with their lives. She was not sure if that was what *she* wanted. Shadow was a mystery to her; she understood nothing about him, and the longer they were together the more enigmatic he became. Her curiosity was getting the better of her. She wanted to know more about him. It would of course be impossible for her to learn more about him if they went their separate ways now. Zia was finding it very difficult to decide if she should trust Yartu's judgment and leave Shadow behind or ask him to continue traveling with them. Fortunately, the decision was made for her.

"This is where we part ways. The people here will help you with whatever you may need. They may not seem the friendliest sort but if you explain that you are lost they will help you find your way to wherever it is you wish to go." Shadow did not look her in the eyes when he spoke, nor did he look towards the town. He seemed as if he just wanted to go away, and he appeared quite uncomfortable.

"You have to go now?" she asked tentatively. Zia realized she did not want him to leave. She may have had problems with him in the beginning but she thought things had changed. For some strange reason she felt they were similar in many ways. In what ways she did not know, but she wanted to find out.

Shadow glanced her way and nodded. "You should be alright from here on. I know there were problems but it was nice while it lasted. You and your dragon take care. I hope you find whatever it is you're searching for."

Zia was a bit surprised by what he said. She gave him a small smile. "It *was* nice. Thank you for all of your help, Yartu and I would never have made it this far without you."

"My life got a little crazy after I met *you*, I can't possibly imagine the effect *I* had on you." The breathtaking smile returned to his beautiful face, "If it is alright with you I would rather we do not meet again. You stay out of my life and I'll stay out of yours. It would probably be safer for the both of us that way."

"I agree completely. We seem to be nothing but trouble for each other. Yartu and I really are grateful to you for getting us this far. You are right, though, we should part ways here. Once again, thank you for all of your help. Goodbye." She started strongly but her goodbye was spoken softly. He was right, she knew that, but it did not change the fact she wanted him to stay with her and Yartu. She wished it did.

He said nothing more. He nodded his head in acknowledgement, turned and walked away. Zia watched him leave, disappointed with herself for wanting him to stay, and saddened by the fact that she would never see him again. It was the first time Zia ever had to watch someone leave her. Normally she was the one doing the leaving. She did not expect it to hurt so much—after all, she barely knew him. It wasn't supposed to be this way, she wasn't supposed to grow attached, she knew better. People were always coming and going in her life, she was used to that. So why did it bother her this time? What made this strange and beautiful young man different? Why did he matter when no one else before him had mattered? It was too much for her to think about at the moment. She had to focus on the situation at hand, and that was exactly what she did.

CHAPTER 10

Zia walked into the town. She did not worry about Yartu, for he blended almost perfectly into her hair. The townspeople watched her approach with suspicion in their eyes. They knew she did not belong there almost as much as she did. Zia tried vainly to find a welcoming face among all the people she saw pass her by. None of them stopped what they were doing to ask if she was alright or needed help, they all ignored her. That is until she walked by, then they watched her go and whispered to their neighbor about who she might be and what she might be doing there.

Whispers: Zia was getting tired of whispers. All her life she had heard whispers. What a strange looking child, doesn't she ever go outside, look how pale, I wonder if she is sick, she could use some sun. Everybody was always whispering about her, though they never said anything directly to her face. She wished they did, it would have made her feel less strange, as if that was even possible.

"Someone is watching us," a voice murmured into her ear.

Watching them? Every single person in town was watching them. Zia knew Yartu would not have said anything if it wasn't important. She discreetly looked about, trying to find the person who was watching her. Every pair of eyes she met fell away from her gaze—that was, all but one.

Hazel eyes met hers. They belonged to a young man who looked to be a few years older than she was. He was handsome—he did not possess the strange kind of beauty that Shadow did, but he was still attractive. He watched her openly and did not shy away from her gaze. He did not look like the other townspeople; she wondered if he might be a traveler just passing through. Zia debated with herself as to whether or not she should ask him for assistance.

It seemed as if the man had sensed her thoughts, for he walked over to where she stood. "You look like you might be lost. Need some directions?"

Zia wondered if her face showed the relief she felt inside. Finally, someone would help her and Yartu get out of this miserable town.

The man smiled. "Guess I was right. It is really easy to get lost in this place. Don't worry, I'll help you."

"Thank you. I do not even know where I am." Zia was extremely grateful that someone was willing to help her.

"Here is an annoyingly remote area about two weeks north of Selia, if you know where that is."

Zia was surprised that they were still so close to Selia. "I would think that Selia would be farther away. This does not look anything like it could belong anywhere near the city."

The man nodded in agreement. "It would seem that way. Like I said before, though, this place is about two weeks north of Selia. Well... north and a bit to the east. You have to cross through that small mountain range to get here. It is a fairly dangerous journey and most don't even attempt it because what's over on this side of the mountains is worse than the trip to get here. You have to be somewhat insane to even want to come here."

Zia was slightly confused by what the man was saying. She knew of the mountains, she had seen them on her way to Selia. She had heard that there were some very small settlements on the other side, but it was crazy to go there. If the mountain pass did not kill you, once you got through to the opposite side, the near-constant storms would. She had not expected this to be what lay beyond the mountains. A strange inhospitable land that was so completely different from the gentle rolling hills, picturesque landscape, and beautiful expanses of ocean that surrounded Selia.

"I guess that makes us both insane, then." The comment was completely random, she meant nothing by it. It was an involuntary response to what the man had said although it seemed to have amused him.

"Perhaps you are right. I know quite a few people who would agree with you. Ironic that *you*, someone I've just met, would come to the same conclusion." A smile came across the man's face.

Zia did not like the look of his smile. Truthfully it was more of a smirk. It made her think twice about how helpful this man might truly be. She wondered how he would benefit from assisting her. She did not believe that he was just being friendly. There was something in it for him, and she wanted to know what it was. It was all too easy, she was lost and there he was ready to help her. She would not deny that he was handsome and charming, but he was too charming and too handsome. Zia became very wary, but she did not let it show.

The man extended his hand to her. "I'm Nicolai."

"Zia Amarra." She had no reason to lie to him, but she also had no reason to trust him. She did shake his hand to keep up the appearance that she was willing to trust him even though she had absolutely no intention of doing so.

There was something wrong with what he said and did. He made her want to trust him. He used his charm and promised to help her. Everything about him invited her in, his voice, his physical appeal, his charm. He was too good to be true, he appeared to be trustworthy but something about him screamed at her to run away. Zia started to get a sinking feeling in the pit of her stomach. *Trust no one but the shadows.* The words spoken to her in her dream suddenly came back to her.

"Zia is an interesting name, not one you hear every day. You are not from this area, are you?" He was smiling this time, no smirk. It did not make her uneasiness disappear.

She tilted her head to the side and arched her eyebrows, "If I was I am fairly sure that I would not need your help finding out where I am."

"Very true. I don't know the name of this wretched little village, never bothered to find out, but I do know where we are. What you want to know depends on where you are going."

Zia closed her eyes and shook her head, "I don't care where I go just as long as it is far from here."

"I know how you feel. My friend and I are actually heading back to Selia. You could come with us if you like."

His proposal stunned her. She barely knew him and yet here he was offering to let her accompany him and his friend on their way to Selia. Was this what he wanted? Why did he want her to go with him? None of it made any sense.

"I am not sure. I have no desire to return to Selia, I have already seen it. I was thinking of going somewhere else. I'm not sure where, but I want to see more of the world than Selia and this place."

He nodded his head, "You thought—oh, no, I meant you could come with us as far as you wanted. You don't have to come all the way to Selia. I understand what you mean about wanting to see the rest of the world. Selia is not everything, regardless of what some people may think."

Something in the tone of his voice made her wonder once more about him. He had started to talk in a normal tone but when he began to speak about Selia he seemed to grow very annoyed. Zia did not let it bother her although she did wonder why he seemed so annoyed by a city.

He had offered to let her come with him as far as she wanted. Was it worth traveling with someone she had just met and risking her and Yartu's safety? Zia could not decide what to do. If she was to travel with strangers there really was no choice but to hide Yartu, even though she knew he would complain about it. There was no obvious downside to going with Nicolai. However, something inside of her kept telling her to stay away from him, that he was not to be trusted. His charming persona was merely an illusion. His handsome face a mask to conceal something ugly. His eyes were what gave him away; cold and unfeeling they held no light, hidden in their depths lay something sinister.

She had no choice, it mattered not what she thought she saw. Maybe she was just imagining things. How could someone who appeared so kind and helpful be as bad as she felt he was? Nicolai had a friendly approachable face, was that a crime? She did not know him, so who was she to judge? He seemed nice enough. What other choice did she have? None.

"I understand if you are a bit uneasy traveling with me, but I assure you no harm will come to you. I'm actually not that bad a person." That smirk had returned, "You can ask Crystal if you want. We will take good care of you, don't worry. So how about it?"

"Crystal?" Zia was confused. Was this Crystal his friend?

Nicolai's smirk stayed in place, "My companion. She is a bit eccentric if that's what you want to call it. In fact, most people do. She's not that bad, got quite a temper but that's about it. She should be here any moment if you want to wait and meet her before you agree to anything." The kind, friendly smile returned to his face. This time it erased all feelings of anxiety. She even gave him a small smile in return.

"No, I do not need to wait. I believe I will take you up on your offer. You have been the only person here who seems to be helpful in any way and I am most eager to leave this depressing place." Zia spoke the truth. She had barely even spent an hour in town and already she wanted desperately to get as far away from it as possible. Nicolai was the only way she could find her way back to somewhere more civilized.

"Nicolai, you no good miserable excuse of a man. How dare you just walk off and leave me alone like that? You know how much I despise these worthless people who are actually crazy enough to want to live in a place like this. All they do is stare at me with their mouths hanging wide open. Do you have any idea how close I came to shutting a few of them permanently?" The voice was full of anger and belonged to a woman. Zia wondered if this was the Crystal that Nicolai had mentioned.

The woman marched right up to Nicolai and glared at him as if she was expecting an apology. Zia got the feeling she would not accept it even if he did. The woman was rather odd looking, her steel gray hair and gaunt face did not match her seemingly youthful body. Her eyes were not tired and dull but bright and appeared to see much and forget nothing. She appeared both young and old at the same time. It baffled Zia to no end.

The woman put her hands on her hips. "Well? Are you going to say something or just stand there stupidly?"

Nicolai laughed, and a strange sound it was too, an empty hollow laugh that carried no emotion. It made Zia wonder once more about him. "I would, but I fear you would permanently shut my mouth too."

The woman nodded in agreement. "I probably would, now that I think about it. If I did I would be doing the rest of the world a favor. You like to talk far more than you should. Some people may like all that charm but I've seen you at your worst, you wretched boy. You not being able to talk anymore might be a good thing." The words were meant to be harsh but Zia could hear genuine affection in them.

"You're probably right." He shook his head. A quick glance in Zia's direction brought that smirk once again to his face. "Crystal, this is Zia Amarra. Zia, this is Crystal."

The woman raised her brow inquisitively, "Zia, eh?" A knowing smile played across her lips.

Something once again put Zia on guard. "It is a pleasure to meet you, Crystal."

"Good gods, at last someone here has some manners. It is good to meet you as well." It seemed as if Crystal had a flair for the dramatic, Zia thought with a small smile.

"I have offered to let Zia come with us on our way back to Selia. She agreed, so it seems someone else will have to suffer the abuse I've had to deal with." The look Nicolai cast in Crystal's direction was rather odd. There was some unspoken understanding that passed between the two.

Zia had not noticed the two and their strange silent exchange. She had been distracted by a slight shift of Yartu's body. She hoped he would stay hidden beneath her hair, out of sight. She was about to return her attention to Crystal and Nicolai when a strange sensation overcame her. It felt as though she was being watched, which seemed rather ridiculous because almost every person in the town had been staring at her. This was different, though. She was being spied on, she could feel it. It was not at all like the innocent curiosity of the villagers—this was something else entirely. Zia felt like she was being hunted, whomever it was that was watching her was the hunter and she was most definitely the prey. She did not like the thought that she was being observed by some unseen stalker.

CHAPTER II

The sound of her name brought her attention back to the others. "Zia, if you are ready, we should probably head out now. If we stay much longer Crystal is likely to destroy the town." Nicolai smiled to show that he was teasing.

A smile and nod of her head were her only response. As the three of them walked out of the town, Zia cast a glance over her shoulder wondering again if she was being watched or if it was just her imagination. She saw nothing, but did that mean that no one was there? Stop it, she told herself silently, you will just make things worse. Paranoia was slowly creeping up on her. It had been ever since that hilltop where she had watched Shadow walk away from her. She did not know why but she had felt safe with him. She knew nothing about him but something made her think he was not so different from her. Shadow had been enigmatic and rather distant, preferring to keep to himself, and yet Zia had been more willing to trust him than she was Nicolai. This made no sense to her at all. Nicolai was the kind of person one was supposed to trust whereas Shadow was the kind of person she should have been wary of. So why was it the other way around?

It was all too much for her to figure out. Zia knew that thinking about it much longer would drive her insane. All she had to do was stay with Nicolai and Crystal until she was on the other side of the mountains. Then she would be on her way with Yartu to the next inn where they would stay until it became time to move on yet again.

"Do you think she knows?" Crystal quietly questioned Nicolai.

He glanced at Zia momentarily before he returned his attention to Crystal, "She doesn't have a clue. It would be shocking if she assumed the truth. She may be a bit unsure about us at the moment but still she came, didn't she?"

"Nicolai, I don't know. There is something wrong with her. I am beginning to understand Lady Yena's fear of her. Just looking at her makes me uncomfortable. I can sense a power in her, but it is one I can't comprehend." Crystal had not meant to reveal so much to Nicolai but she couldn't stand it anymore. The girl was definitely odd. Crystal had been on edge ever since she had laid eyes on Zia.

The girl was so pale it appeared as if she had never seen the sun in her entire life. Her long hair was as black as a starless night and her blue eyes had strange streaks of silver in them, almost like lightning flashing through a storm cloud. It was not her appearance that unsettled Crystal, at least not much. Crystal could sense a strange power dwelling deep inside of the girl, and she wondered if Zia even knew about it. It was highly doubtful, and yet... what was it that Nicolai had told her about the girl and the unusual events that had occurred when she met the Magic

Council? Maybe the girl's power was awakening; if it was, Crystal had a feeling that she would want to be as far away from Zia Amarra as possible. What scared the Magic Council and Lady Yena was not good for a witch either. Crystal considered herself a sensible and rational witch, but something about Zia made her fearful, which of course made her worry even more.

Nicolai's trademark smirk showed up once again, "Crystal, you are worrying about nothing. We know about her *strange* power, we have known for quite some time."

"I know that," Crystal snapped, "We know she has a strange power. We just don't know what it is. That's what worries me. It is unlike anything I have ever come up against."

The smirk stayed in place. "Don't let it bother you. If anything happens, I will protect you."

"Nicolai, the hero? I would be safer with Lady Yena guarding my back." Crystal wanted nothing more than to swipe that awful smirk right off his face. To make matters worse she knew he was right, she would be safe with him, but she would never admit it.

Nicolai had helped her out of many a difficult situation when she had thought there was no hope for her. He was extremely useful when one was in trouble. The worse things got the better off you were normally, the only problem was figuring out whether he was on your side. Nicolai was an extremely dangerous man who enjoyed keeping everyone around him on edge. Many who placed their trust in Nicolai wound up dead, most of them by his hands. He would turn on just about anyone if the mood came over him. The man did whatever pleased him, and often there seemed to be no logical reason for it. Crystal knew otherwise; he did everything for a reason, though whatever the reason was he never told her. She knew she could trust him, at least to a certain extent. For some unknown reason he seemed to like her and possibly even trust her. Crystal knew she was the closest thing to a friend Nicolai had, but that was only because it suited him to have things that way. The witch knew that at any moment he could turn on her if he felt like it. She also knew that he would not blame her if she suddenly decided to do the same. It was a strange relationship the two had and oddly enough it seemed to work.

Zia had been so immersed in her own thoughts that she did not notice the quiet conversation going on in front of her. It surprised her when Crystal turned to her and told her that they were going to stop for the night. She did not realize that so much time had passed. The two did not ask for her help in preparing the camp, they managed everything quite efficiently on their own. Zia got the feeling she would only be in the way if she tried to help, so she did not even offer. She watched them as they went about setting things up; it was rather strange. Each seemed to know exactly what the other was supposed to do and did not bother with anything but what they were doing. It did not take long for everything to be ready.

"You can sit, you know. It has been a long day, and tomorrow will be even worse," Nicolai said with a smile.

Zia was glad it was just a smile and not that strange smirk of his. His smile was warm and inviting and banished all the terrible thoughts she had been having about him. "I am grateful to you both for inviting me to come with you. I do not believe that I would have made it very far if I had been on my own. You see, I am more used to traveling on the main roads, so I fear I would have been completely lost if it were not for you two. Even getting this far from the village would have proven difficult." She wanted them to know that she was appreciative of all their help, even if she had been thinking some horrible things about Nicolai. She was thankful he had offered to let her come.

His smile was her answer. "You don't have to thank us. I am actually glad you decided to join us. I think I would have lost my mind if I had to spend the whole trip back listening to Crystal complain. You at least grant me some measure of peace."

Zia was not sure what to say so she smiled in return. Crystal remained silent and just shook her head. Poor girl, so easily fooled by a handsome face and charming smile... if only she knew.

"What would you do if you knew the truth about him?" the witch wondered, muttering to herself so no one would hear her. "What could you do? You would not be able to overpower him. He is stronger and far more cunning than you. Where will you run when you finally discover the truth? Lady Yena has done something far worse than you could possibly imagine." The witch closed her eyes and hung her head in regret, "Even if you manage to escape him now, he will find you again, you will never be free of him. No matter where you run, no matter how far, he will be there waiting. Death would be more pleasant than to have Nicolai haunt you for the rest of your days. Be a good little girl and don't try to escape. Go to Selia and be the Magic Council's experiment, it is a far better fate than what awaits you should you run from him."

CHAPTER 12

The next two days were long and painful ones for Zia, who was unused to the harsh conditions of the area. She hurt everywhere and wished for nothing more than a long warm bath to cleanse her skin of the dirt she had accumulated on the road.

Worrying about Yartu did not help matters either. Shortly after they had left the town, he had left his hiding spot beneath Zia's hair to remain a secret from Crystal and Nicolai. She knew he was following her, she could feel his presence close by. There was another, though, something else was watching her besides Yartu. The same feeling she had of being hunted in the town was still there. Each move she made in every moment was being watched.

Hunted. Who would be hunting her and why? Regardless of how much she tried to figure it out she could not. Was it the Magic Council or something else? The thought that she was losing her mind kept returning to her. Of course, this was when she wasn't thinking of all her other problems. *Insanity.* She did not treasure the thought.

"Is something wrong?" Nicolai's question was a welcome distraction from the disturbing turn her thoughts were taking.

Zia shrugged her shoulders. "I am in more pain than I can ever remember."

She missed Crystal rolling her eyes as Nicolai's laugh filled the air. "This place is the worst when it comes to traveling. I think it is because no one is crazy enough to want to come here, so why make the roads safer and more accessible?" The sarcasm was clearly heard in his voice.

Zia felt herself smile in response, "You truly do not like this part of the country, do you?"

The smirk that always seemed to be ready to make an appearance showed up. Zia almost wished it hadn't. She had become accustomed to it but it still put her on edge for some reason. She liked his smile much better. "I hate this place more than you could possibly imagine."

"I can't see why."

"You have only been here for a few days. I have wasted more time in this vile place than I'd like to remember." He spoke casually but disdain and contempt oozed from every word.

Zia found herself wondering what would make him spend so much time in a place he so clearly detested. "Did you live here? I cannot imagine another reason why someone would be here."

Nicolai shook his head, "I understand why you might think I had lived here, and in a way I guess I did. I first came here a couple of years ago; unfortunately I was crazy enough to stay for a while."

"Do you mind if I ask why?"

He stopped walking for a moment, "I was looking for something. Someone asked me to find something for them."

Zia stopped next to him, "What were you looking for?"

"A person." The smirk disappeared. It was replaced by a cold and deadly look that frightened Zia.

A person, he had been searching for a person? She half expected him to say treasure; she had thought that Nicolai and Crystal were adventurers. She was unsure why but she wished he had said something other than person. All the strange thoughts that she had pushed out of her mind about Nicolai suddenly resurfaced. The uneasy feeling came back in a rush and she felt as if she was going to be sick. A part of her longed to see his friendly smile, she would have even accepted the smirk, anything but that terrible look. It transformed his handsome face into something cruel and terrifying.

"Why would you be looking for a person?" She spoke calmly, easily masking the fear she felt inside. Hiding her true emotions had always been a talent of hers. Zia had perfected early on in her life how to appear calm and in control when she was screaming on the inside.

The smirk reclaimed its rightful place upon Nicolai's handsome face. "For the usual reasons. It doesn't matter anyway; I didn't get what I wanted." He turned towards her and a smile replaced the smirk, once again dispelling all negative thoughts about him from Zia's mind. "We better catch up with Crystal. She is not likely to wait for us."

She nodded in agreement. They found Crystal not too far up the road. She was standing in the middle of the road with her arms crossed. She did not look pleased to see them.

"It took you long enough. Do you have any idea how long I have been waiting?" She glared at the both of them.

Nicolai rolled his eyes, "Always so dramatic. We were not that far behind you."

"Maybe our friend is not so far behind either." Crystal's comment caused concern. Nicolai kept his expression calm for he did not want Zia to become anxious.

"Friend? Is a friend of yours following us?" Maybe that was it, Zia thought, maybe that was the strange sensation she was having of being followed. Perhaps Crystal and Nicolai had forgotten a friend back at the town and they were trying to catch up.

"We don't have any friends, girl." Her remark did not make Zia as nervous as it should have.

Zia was mainly concerned about the fact that she felt someone seemed to be following them. Part of her was relieved that Crystal had noticed it too, that meant it was a real person and not her imagination.

"How far?" Nicolai asked. He wondered why Zia did not ask more questions or why she did not panic. Most girls her age would have if they found out they were being followed, but then again Zia was not most girls.

"Too close."

"We can't do anything yet. Whoever it is has lasted this long so we might as well wait for him to show himself."

Crystal shook her head vehemently, "I don't like it, Nicolai. We can't just stand around and twiddle our thumbs waiting, it'll be disastrous. That person might just want to kill us, did you think about that?"

Nicolai raised a hand to rub at his temple in a bored gesture, "Yes, I have. If they wanted to kill us, they would have tried to do so by now. Whoever it is wants something else."

"The girl?"

This got Zia's attention, "What do you mean?" The Magic Council immediately came to mind. Were they searching for her?

"Nothing. Crystal has a tendency to overreact, don't pay any attention to her." He gave her a reassuring smile. It did not work.

Zia was getting that feeling again and this time it was accompanied by the feeling that her companions were hiding something from her. "I want to know what is going on, and now. You do not seem surprised that someone is following us, and if either of you know who it is or why they are there I want to know. Crystal would not suggest that our unseen stalker is after me if she did not believe it was so. I want answers and I want them now."

The witch snorted, "Not too demanding, is she?"

"And, unfortunately for her, far too clever." Nicolai smirked at Zia, which caused her to take a few cautioned steps back. "In response to your question, no, we do not know who is following us or why they are doing so. What is going on is a completely different story."

Zia tried to remain calm. Her mind was once again screaming at her to run away as fast as possible. Don't trust anyone, the words from her dreams kept coming back to her, don't trust anyone. Her mind was reeling. "What kind of story?" She was surprised that the words came out as steadily as they did.

That evil smirk stayed in place, "The story about a girl and how she escaped the Magic Council. Where's Yartu, Zia?"

Her eyes went wide. Yartu. They knew about Yartu. The Magic Council had sent them to find her and Yartu. "You... you work for the Magic Council." Her voice was shaky; she could feel herself start to fall apart on the inside.

"I do not work for the Magic Council," Nicolai practically shouted at her, making her jump in the process.

He seemed to enjoy seeing her nervous. Zia would have become even more distressed if she knew just how much he liked the fact he had upset her. Why not have some fun before I return her to Lady Yena? he thought. This girl made his life hell; the last thing he had wanted to do was get involved with the Magic Council again, but because of her he had. She had inconvenienced him. Now it was time to make her suffer as much as he.

"Lady Yena hired me against her better judgment to find you. She thought you were troublesome, so she assigned me to come after you. You see, Zia, you are going back to Selia whether you like it or not. That is what we are doing right now." His words seemed intended to mock her and at the same time frighten her. It worked.

Zia was shocked at how easily and quickly the charming façade faded from sight. She did not like what was underneath. Everything she had felt was true. [Run,] a voice inside her mind insisted. She shook her head, trying desperately to sort everything out.

"Oh, poor little Zia Amarra; is it that hard for you all alone without your dragon? Didn't your parents ever tell you not to talk to strangers? Here is the perfect example of why you should not go off with strangers. They just might be taking you to the Magic Council. Whatever will you do, Zia?" Nicolai was taunting her and enjoying it immensely.

"Nicolai, now is not the time. We have to get going. We still have someone following us, don't forget." Crystal was worried, someone was out there and they did not know what they wanted. It was dangerous to stay in one place for too long, especially in this wild land. That was not what worried her the most. Nicolai had been developing a deep and powerful resentment and hatred of Zia while they had been looking for her. It only seemed to intensify once they had finally met the girl. Now he was unleashing all of the pent-up anger that had been simmering below the surface for days. It was not a good time for this and, to make things worse, the witch was beginning to think the girl was not going to make it to Selia if Nicolai kept going on the way he was. Nicolai was difficult to handle and extremely dangerous when he got like this. Crystal almost felt sorry for the girl, she was just standing there with her eyes tightly shut shaking her head in denial, as he kept telling her horrible things about what the Magic Council was going to do to her. How they would separate her from her dragon and how much it would hurt. The witch wondered how the girl kept from crying.

Zia did not cry because her mind was reeling and it took all of her strength to keep her thoughts from overpowering her. It was so hard to remain in control, she wanted to scream. Don't trust anyone, her dreams had warned. The words kept running through her mind over and over again. Nicolai's voice cut through her thoughts like a knife, causing pain. Where was Yartu? It was too much—she could not hold on anymore. The world was crashing down all around her and she was falling, there was only air, she was drowning, she could not breathe. Darkness began to envelop her.

# CHAPTER 13

[Run,] the voice inside her head said again. [Damn you, just run.] The voice was annoying her. It fought the darkness, refusing to let her slip away in its embrace.

Leave me alone, she told it.

[No, if you don't get out of your mind you are truly lost.]

What do you mean? she asked. The darkness was once again pulling at her, welcoming her, offering her an escape.

[Fight it! Don't go with it, things will only get worse if you do.]

It wants to help me. I can go far away, somewhere no one will ever find me.

[You won't even be able to find you.]

I do not understand.

[Your mind is broken. If you go with it now, you will be not be able to regain yourself. You are not strong enough to fight it. It will consume you.]

Consume me?

[You will be lost to the darkness. Your body will become an empty shell while your consciousness slowly fades away into nothingness.]

It wants to kill me.

[No, it simply wants you. It does not understand the concept of life and death, the darkness is eternal.]

Why does it want me?

[I don't know. Damn it, we do not have time for this. You have to focus, don't let the promises of the darkness seduce you. Fight it and, when you break free of the confines of your mind, run.]

Zia tried to fight it. She tried to break free of its hold, but she could not. *I can't, it is too powerful,* she told the voice.

[Wonderful, more for me to do.] The voice was not only annoying but seemed to be quite sarcastic.

Zia felt the darkness pull away suddenly. Something was holding it back, keeping it away from her. The chaos that was her mind only moments before disappeared. Things were returning to normal.

Her eyes flew open. She saw Nicolai and Crystal; neither seemed to have noticed that anything had happened to her. They also appeared to be in the same place they had been in before she had closed her eyes. How much time had passed? she wondered. Did the strange conversation she had with that mysterious voice inside her mind really happen? I am losing my mind, she thought.

Nicolai reached out and grabbed her arm. Zia let out a small gasp of pain when he pulled her toward him. "Are you listening to me? I really hate being ignored." Zia could hear the threatening undertone in his words.

[Run; this time I really mean it.]

This time Zia obeyed the voice's command. The small dagger she kept hidden was in her hand in the blink of an eye. She slashed Nicolai's arm and as he cursed in pain and glanced at the wound, Zia pulled her arm out of his grasp. She did not hesitate for a moment. The instant her arm was free she turned and ran as fast as she could.

"Crystal, get her!" Nicolai shouted as he began to run after Zia.

The witch was already in motion; she spoke the words for one of her spells. While she was busy doing that Nicolai had almost caught up with Zia. She was infuriatingly fast, but he was the faster. The terrain itself seemed to be working against her and aiding him.

Zia's entire body ached and the constant stumbling slowed her more than she wanted. She knew she would not be able to outrun Nicolai in the open. He was used to this land; she had to use it against him as best she could. She noticed the forest was not too far away. If only she could make it that far. She turned towards the trees all the while trying to figure out how she would escape him.

Zia was only a few feet away from the forest when she fell to the ground hard. Nicolai was almost upon her, his sword drawn. She tried desperately to get up but her efforts were in vain. He advanced slowly, knowing she was defenseless; he wanted to make sure she knew that great pain awaited her.

"It seems you are not immune to the spells of a witch. Let's see how you are against steel." His trademark smirk seemed to make him even more threatening, for Zia now knew what it was that was hidden behind it, cruelty and hate.

Crystal walked calmly to his side but did not stop him, "Don't kill her, Lady Yena wants her alive. Try not to make it too messy. We still have to get her to Selia."

"I won't hurt her that much; just enough to keep her from running away again."

Zia did not know what he meant, nor did she wish to find out. She tried again to get up, but it was useless, she could not even move. She could do nothing but watch as he raised his sword. She closed her eyes for only a moment, wishing Yartu was there with her. Cursing and the sound of flapping wings made her open her eyes.

Yartu had flown out of his hiding place in the forest to rush to Zia's aid. He attacked the man who was trying to hurt his Zia. No one hurt Zia. The miniature dragon was a flurry of leathery wings and sharp talons that searched for whatever tender human flesh was closest. The human did a frustratingly good job at protecting himself from the dragon's assault. Yartu fought valiantly but to no avail; he managed to keep Nicolai away from Zia for only a few moments. Crystal cast a spell to immobilize him. It worked only long enough for Nicolai to knock the miniature dragon to the ground. The witch was surprised that it did not have a more lasting effect, as it had with Zia.

Zia could only watch as Yartu tried to protect her from Nicolai and Crystal. Nicolai had hit Yartu so hard when he fell to the ground she felt as if her heart had been ripped out of her body. No, she thought, this was not how it was supposed to be. She would not let this happen. She had to get to Yartu. She struggled against the spell, trying as hard as she could to reach her dragon's side. Zia cried out when Nicolai stepped on one of Yartu's fragile wings. The pain was excruciating but it did something to her, and somewhere deep inside of herself she found the strength she needed.

"Nicolai, she's moving," the witch shouted.

He spun around to face Zia standing. It was not possible; Crystal's spells normally lasted much longer. It didn't matter, he thought, as long as he had Yartu he was in control. The dragon's pain had to be getting to her, Nicolai had broken his wing. Zia was not a threat; he had won.

Zia was not sure what she was going to do, she only knew she had to do something. Her dagger would be useless against Nicolai, who had a sword, and obviously knew how to wield it. It didn't matter. She had to get Yartu away from him. She knew failure was inevitable, both she and Yartu would be taken to Selia where they would be separated forever. She also knew she would not let Nicolai take them without putting up a fight; she would cause more trouble than she was worth. It did not matter anymore, her whole world was about to be destroyed because of that deceitful and cruel man. She would make him feel all the pain he was going to inflict upon her and her precious Yartu. Zia just wished she knew how.

Nicolai noticed her dagger was in her hand once again. Her entire body was trembling—from pain or fear, he neither knew, nor cared. "Are you going to fight me, Zia Amarra? I thought you were smarter than that."

"I will do what I must." Her voice was trembling just like the rest of her, yet the words held a certain strength.

He laughed, "Just be a good girl and do as you're told. If you do, I might not hurt your little lizard anymore. You see, I can be nice." The last was more to Crystal than to Zia.

"I would listen to him if I were you, girl. That is the nicest he is going to get," the witch warned.

Zia looked at Yartu lying helplessly on the ground, his limp broken wing spread out beside him. The fire burning inside of those shimmering red eyes told her all she needed to know. "When I want your advice, I will ask for it, witch." She spoke with conviction and the look in Yartu's eyes further convinced her she had made the right decision.

"Fine. I almost wish you hadn't said that, for your sake. It will be more troublesome for me this way, but far more fun." The smirk promised her a great deal of suffering. He walked to her slowly, making her tense up in anticipation of the pain he had promised. Zia waited for the blow. It came but it did not land on her.

The moment Nicolai raised his sword, a dark figure suddenly rushed in front of her. The sword struck air and nothing else. It brought the image of Yartu hitting what could only be described as an invisible wall of air to Zia's mind. While Nicolai tried to recover, a booted foot connected with his chest, causing him to reel backwards. Crystal rushed to his aid but fell to the ground for no apparent reason.

The dark figure glanced over his shoulder at Zia. "Get Yartu. Take him into the forest. Go! Now!" Zia would have done as he said except for the fact that she was in shock.

Shadow. He was there. He was helping her. For some reason her mind kept thinking that he had come to rescue her. She did not like that; she did not need anyone to rescue her.

He looked at her again and threw his hands up in disgust. Shadow hurried to Yartu, picked him up and ran back to Zia. "Go, damn you. Don't you ever listen?" he said as he thrust Yartu into her arms.

"It's you!" Nicolai had finally noticed who it was that had come to Zia's aid.

Shadow turned back to meet his eyes, and Zia felt as if Nicolai and Shadow somehow knew each other. "Zia, go now!" he shouted.

This time Zia did listen. She ran as quickly as possible to the trees only a short distance away. She held Yartu as close as his injured wing would allow, cradling him in her arms. As she ran, she heard the sounds of fighting behind her as well as chanting. Zia realized the witch was about to cast a spell. She prepared herself for whatever the witch was about to throw at her. Instead she heard the words for the spell turn into a colorful string of curses.

She made it to the forest, surprisingly without any incidents. Zia turned as the trees formed a barrier between her and the fight going on behind her. What she saw amazed her. Shadow had somehow managed to gain the upper hand in the battle. She watched as he effortlessly held off Crystal while still managing to keep Nicolai at bay. Every spell the witch threw at him seemed to have no effect. Nicolai seemed to be faring better than his companion, although not by much.

All of Nicolai's attacks were masterfully avoided by Shadow, who even managed to get a few shots in himself. Shadow used no weapons other than his fists and feet, and those seemed dangerous enough. Zia did not want to know what would have happened if he had a real weapon. Each punch and kick somehow succeeded in connecting to a body part. It was all too strange, for even when he did not physically touch Crystal she was still falling down and acting as if she was being attacked. It was as if some unseen force was focusing on keeping her occupied long enough to prevent her from casting any spells. The witch was definitely not doing as well as Nicolai was; every time she tried to get up she was knocked back down.

A swift and powerful kick to Nicolai's abdomen made him stagger backwards, his breath coming in short ragged breaths. Shadow did not wait for him to recover, he ran swiftly to the forest's edge where Zia was waiting.

"Come on," he said as he slowed down to a walk, "They won't follow us in here."

Zia looked back for a moment past the trees to where Crystal and Nicolai were now both standing. She felt as if

Nicolai could see her, although it would be almost impossible for him to do so considering how close the trees were to each other. She could see the anger and hate in his hazel eyes. All his hate and rage was focused on one thing, her. She was not sure how she knew this. Zia only knew that Nicolai would not let her get away that easily. He would come after her. She understood that she was now indeed the prey and Nicolai the hunter. Her gut instinct told her that he would never stop until he had her in his grasp. A chill ran down her spine. She turned and followed Shadow deeper into the dark forest.

CHAPTER 14

"Are we going after her or not?" Crystal asked Nicolai once again. He had not moved at all since the girl and her mysterious rescuer had disappeared into the forest. He was actually starting to worry her.

He shook his head, "We can't follow them in there. It is too dangerous." Not now, not yet. They had to wait, be patient. If she didn't come out then he would follow her into the forest, but until then he would wait.

"What do you mean? Is that it? Are we just going to give up?"

Nicolai met the witch's gaze and, when he spoke, it was eerily calm, far calmer than he ever sounded. "We are not giving up. That forest is cursed, no one knows their way around it. They cannot stay in there for long or they will be lost in the forest forever. He knows this. He will stay in there only as long as he has to. The dragon will also need healing. She will not let him go without treatment. They will come out eventually and we will be waiting."

Crystal did not like the way he was acting. It was not like him. Nicolai was never at a loss, or if he was it never lasted more than a moment, not like now. "Nicolai, do you know who that man was?

"Shadow." There was no emotion in his voice when he said the name.

"The boy you were tracking down a few years ago?" Impossible, the witch thought. Nicolai had told her about a strange boy he had spent two whole years trying to find. He had said he had gotten close a few times but the boy had always managed to escape. Nicolai had informed her that the boy had displayed unusual abilities. Crystal had not believed him at the time, but now she understood a bit more. He can move things without touching them, Nicolai told her. He had also spoken of other things he had seen the boy do that could not be explained. "What is he doing with the girl?"

"I don't know. He does nothing without a reason. She must be of some importance to him for him to help her like that. He is not the heroic type." Nicolai was not answering Crystal's question, he was just thinking aloud.

"Do you think it might be the same reason Lady Yena wants her?" she asked.

He turned away from her to gaze into the distance, not really looking at anything in particular. "Maybe. It is not like him to do something like this. He normally stays away from people, he is almost completely antisocial. He must have been the one following us. There is no other explanation as to why he was here. If he had just happened to come along he would have turned around and gone in the other direction."

"Do you think it was you he was following?"

"No. He was tracking her."

"How can you be so certain?" Crystal questioned.

Nicolai glanced back at the forest. "I know. He wants her, for whatever reason I don't know, but he would not have interfered unless she was important to him. Me, he would have run from the second he saw me, old habit."

Crystal seemed to be content with that for an answer, Nicolai was glad for he would have offered no other and he was not in the mood to argue with her at the moment.

"What is it you want with her, Shadow? Who is she to you?" he whispered to the trees and the young man hidden within them. He glanced down to his arm; blood still flowed from the wound she had inflicted, and it would scar. He wanted it to. It would serve as a constant reminder of her. "Run while you can, you will soon grow tired and when you do I will be there. He will not be able to keep you safe from me. You are mine, Zia Amarra. Your new friend won't be able to save you. No one can."

Shadow had not spoken a single word to Zia or Yartu since they had left the forest's edge. She wished he would have said something, anything that would explain how and why he had been there to help her. Zia also wanted to stop for a moment, not just because she was tripping over everything in the forest, but for Yartu. They had been walking for a while and every time she lost her balance she could feel the acute pain that shot through Yartu. She needed to examine his wing. It was never a good thing when a dragon's wing was broken. It was extremely painful and could cause serious problems to their balance and overall health. Zia was not about to let anything happen to Yartu.

"Shadow, can we please stop?" she asked, more like begged.

He ignored her. Shadow did not seem overly concerned with either one of them. Wonderful, that is some rescuer we have, she thought. He did not even glance back to see if she and Yartu were alright. The strange young man acted as if he had forgotten about them completely. Zia had had it, she was tired, sore, and worried about Yartu, she was not in the mood to be ignored. She sat down right where she was standing.

Shadow stopped walking as if he knew she was not following him. He ran a hand through his hair in annoyance. "Why did you stop?"

"Oh, you noticed, I am so flattered," she said sweetly.

He turned towards her. "Sarcasm is not going to help you."

"No? Such a shame. It did seem to get your attention." Zia was tired of being nice.

He raised a brow in response, "I was not aware you were so desperate to get my attention. I guess it is my turn to be flattered." He spoke just as sweetly as she had and with even more innocence.

Zia's eyes narrowed as she glared at him. "Considering the fact that you have been ignoring me ever since you showed up I should think that flattery is not to be expected. I am tired and have no idea where we are. Yartu's wing is broken and I need to know how bad the break actually is. We need to stop, if only for a moment, I should think that was obvious. Perhaps you had not noticed our injuries, or that I have been stumbling over tree branches and roots, making Yartu even more uncomfortable than he already is. Since you do not appear to notice or care about us or our well-being I decided to take matters into my own hands."

He came over to her and crouched down to examine Yartu. "It's not that I have not noticed you both are injured, I just wanted to get you away from him." He paused for a moment, "You taking matters into your own hands is not a good thing, look what happened last time. I leave you and you end up with *him*, you should not be trusted to make your own decisions."

"How dare you?" She could barely speak she was so angry, yet the words still managed to find a way to escape. "We had agreed to go our separate ways, do not act as though you have done me some great service by coming to my assistance back there. I had no choice but to go with Nicolai and Crystal, there was no one else who seemed willing to help Yartu and I get out of this miserable godforsaken land. How was I supposed to know they were after me? You sit there as if this was all some minor inconvenience, like this is my fault. If you were so concerned with who I would get to help me once I got to town then you should have suggested someone you thought reputable or offered to assist me yourself."

Her words seemed to have hit their mark. The beautiful young man lowered his gaze to the ground. "You are right. I should have tried to get you away from him the moment I recognized him. You would have been spared a great deal of pain and trouble and Yartu's wing would be fine. I am the one at fault, not you." He spoke softly, his voice filled with shame.

Zia began to feel bad for him, she had been rather harsh. She had not expected him to react the way he did, it surprised her. Something was bothering her, though. "You know Nicolai?"

His dark eyes met hers. "Yes."

"How? I mean...," She trailed off, unsure of what it was she was trying to ask exactly or if he would even tell her.

"He was after me a few years ago, much like he is after you now."

Zia remembered what Nicolai had said about why he knew this area so well. "You are the person he was looking for?"

Shadow nodded, "I never found out the real reason he was after me. I didn't really want to get close enough again to ask. I haven't seen him in three years either. You must have done something to upset someone a lot for him to be tracking you."

Zia buried her face in her hands, "It is complicated."

"It's not as if we don't have time to sort it out. You and I are stuck with each other for the moment whether we like it or not." He smiled and Zia felt her heart skip a beat.

"Do you know anything about mending broken wings?" she asked.

"Not as much as I should, given the current situation." He reached out and ran a gentle finger along Yartu's injured wing. The miniature dragon did not even flinch. He barely felt it or anything else.

Zia was so worried about him. "Please, if you can do anything to help him, I do not know anything about healing, I..." She lost the words, unable to find the right ones. She pulled Yartu closer to her, hoping that somehow, she could offer him some small amount of comfort. Unshed tears glistened in her eyes.

Shadow placed a hand on her shoulder. "I have some experience with mending the wings of birds. I know a dragon is completely different from a bird but I could still try if you want me to and if Yartu will let me."

She wanted to throw her arms around him and cry. "He will not mind, if you can help."

The young man flashed his dazzling smile at her, "You're sure? I am not Yartu's most favorite person in the world."

Zia gave him a small smile. "You just might become it if you are able to fix his wing."

"All the more reason to do it, then."

She gently placed an almost unconscious Yartu in the young man's arms. She watched him examine the wound for a few moments. She desperately hoped that he could mend Yartu's wing, the miniature dragon would be devastated if he was unable to fly again. If his wing healed the wrong way flight would prove impossible. Zia wished for her dragon's sake that Shadow would be able to help.

Watching him tend Yartu's wing Zia noticed she was more comfortable around the young man than she had been previously. She was grateful to him for saving her, far more than she would have admitted. Showing up the way he had, though, made her wonder. How was it that he was there at the exact moment she had needed him? Her thoughts began to center on the sensation she had that she was being followed. Was Shadow the one who had been following her? He had said that he should have warned her about Nicolai the moment he saw her with him. Did that mean that he had seen her talking to Nicolai in the town, or had he seen her leave with him and Crystal? Zia wanted to ask him but she knew it would be better to wait. He was concentrating so hard on Yartu she did not want to disturb him. One more thing she would have to thank him for, she thought. It was going to be alright, Shadow would help her and Yartu, everything was going to be fine. She had to believe that. Zia's gaze fell to her dragon's unconscious form, and as it did so she felt a sharp pain course through her entire body. Her head began to spin and darkness overcame her.

CHAPTER 15

The shadows enveloped her. The pain was gone. There was nothing but the darkness. It was so glad to have her back in its shadowy embrace. The darkness wanted her to stay with it, never leave again. Alone, the shadows were so lonely. They wanted her to stay with them; no one ever wanted to spend time with them. The darkness promised her everything she could have ever wanted; in return all she had to do was remain here with it.

"Give up all your pain and sorrow, you will never be alone again," whispered the voice within the darkness. It was the same voice that had spoken to her twice before. It was not the annoying voice that had tried to keep her from the shadows.

"You must do as I ask, my child. Time is running out. Every moment that passes is critical. Why do you not seem to understand this? I can understand your slight fear of the darkness, it can be a little overzealous at times, but the shadows it sends to you are your friends. The darkness only wants to help you, take care of you. It cannot do so if you are constantly fighting it. You must give in before there is no more time left. The shadows need you just as you need them. Please, you must hasten to my side. I will not be able to help you if you do not give in."

The shadows began to pull at her; their urgency was disturbing. The darkness pulled and pushed, wanted and needed, it would not leave her alone. No, Zia thought. She struggled to break free of the hold the darkness had on her.

"No. Don't fight. Give in; the shadows will not harm you. Why must you always fight? The darkness needs you, please stop fighting it. You know I speak the truth. Why do you deny it?"

She had to get away. They would not let her go. Zia fought desperately to escape the cage that the shadows were building around her. No. She would not let them have her. She would not let the darkness consume her. She tried to think of something other than the darkness. She no longer listened to its promises, the secrets it whispered to her. She had to break free. Her struggles were in vain. The more she fought the more the shadows tried to surround her. The darkness wanted, needed and had to have her, it would never stop. She could not win. She was so tired and the shadows promised her the chance to rest. They promised her everything she had ever wanted. They would make everything better, they would help her. The shadows were her friends. The darkness would hide her away and keep her safe. Give in, give up. She felt herself losing the battle of wills. The darkness was eternal—how could she possibly fight it?

It does not understand the concept of life and death, darkness is eternal. That was what the annoying voice had said. Where are you now? she thought. The voice had helped her escape before. Why did it not help her now? Was it just going to leave her alone to fight on her own? How could it do this to her? Help her once and then leave her; she would not tolerate it. Her anger towards the sarcastic and infuriating voice began to drown out the whispers of the darkness. How dare it abandon her? She promised herself that she would give it a piece of her mind when it came back.

[What are you doing?] the voice asked harmlessly. It was back. Zia was going to make it pay for leaving her alone for so long.

What am I doing! I am fighting the darkness all by myself, thanks to you. What, were you unable to come sooner, someone else you had to annoy?

[I'm here now, aren't I? I have better things to do than bail you out of every messy situation you get yourself into.]

Fine, leave then. I do not need you. I can take care of myself.

[Right. You are doing such a wonderful job of it too. Do you want me to write your eulogy now or later? Better to be prepared, you know.]

Why don't I write you a eulogy? You are going to need it if you don't help me.

[I see the fight hasn't gone out of you completely.]

Oh, what I would do to you if I could get my hands on you.

[Your anger is misplaced. I think it would be best if you directed it at the darkness and not me.]

I do not need you to tell me what to do. Just get me out of here. Zia had lost all of her patience. The voice was doing this on purpose. The longer it spoke the louder and more insistent the shadows became. If it was waiting for her to beg, it was going to have to suffer, even if it meant losing herself to the darkness.

[You are willing to succumb to the darkness just to prove you don't need me? I think you are insane.]

If I wanted your opinion, I would have asked for it. As for me being insane I completely agree with you. I am fighting the shadows and talking to a disembodied voice inside my head. I think it is safe to assume that I have definitely lost my mind.

[I am *not* disembodied. I have a body, it's just not here.]

Oh, really, I thought for a moment you were my conscience. I guess I am not special enough to have one. I get stuck with you. Who would have thought that the little voice inside my head was real, and belonged to a real person? I am fairly sure no one will argue with the insanity claim.

[I did not ask to be here. I don't want to be here anymore than you want me here.]

All the more reason to help me get out of here. Once that is done you can get out too. I do not like having to share my mind with you.

[We are not really sharing. It isn't so much sharing a mind as visitation. Normally, I have control over this sort of thing, but for some strange reason that doesn't seem to apply here.]

How did you get in here, then? Did you want to visit my mind? Do I know you?

[No. This was an accident. I was not meant to connect with your mind, I really don't know how this happened or why.]

The darkness was tiring of cajoling her, it decided it was going to take her, she would forgive it later. Shadows crashed down all around her. Darkness surrounded her. There was no escape; they would not let her go. She belonged to them and no one else. She had to come with them, they would make her see.

Zia could not break free. She felt as if she were suffocating. The shadows had never been this bad before. It was becoming difficult to breathe, and she was falling, losing herself. The darkness was going to consume her. She would never be free of her nightmares. Fear took over her.

[No! Don't! You'll kill her!]

The words were barely audible. She did not know anything anymore. The darkness had taken her mind from her.

[Damn. How the hell am I supposed to fix this? That's it. Hold on, Zia, don't let go.]

It was too late. The shadows had gained control. She let them envelop her, hold her gently. The whispers of the darkness lulled her into sleep. It would keep her safe, she had nothing to fear. Come with us, it whispered. Yes, go with them, that was what she was meant to do. Why had she fought her friends so hard? She hoped they would forgive her, she had not meant to be so cold to them, her friends, the shadows and darkness.

A single thought escaped the darkness. A thought it could not contain, the image of a beautiful young man, Shadow. He wrapped his arms around her. The darkness could not keep him away. The thought had more power than it should have and far more control. Zia felt the embrace. She could feel the warmth of a body next to her. The darkness was trying anxiously to regain its hold on her.

He kept the shadows at bay. The darkness could not reach her. She was safe in his arms. Her palms were pressed against him and her forehead came to rest upon his chest. She could feel each beat of his heart. The sound began to drown out the whispers in the darkness.

Everything disappeared, nothing else existed but him. The darkness was gone, the shadows were fading. The shadows tried once again to reach her but their attempt to do so failed. He had stolen her from them. Within the darkness two hearts had become one.

CHAPTER 16

It was difficult to open her eyes. She did not know where she was, she was even unsure of who she was. Her thoughts were in complete disarray. She was leaning against something; it was warm and moved. A person? A sound reached her ears, the fluttering of wings. Where was she? Who was she?

"Zia?" A voice broke through the confusion.

Zia. That was her name, Zia Amarra. There was more, though, the where and the why, she had found out the who. She could not sort through the confusion in her mind.

[Your dragon is a little anxious. You should tell him you are alright.]

That voice, she knew it, annoying and full of sarcasm. Where had she heard it before? Wait, dragon, she had a dragon? The image of a small dragon with black scales edged in silver came to her. Yartu. It all started to come back to her.

She opened her eyes to darkness. She fought back the panic that started to rise. She took a deep breath to calm down and looked again, not darkness but black cloth. Zia tilted her head slightly to the side. She could see light filtering down from above. Trees, she was in a forest. "Yartu?"

Something nudged her arm and she glanced down and saw him. Yartu's wing had been wrapped tightly to his side, making any but the slightest of motions impossible. His uninjured wing was flapping as he tried to maintain his balance. He would have to get accustomed to having the use of only one wing. She reached out a hand to stroke him.

"Are you going to move? I don't think Shadow wants you to stay there forever." Yartu seemed to be perfectly fine. She could hear his dislike of Shadow in the tone of his voice. That would most likely never change, Yartu would probably never change.

Zia looked up and noticed that she was leaning against Shadow. His arms were around her, and he did not appear to mind that she was still there. A part of her did not mind either. The rest of her was so quick to get out of his arms that it sent her reeling, only to lean on him once again.

"You should be more careful. You were out for a while." It was the first thing that Shadow had spoken since she had awoken. Hearing him speak reminded her of someone or something, she could not figure it out, though, so she ignored it.

Yartu snorted, "It would be best if she tried to sit on her own."

"What happened?" she asked tentatively, uncertain she wanted to know.

Shadow helped her to sit up on her own by leaning her against a tree for support. "I was doing my best to mend Yartu's wing... You seemed fine in the beginning but then you lost consciousness. You were out for quite some time, I'm not sure how long exactly."

Zia attempted to remember what had occurred. Memory flooded her mind. The darkness had been there, another dream. Had it been a dream? Her thoughts whirled out of control. Had they all been dreams as she had originally thought, or were they something more? What was happening to her? Was she losing her mind? Everything was wrong; nothing seemed to make sense anymore.

[Calm down. Don't over analyze this. The darkness is gone for the moment but it will come back eventually. If you keep freaking out it will claim you a lot faster.]

The voice was right. She took a deep breath and forced herself to calm down. The darkness, her dream, must have come when she had blacked out. She would have lost herself had it not been for the voice. The voice inside her head, which was not her conscience; at least that was what it had claimed. How was she to know? Maybe her conscience did not want to admit it belonged to her. If that was so, she really didn't blame it. The little voice inside your head was not supposed to be real, not the way it claimed it was anyway, or so she thought. Zia could not help but wonder if her life had always been this complicated or if had just gotten worse.

"Are you alright? You seem a little unsteady," Yartu asked with great concern.

She gave him a small reassuring smile. "I am fine. I need to rest for a while, if that is alright with you and Shadow."

Yartu cast a baleful glance at Shadow. "We will rest here. You need to rest, as do I." His tone clearly stated that it did not matter if Shadow agreed with him or not.

"I don't think it is a good idea to stay, but I have no choice, do I? You will not listen to me, even though I know this forest and how dangerous it is. Why should I even try to change your mind?" Shadow was not pleased that the miniature dragon had decided that he was in charge.

"Dangerous, just how dangerous is it?" Zia was a bit apprehensive; if Shadow claimed the forest was not safe to be in, she felt it had to be really bad. He never seemed to be fazed by anything, so if he said it was dangerous to stay she believed him.

He ran a hand through his hair. "You would not believe me if I told you."

Yartu rolled his gleaming red eyes. "Try me."

"The forest is supposedly haunted, by what I don't know for sure. I have spent a lot of time in here and, trust me, it is really strange sometimes. More people have died in this forest than you could possibly imagine. Died or lost, not sure which truthfully, I do know that almost everyone who enters this forest is never seen again." The way he spoke made her believe every word he said.

"Trying to scare us, are you? Well, sorry to disappoint you, but I don't believe you. This is a forest just like any other, I can see no difference. You better save your ghost stories for frightening little children." Yartu was a cynical dragon and was not likely to believe anything he heard, even if it was true, until he had proof.

Zia did not agree with her dragon. "Yartu, I don't know. He seems to know what he is talking about. I think we should listen to him."

Both the miniature dragon and the young man stared at her in shock. "You are siding with him, Zia." Yartu was so stunned he could barely find words to speak.

"I am not siding with anyone. Shadow obviously knows this land better than we do and if he feels it is not safe for us to stay in the forest then we should not. Yartu, he has proven that we can rely on him. Why would he lie to us about such a thing? Why would anyone make up a story like that unless there was some measure of truth behind it?"

The dragon grimaced, "I don't know, Zia. If you feel like we can trust him then I won't argue, much."

She smiled at him, "You will never pass up a chance to argue, but thank you." She looked at Shadow, "If you take things a little slower this time it would be a lot easier on Yartu and me. We can move, but not very fast or far. I apologize for any inconvenience."

He shook his head, "Don't be sorry, you both have been injured and I wasn't very understanding. We aren't going much further, I want to get a little deeper into the forest and then we can stop for the night."

"I thought you wanted to leave the forest," Yartu snapped.

Shadow closed his eyes for a moment, "We are going to get out of here, I just have to find the way out."

"Find the way out? I thought you knew this forest better than anyone. I think I'm losing what little confidence I had in you. What about you, Zia, beginning to lose your faith in him?"

She met Shadow's gaze and found she could not turn away, "No, I trust him."

Zia heard Yartu mumble something, but her eyes did not leave Shadow's. She was unsure of why she could not look away. His dark gaze seemed to have captured her, trapped her better than even the shadows themselves had. It frightened her more than the shadows and she could not figure out why.

Shadow broke the strange, almost hypnotic, hold he had over her, and when he rose to his feet he held out his hand to help her up. As Zia took his hand a shiver ran through her. Yartu felt a strange sensation as Zia was helped to her feet by Shadow. It came from her and it made the dragon dislike the young man even more. He would not take his Zia from him.

Night had fallen and the forest had become very dark. During the day the forest was dark enough but at night there was almost no light to see by at all. A thick fog blanketed the ground and the sounds of the night seemed amplified. There were other things that could be heard as well, things that made shivers run down your spine and dark thoughts race through an unsuspecting mind. Zia's thoughts were dark, but not because of the forest and its eerie atmosphere.

Yartu had fallen asleep almost immediately after they had stopped for the night, but the idea of sleep terrified her after the day's events. She wished he was awake; she wanted to talk to him about what had happened. He might not have been able to explain it but he would have at least comforted her. She thought about waking him but did not, for he needed to rest, his wing would not heal properly otherwise.

Zia had always been at ease when night had fallen. She seemed to just disappear in the dark. She had never questioned it before, just as she had never wondered if her dreams might be something else. Could a dream be more than just a dream? What if dreams were real? How else was one to describe what she went through almost nightly? Zia's dreams had always felt real, as if she was experiencing a whole other world when she closed her eyes; a world where nothing else existed but the darkness and her. Then everything changed, a voice had spoken to her from the shadows. A voice that wanted her to come to it, begging her to hurry before time ran out. As if that wasn't enough, she had a dream while she had been awake, something that had never happened before. As bad as all this was, the worst was the other voice that had started to speak to her, an irritating and often sarcastic voice that seemed to take great pleasure in annoying her. It did not even have the decency to come to her in a dream first; it had to speak to her when she was wide awake. It even had the nerve to call her insane. No matter how hard she tried she could not figure out where the voice had come from or what it wanted. It seemed to have the ability to sense her thoughts and acted as though it was blaming her for being connected to her mind. She wished she could talk to Yartu. She got her wish, with one minor change.

CHAPTER 17

[Do you ever sleep?]

Wonderful, she thought, *it's back.*

[I didn't really leave.]

Are you ever going to? Didn't you say you have a body? I am sure you must miss it. Go back to it and leave me and my thoughts alone. I am fairly certain that you are not supposed to share your mind with a disembodied voice.

[You're not.]

Then why are you here?

[I don't know.]

I do not want you here. My thoughts are my own. Get out.

[I would if I could.]

So you can't fix this? I am going to be stuck with you in my mind forever? I do not cherish the thought. Don't you want your body back?

[I have my body.]

Then your consciousness is here? Is your body just lying around somewhere?

[No, I'm in my body. I am connected to your mind. I'm not actually living here. Trust me, I do not want that. Your mind is somewhat scary; I have no idea how you can stand it. It is probably a good thing that I'm here. You should not be left in here alone.]

I did not ask for your opinion of my mind. How did you even get in here in the first place? How is it possible for you to be here and in your own body at the same time?

[I thought that we had already been over the how did I get here thing. Once again, I don't know. I somehow linked to your mind and established a permanent connection. This is as new to me as it is to you. As for the whole being in my body and in your mind at the same time, I can explain that better.]

Then please do so.

[I am able to read people's thoughts. I don't leave my body. I can do this with anyone I am near. The thoughts just enter my mind whether I want them to or not. Entering the mind of someone else is a bit more complicated, it is different because I am going deeper into the person's consciousness. The thoughts I am able to read are floating around the top, they are what the person is thinking of at that moment. When I enter a mind I can see everything, not just thoughts. I am able to see all their memories, every thought, every emotion. I can learn anything I want and they would not know I was there at all.]

So you know everything about me? Zia was afraid, her thoughts and feelings were not meant to be seen by anyone. They were private and to be shared only if she wanted to share them.

[I'm not invading your privacy. This was an accident. I swear that I have not delved any deeper into your mind than was necessary.]

How deep is necessary? Accident or not, you are still in my mind. I don't want you in here. I have enough problems; I do not need this. Please, just go away.

[I wish I could. I don't want to be here, it feels wrong. I don't know how to break the connection, I don't even know why or how I got here. I was not trying to do this on purpose. If it makes you feel better, I have only stayed on the outskirts of your mind. I have only seen your current thoughts and have only sensed your more recent feelings.]

The voice sounded as if it were truly sorry, though Zia did not know if she could forgive it.

[I am sorry. I don't expect you to forgive me. I promise I am trying to find a way to break our mental connection. I will be gone as soon as I do.]

I guess that has to be enough.

[There can be benefits to having me in here, you know.]

Like what?

[I can help you with your little problem involving the darkness. I have already done so twice. I can be useful.]

I guess I should thank you for that.

[Don't worry about it. I seemed to have caused more trouble than I wanted to.]

Why do I get the feeling that you seem to like causing trouble?

[I don't really. I just like annoying you. You are extremely amusing when you get mad.]

I am so pleased I am able to entertain you.

[Sarcastic much?]

You're one to talk.

[Maybe. You should try to get some sleep; you've had a long day.]

Zia did not want to sleep. She knew she should, but she was afraid; what if she had another dream? The darkness might try to come for her again.

[Sleep. I will keep the shadows away.]

That is very kind of you. I guess it might not be that bad to have you here for a little while longer.

[Told you I'm not all that bad.]

I will have to take your word for it. By the way, what is your name?

[My name?]

Yes, you have a name, don't you? If you are going to be in my mind for a while I can't keep calling you the voice.

[Why not?]

I will not do it, that is why. It is my mind, so you should do as I say.

[Fine, your mind, you win. I am not going to tell you my name. I will tell you I am a man.]

A man? Young or old?

[Young.]

How young?

[Not much older than you. Will you go to sleep now?]

She wanted to ask him more questions, but she had a feeling he would not answer. There was still much that needed to be explained, though it could wait until later. She began to feel drowsy and soon slipped into sleep.

Dragon and girl slept deeply, neither one noticed that one had remained awake. Shadow watched them for a moment, the dragon curled next to his human. They both seemed so peaceful; he wondered how long that would last.

The fog almost covered them completely. The silvery mist swirled around them trying to devour the two helpless and warm bodies. Shadow waited for it to come.

An indistinguishable form appeared within the mist. It reached out to the two unsuspecting forms with a ghostly hand. The apparition gently brushed away a strand of Zia's hair from her forehead in a disturbingly affectionate gesture. Its hand trailed down her face to her neck and then down to the chest where one could feel a soft heartbeat. It wanted and needed the warmth, the life held within. The ghostly hand reached into the body of the human, preparing to take the warmth from it. A few fingers were all that entered Zia's body.

"Don't even think about it." Shadow spoke to the apparition without any fear.

It turned towards him and spoke in a faint watery voice, "W-warmth. L-life. N-need."

Shadow shook his head. "Not hers."

"M-must have. N-need," the thing protested.

"Find another victim, phantom. You will not harm her or the dragon who rests at her side." He spoke with authority as if expecting it to obey.

The apparition held out a hand to him. "I will claim the h-human. Then I will take your l-life."

A faint smile played across his face. "Try. You will never again have to search for warmth. You will not need it where I will send you."

The ghostly being thought this over for a moment as it stared at the mortal who was trying to take its prey. It could feel the heartbeat of the one behind it. The apparition was not going to give it up. It reached once more for Zia's heart.

"One last chance. Leave her alone. You will not claim her life this night or any other."

The apparition looked back at him intending to watch the mortal as it took the life from the one it was trying so hard to protect. It had not expected to see what it saw at that very moment. "F-forgive me. I-I did not k-know."

"Now you do. Leave at once. If I ever see you near her again it will be most unpleasant for you." He eyed the creature coldly.

The apparition knew when it was in danger. It knew when it had lost. It faded back into the mist. Shadow watched it disappear. When he was sure it was gone he knelt beside Zia. She was still asleep, completely unaware of the danger her life had just been in. He wanted to keep it that way. The last thing she needed was to find out a ghost had wanted to kill her, the last thing he wanted was to explain to her or Yartu how he had prevented it from doing so.

A small moan came from the sleeping girl. She had become restless, another nightmare. During the time in which they had traveled to the town he had seen her experience many bad dreams. Yartu had always kept him away from her; the dragon did not let him wake her. Shadow didn't really care. The girl was nothing but trouble. Why, then, did he feel responsible for her? He should have just left her to fend for herself and her infuriating dragon, but no, he had to help.

Don't get involved, he had always told himself, people were nothing but a waste of time. He had always stayed away, never gotten close, he liked being alone. Then she showed up and his life had become more complicated than he wanted or expected. Things were bad enough for him on his own and now he had to take care of an annoying girl and her pet dragon. The worst thing of all was Nicolai. What did he want with Zia? Shadow wondered how he had gotten himself into this position. There goes peace and quiet, he thought. Life was definitely going to get interesting.

CHAPTER 18

The forest was just as creepy during the day as it was at night. The trees were old and very large; they were also too close together in many places. What little sunlight managed to find its way down through the massive trees gave the forest an eerie dark green glow. It was difficult to see and the dim lighting made it nearly impossible to walk without falling.

Shadow moved with ease through the forest, but Zia did not fare as well. The deeper they went the worse it became. Yartu's incessant complaining and his demand to be constantly carried had put Zia in a dreadful mood. She loved her dragon dearly but she wanted nothing more at the moment than to be far away from him. The same went for how she felt about Shadow. He was leading them farther into the forest and did not seem to notice the rough time she was having. The first day they spent in the forest together she thought they had finally begun to get along, maybe even started to understand each other. Zia did not think that way anymore. Shadow remained just as distant as he had been when she first met him. The only person who spoke to her without hesitancy or demanding something was the voice.

He did not speak to her on a regular basis; the voice came and went as it pleased. Normally it was just to annoy her. Zia attempted on several occasions to learn his name but he would change the subject or stop talking to her. The more she spoke with him the more she wanted to know about him. He had to be the most infuriating person she had ever spoken with, but something about him intrigued her. There was so much he knew about the darkness and he had the strangest ability. She also wanted to know how he had forged a connection with her mind. There was so much she didn't know about so many things. Why does everything have to be so complicated? she thought.

[Not everything is complicated, you make it that way.]

Zia suppressed a smile, he always seemed to be there when she least wanted him. She had gotten to the point where she could tell when he would interrupt her thoughts. Oddly enough she was on better terms with the mysterious voice inside her mind than she was with Yartu and Shadow at the moment.

[It's always nice to know I'm appreciated.]

She could not help but roll her eyes.

"Something wrong?" Yartu asked from his normal position, wrapped around her neck.

"No." Zia had not told Yartu about the voice; a part of her wanted to, but she did not think it was a good idea. The last thing she needed was Yartu to start worrying about her more than he already did. He would consider the voice to be just as bad as her dreams.

A small reptilian head stretched out to get a better look at her. "Zia, I know when you are lying. What is it you are hiding from me? You know you can tell me anything, we are Bonded."

Tell him everything? What was she supposed to say? "Yes, I know Yartu, I'm fine, really." No, I am not, were her unspoken words.

Yartu did not believe her, but he didn't push. He knew she would tell him when she was ready. He was quite worried about Zia. Ever since they reunited with Shadow she had become more withdrawn than usual. The human was seriously beginning to annoy Yartu. The miniature dragon had thought that he was out of their lives for good, and now they had to rely on the human once more. This was not what Yartu had planned or wanted, he wanted Shadow gone. It did not matter to him that the young man had saved him and Zia or that Shadow had mended his wing. The only thing that mattered was that he was a threat.

A rustle above caused Shadow to stop where he stood; he motioned to Zia to do the same. She did, although she did not understand why. It was most likely a bird, nothing too serious. Shadow watched the branches hanging above them intently. He seemed to be looking for something. Zia was confused by his behavior. What did he think might be up there, even worse what did he think it would do to them?

She did not hear anything, but something did not feel right. Zia would have been unable to explain the feeling she had, something just felt wrong. Yartu had also become restless; she could feel his talons digging into her shoulder. What was out there? Her question was answered.

"Leave at once. It is forbidden for your kind to be here. If you go now, we might let you keep your lives." The voice came from everywhere, making it impossible to determine where the speaker was.

Shadow moved to the base of one of the massive trees. The voice spoke again, "How did you even get this far? Why didn't the phantom kill you?" It sounded just as confused as Zia felt. When she first heard the speaker she was unable to determine whether or not it was male or female, but this time she heard the masculinity in the voice.

She did not understand what he meant by phantom, but she felt it was a good idea to leave. She was about to suggest this to Shadow, but he was nowhere to be found. Zia knew she should have been frightened but all she felt was anger. She could not believe Shadow would abandon her and Yartu at a time like this. Now, she had to deal with the person herself; could things possibly get any worse?

The sound of something crashing to the ground behind her made Zia jump. She spun around, her dagger in hand ready for anything, well, almost anything. Nothing could have prepared her for the sight that met her eyes. A body was sprawled out on the ground. The faint moans of pain were all that suggested it was still alive. She moved to the person lying on the ground before her. When she got close enough to see, something dropped in front of her.

A small cry escaped her lips, before she realized who it was. "Don't do that!" she exclaimed.

Shadow shook his head. "Do what? I got him, didn't I? You should be grateful."

Zia tried to suppress the urge to hit him. "Grateful? You scared me, I thought you had run off and left me here to die. What exactly is it I am supposed to be grateful for?"

"He wouldn't have killed you. He is a novice, doesn't know what he is doing. I'm surprised they let him come out here on his own." Zia had no idea what he was talking about, and his cavalier attitude made her mad. So she hit him.

"Next time I would appreciate it if you would at least give me some sort of sign to let me know that you are not going to leave me to die," she snapped.

Shadow rolled his eyes. "His attention was on you, not me. I was in a position to be able to change our situation. I did not leave you, why would you even think that?" Zia could hear the disappointment in his voice. She said she trusted him, how could she have thought that he would abandon her?

She started to apologize but a groan interrupted her. Zia's attention returned to the unconscious form lying on the ground. He was young, her age or a little younger, with dark brown hair and lightly tanned skin. He wore dark pants and a high-collared leather vest; an intricate tattoo encircled his upper right arm. She leaned in closer to get a better look.

A hand reached up and pulled her to the ground; unable to fly, Yartu was flung from her shoulder and crashed into a tree. A fresh wave of pain shot through her body—barely clinging to consciousness, she felt something cold press against her throat. Her vision began to clear only to reveal an unknown man on top of her holding a dagger close to her, far too close for comfort. Instinct took over and she struggled to get out from under him, only to have his dagger press deeper into her neck.

"I don't think you should do that." Shadow spoke calmly, as if he was just giving friendly advice to a friend.

The dagger did not move. "Shadow..." Zia's voice was shaky. Why did he just stand there? Wasn't he going to help her?

"He won't do anything, Zia. He's just trying to scare you." His voice remained calm; she wished it worked.

A small laugh met her ears. "I will most definitely do something. You are not supposed to be here. You have trespassed and you will be punished."

Zia once again tried to push him off her but was unsuccessful. Luckily, she didn't really have to. Shadow had grown tired of watching Zia in danger; every time he turned around her life was being threatened again, and it was getting annoying. He reached out and pulled the boy off of Zia. She was surprised at the amount of force Shadow used. He practically threw the young man into a tree.

CHAPTER 19

Shadow helped her to her feet, and as she stood she felt his fingers brush her neck. "What are you doing?" she squeaked.

A single brow shot up. "I am making sure he didn't hurt you. I might be mistaken, but didn't you want me to worry about you more?" The tone of his voice was slightly mocking. Zia was unsure why but it reminded her of someone or something.

"I am fine, no thanks to you," she snapped.

Shadow ran a hand through his hair. "Why don't you check on Yartu? I'll take care of him." He gestured to the boy.

Yartu. She had almost forgotten. She went to him, and cradled him in her arms. "Yartu, are you alright? I am so sorry."

"For what?" Yartu answered with a weak response. "How were you supposed to know that he would attack you?"

"It doesn't matter, you are alright." She gently stroked him, "You must be tired of getting hurt. I know I am."

"You have no idea." The dragon muttered. He snuggled closer to her and promptly fell asleep.

Yartu was safe, so now she could focus on the stranger who had attacked her. Shadow dragged the boy to his feet. "You are a pitiful excuse for a Guardian. Have you even passed the test yet?" Shadow shook his head, "I don't know why they would let you out here alone. It is suicide for one as inexperienced as you obviously are."

The boy pulled his arm out of Shadow's hold. "I have every right to be here, and you don't, so leave," he said petulantly. A confused expression crossed his face. "Wait, did you say Guardian? How do you know about Guardians?"

"If you were one you would know."

The boy looked even more confused than before. He looked at Zia as though she might answer his questions.

"Don't look at me. I don't know what he's talking about either."

"If you don't know about Guardians how come he does? Who are you people?" The boy's frustration was clearly heard.

Shadow ignored him. Zia almost felt sorry for the boy. He wanted answers that Shadow was unwilling to give; she knew how he felt. "This is Yartu," she said pointing to the sleeping dragon, "I am Zia and the cryptic one is Shadow."

The boy seemed to have noticed Yartu for the first time, and a smile lit up his face, "You have a dragon. You're really lucky, I've been trying to find one but it is impossible. I don't understand it, they used to be everywhere you looked but now it's a miracle if you see one."

Zia was taken aback for a moment. "I am afraid I do not understand. Miniature dragons may be rare, but it is not impossible to find one. If you know the right people, anyway." Did miniature dragons not exist in the wild? Honestly, Zia didn't know, but she did wonder about Yartu herself sometimes.

"He's the first one I have ever seen. Maybe they just don't live here anymore. The dragons might have decided to leave the forest." He looked at Zia with something close to reverence. "You must be really special to have Bonded a dragon. They have only been known to Bond with important people."

She could not believe what he was saying; she wasn't special, although she believed Yartu was. True, only the rich and powerful could have a miniature dragon if the Magic Council approved. They didn't approve of her, but that was not something he needed to know or something she was willing to discuss with a total stranger. "You do not know much about miniature dragons, do you?"

The confused look returned to the boy's face. "I know a lot about dragons—I have to."

"Why do you have to know about dragons?"

"It is part of his training as a Guardian." Shadow answered for him. "They must learn about that which they have to protect."

The boy looked at Shadow with a mix of fear and apprehension. "How do you know so much?"

Shadow met his eyes. "I am going to ask the questions and you will answer them."

"But..." the boy protested.

"What is your name and why are you out here alone?" Shadow's tone suggested he was bored with the boy and was only talking to him because he felt he had to.

The boy hesitated momentarily. "My name is Thorn. I am here because I have to protect the forest."

"I'm not stupid, you are a novice. I want to know why you are out here alone."

Thorn glared at Shadow. "How do you know so much? No one knows anything about this forest or Guardians, why do you?"

Shadow returned Thorn's glare with an icy stare of his own. "I am quite knowledgeable about this forest and the people who protect it. If you were an actual Guardian instead of just a novice you would know that, as well as who I am."

Thorn's gaze fell to the ground. "They won't let me take the test," he said sullenly. "I am ready. I don't care what they say."

"So you came out here alone to prove that you are capable of handling the responsibilities of a Guardian. Do you have any idea how stupid that was? There are things in this forest that will kill you and not think twice about it. It is dangerous for anyone but a Guardian to walk in this forest alone; coming out here proves nothing." Zia was surprised by the anger she heard in Shadow's voice.

"I had to do something. I am so sick of them babying me. They won't let me do anything." Thorn buried his face in his hands. "I just wanted to do what I am supposed to do. I should be a Guardian by now. Why won't they let me become one? I have done everything that was expected of me and more."

Zia was not sure what was going on. She did not understand any of the conversation that was taking place before her. She did not have to know what they were discussing in order to see that Thorn desperately wanted to be a Guardian, whatever that was. She could hear the pain in his voice and the desperation. "I may not know what a Guardian is, but if they are meant to protect this forest I think that you are quite capable."

Thorn looked up at her. "Really?" he asked softly.

She smiled and nodded. "You did an excellent job of scaring me, trying to get me to leave. Shadow does not count, nothing bothers him. Even one of your Guardians would be unable to scare him." Zia paused for a moment and rolled her eyes, "You would have had to literally drag Shadow out of here in order to make him leave."

"I am flattered that you think so highly of me." Shadow said dryly, "Now if you don't mind we should be going."

"Fine, can we go a little slower this time? Yartu is asleep and I don't want to wake him, he needs his rest." She walked over to where Shadow stood and looked at him expectantly.

Shadow nodded in agreement, but as they turned to walk away Thorn spoke: "You aren't going anywhere. If it is so dangerous for me to be here alone then how is it safe for you? I have spent my life growing up in this forest. I know the dangers and how to survive them. With all due respect I can't let you go off on your own, what if you get yourselves killed? I would only blame myself for your deaths, then where would I be? I insist that you come with me."

"I am afraid that we are going to have to refuse your offer, Thorn," Shadow said evenly.

"It wasn't an offer."

Shadow shook his head in disbelief, "How naive are you? You really don't want to fight me."

"As a Guardian of this forest I cannot let you leave. You have violated an ancient law by trespassing; you must answer for your transgressions. I will see to it that your punishment is lenient if you come willingly." Thorn spoke confidently, unafraid of Shadow's previous threat.

Zia wanted to scream. Why was it that she always seemed to be getting in trouble? Why did everyone want to punish her? She could not remember doing anything that caused her to be deserving of such violence. It was all Shadow's fault. He had led her into this deathtrap of a forest.

[Is that how you truly feel?]

Wonderful, she thought, the last thing I need at the moment is *Him*. She ignored the voice and hoped that Shadow would get her out of the mess he had gotten her into.

[It is nice to know you still have faith.]

Shadow shrugged. "Zia and I will not be going with you. I am far more capable than you are when it comes to surviving in this forest. Try and stop us."

[Things are getting interesting. I'm surprised the would-be Guardian has let things get so out of control. He really is a novice.]

How does the voice know what a Guardian is? she wondered.

"I will do whatever is necessary to detain to you. You have broken the law of this forest." Thorn remained calm under Shadow's dark gaze.

"Tell me, if the phantom failed before you, how do you intend to punish us for our crimes?" Shadow asked innocently, a small knowing smile playing across his face.

Zia wondered why Thorn looked so ill, and what was a phantom? A phantom was a ghost, wasn't it? Ghosts do not exist, she told herself.

[Of course they do. There are quite a few in this forest too. All those rumors about this place being haunted are true, believe it or not.]

Zia did not believe him; ghosts did not exist.

"How did you escape the phantom? No one ever does." Thorn's voice had become a bit shaky.

That knowing smile remained. "I did not escape the phantom." At this point Thorn looked as though he was about to be sick.

[Do you find this as entertaining as I do?]

"There is only one being in this entire forest who has the power to call off a phantom. Not even the Guardians can stop it when it has marked someone for death." Then Thorn gasped: "You are the Fallen One."

CHAPTER 20

The smile faded from Shadow's beautiful face; he said nothing in response. Zia did though, "What is the Fallen One?"

Thorn looked at her—he had forgotten for a moment that she was there. "The Fallen One. Don't you know anything?"

"Leave her alone." Shadow's voice was cold. "She does not need to know. I suggest you let us leave now."

"I do not need to know what, exactly? What are you hiding from me?" Zia was beginning to worry. She had placed all of her trust in Shadow and he still refused to tell her anything about himself. What if he was not trying to help her, what if...?

[Would you stop it? It is not easy for some people to trust, secrets may be kept in order to protect oneself. You have been given no reason to mistrust. Why do you insist on doing so?]

Zia's mind was reeling, it was all too much. She wanted desperately to trust Shadow, but how could she when he did not trust her in return? The voice said that he may have his reasons. She had many reasons not to trust anyone as well.

[Maybe you do not trust as completely as you believe. Secrets are being kept on both sides. How is one supposed to trust the other if both are unwilling to take the steps necessary to build that trust? Perhaps you and this person are more afraid than you realize.]

"Will you ever leave me alone?" She wanted to drown the voice out; he was saying things he knew nothing about. He knew nothing about her. How dare he speak to her as if he did? In her desperation to ignore the voice, she had spoken out loud.

Thorn looked at her inquisitively. "Who is she talking to?"

"Does it matter?" Shadow asked.

Zia's shout woke Yartu up in time to hear Thorn's question and Shadow's dismissal of it.

"Yes, it matters," the dragon snapped at Shadow, then he returned his attention to Zia. Yartu spoke in a more soothing manner to her: "Calm down and explain yourself."

His words cut through the confusion. Oh no, she thought. She had spoken aloud and had not even realized it. Yartu and Thorn were staring at her. Shadow was not staring like the others. He was watching her with a carefully guarded expression. She decided that Shadow's reaction was the worst. People had stared at her before; she was used to it. The look on his face she never wanted to get used to.

"Zia, who were you talking to?" Yartu asked again.

She couldn't tell him, he would think that she was insane. She was insane, she spoke to a voice inside her mind that only she could hear. How was she supposed to explain to Yartu that the voice was a real person when she was unsure if it was true herself? She did not know what to do. The darkness began to close in on her.

"*Zia.*" Her name echoed in her ears and throughout her mind, expelling the darkness. It happened so fast and so powerfully that it caused her to lose her balance. She would have fallen if Shadow had not caught her.

Yartu had leapt to the safety of the ground when Zia had lost her balance. He now stood there glaring at everyone who towered over him. "What is going on? I want to know and I want to know now," he demanded. "Do you hear me?"

Zia barely heard him; her mind was in complete chaos. The darkness kept trying to get in, it knew she was weak. The shadows knew that they had to wear down her defenses now or they might never get the chance again. The only problem was that irritating person keeping them at bay, but it did not matter, he would tire eventually, the darkness never would. They would have what was rightfully theirs. It was only a matter of time.

"Zia? I do not appreciate being ignored," Yartu said crossly. The miniature dragon wanted to know what was going on with her. Ever since the fight with Nicolai she had been acting strangely and he wanted to know why. He had a feeling it had something to do with Shadow.

"She can't hear you." Shadow spoke softly.

Yartu did not like the fact that the young man was holding Zia so close. "Don't be ridiculous. She can hear me, she is simply choosing not to. It is rather rude and I am growing tired of this, Zia."

"She cannot hear you. Do you ever listen to anyone but yourself?" Shadow had lost all patience.

Yartu started to protest when Thorn spoke. "What is wrong with her?"

Shadow's eyes closed. "The darkness is trying to take her."

"What? That is impossible, the darkness has remained dormant for many years. Why would it awaken now? What would does it want with her?" Thorn was in shock, the darkness was something that was never discussed, not ever.

"I need to get her somewhere safe, a place where I do not have to constantly worry about getting killed."

Thorn considered this for a moment. "I can lead you to the edge of the forest, it is not far and you will be safe there."

"No, that's not good enough. I need you to lead me to the ruins." His dark eyes met Thorn's, silently telling him he had no choice. If Thorn did not take him to the ruins he would make him; resistance was futile.

Thorn had heard of the Fallen One and his power, and decided that betraying his people was better than what the Fallen One would do to him; they would get over it eventually. He nodded in agreement.

"Good choice. You take Yartu. He is unable to fly, so you must carry him." Shadow picked Zia up. She was oblivious to the contact. So much of her consciousness was trapped by the darkness in her mind.

Yartu felt Thorn grab him; he did not resist, for he could not follow on foot, but he still did not like anyone other than Zia holding him. The dragon could do nothing but watch as Zia's arms wound around Shadow's neck. He would have been furious except for the fact that Zia did not seem to be aware of anything that was going on. Her eyes were unfocused and her body was limp. Yartu could not feel her, she seemed so far away, somewhere he could not reach her. The dragon was worried about her, and his concern for Zia's well-being took precedence over his animosity towards Shadow. So he let the strange boy carry him without complaint, all the while keeping a close eye on Shadow, who held Zia close. Yartu hoped that these ruins were close by.

CHAPTER 21

The shadows swirled around her and whispered dark secrets in her ears. They would disappear for a moment only to come back stronger than before. There was something else, someone hidden in the darkness that called out to her. The darkness was trying to suppress whatever it was. She could feel the anger and frustration of the shadows. They could not keep what was trying so hard to reach her away.

Her mind had become a battlefield; the shadows against an unseen enemy. The darkness had the upper hand but no matter what it did it could not expel its foe from her mind. The shadows had to both seduce Zia and battle the one who attempted to take her.

[Don't listen to it. Fight, that's what you do best.]

She recognized the voice. It came and went along with the shadows' whispers. Promise after promise, protest after protest, it was difficult for her to determine who was actually saying what. It was all a blur. The darkness, the voice, who was she supposed to listen to?

Us, the shadows whispered. They reminded her of all the pain that had been inflicted upon her. They had always been there protecting her, they had always been her friend. They had loved her when no one else had, they still did. She was perfect, everything they had ever dreamed of. Why would she want to go back to that cruel world?

[Life is cruel, but at least it is life. The pain and suffering that you have endured makes you strong. Do not let the darkness take you. You will lose that which is the most important thing of all.]

What is important? Everything I have been through, is life really worth this? Zia was tired, it did not matter anymore. Nothing did.

[No. Zia, listen to me. I know what it is like to be alone, to have endured so much and still have no one. You cannot give up this easily, what of Yartu? You may think that you are alone, but you have him, he is a part of you. He has been with you through so much, are you just going to leave him? What will he do without you? You know that he will not survive. Everything you two have shared means nothing if you give up now. Are you really so eager for a way out that you would sacrifice everything he has done for you? I guess you don't care about him; after all he is just a dragon.]

Yartu; memories flooded her mind. He was hers, he had always been there. She could barely remember the time in her life before the dragon. He had been with her since she was a child.

The darkness sensed the path her thoughts were taking. It did not like it. It whispered to her of all the pain that had been caused by the dragon. How he had caused more problems instead of resolving them. What good would it do if she went back? There were those who were trying to separate them, and the separation would cause her so much pain and agony. It would be better if she let the darkness take her; there would be no pain, she would feel nothing.

Nothing. What would it be like to feel nothing at all? No pain, no sorrow, no fear.

[Nothing is nothing, Zia. You will not feel sorrow or pain, you will never be afraid again, but you will never feel joy. You will be emotionless, like the darkness. It cannot feel, Zia. That is why it wants you. An empty promise from something that can never begin to understand what it is like to feel. Having no emotions is not as wonderful as you might think. You will never laugh or cry, you will never experience love.]

Love, her mind centered on the word. What was love? she wondered. The darkness claimed it loved her, Yartu said he loved her, but there had to be more. Were a dragon and the darkness the only things that would ever love her? They were all that ever had. No one had ever cared, from the parents who had abandoned her to the various people she had met in her life. She had been ignored, unloved, and forgotten.

[You are not alone, Zia.]

No, she thought, I am not. The darkness has always been there. The shadows comforted her when no one else did; they were the ones who held her gently as she fell asleep. They were the ones who dried her tears, erased her fears. Her earliest memory involved the darkness. It had been a part of her since the beginning.

The shadows rejoiced. They were winning. The foolish mortal who was trying to take her from them was being pushed to the farthest reaches of her mind. She was no longer listening to him, she had seen the truth. She was giving in.

[Damn you, Zia. I thought you were stronger than that. You will lose everything and gain nothing. The darkness used to scare you. Remember your nightmares? How easily you have forgotten. Are you going to let the shadows control you, consume you?]

Shadows. Shadow, beautiful, a stray thought drew her attention away from the darkness. The shadows became the gentle warmth of a body in dark clothing. The darkness transformed into a beautiful face framed by soft black hair. She reached out to touch the face, unsure if it was real. She was surprised to see her own hand. She had never before been able to see herself when trapped in her mind.

Zia was no longer a part of the darkness. She stood within it. The shadows surrounded her, but did not touch. She was alone amidst the darkness.

[Not alone, never alone.]

She turned around and saw the voice, or rather the person who spoke to her in her mind. Shock mingled with fear. It was not possible, she thought, how...?

[Long story. I guess we are going to have to tell each other our secrets now.]

He was in her mind. He was the voice. He was the one that had saved her from the darkness. How could she not know? Both had a complete disregard for her feelings, and there were other similarities. It made sense in so many ways and at the same time no sense at all. She knew now why the voice had never told her his name. Zia already knew it. Shadow.

[Like I said before, you are funny when you get mad. The darkness does not seem too amused by it but...]

That's it? She shouted, at least she thought she did. *You are in my mind and all you can say is that I am amusing you?*

[I'm only trying to help you.]

Zia buried her face in her hands. She could feel tears behind her eyes. Help her? He wanted to help her. He was in her mind, how much had he seen? What had he seen? Did he know her thoughts about him? She wanted to run, but she couldn't. She was trapped in her mind by the darkness with the last person she wanted to be there with.

[You are trapped here as long as you let the darkness keep you here. You have to fight it. Where is that stubbornness of yours?]

She looked up at him, and a single tear fell down her face. *How could you?* she whispered.

Shadow touched her face where the tear had fallen. She thought she saw sadness in his eyes. [It was an accident. I never meant for this to happen. Your mind drew me, just like you did. I cannot leave your mind anymore than I can leave you. I tried; when I left you at the village I had no intention of ever seeing you again. Fate had other things planned, it seems. You need me, Zia. You need me to keep the darkness away. You can't do it by yourself. You almost let them have you. I did not think that my words would get through to you.] The brilliant smile lit up his face. [I guess that insulting you worked.]

She would have laughed but she could only stare. He was there in her mind fighting the darkness. All the anger and fear disappeared. He was doing it for her. She placed her hand over the one on her cheek and pressed it closer. He seemed startled by the contact, but he did not pull away.

[I guess we are friends.]

Zia closed her eyes. He protected her from the darkness. He was the reason she had been able to escape before. Shadow confused her and frightened her. She did not understand anything he did or why he did it. He made her feel things she could not even begin to comprehend.

The shadows were angry. He had found a way to get through to her. His presence had become too strong, they could not fight him. He was taking her from them. No, she was already lost to them. He had won this battle. The darkness had to wait once more. It knew it would get another chance. She was weakest when she slept. It would take her then. He could not keep fighting, she was meant to be with the darkness. She belonged to the shadows.

She could feel the pull of the darkness. It was not nearly as strong as it had been before. Shadow was keeping it away from her. He was helping her fight her nightmares. *Take me back. I don't want to be here anymore.*

[I don't either.]

CHAPTER 22

When Zia opened her eyes, she was forced to close them once more. She fought back the dizziness when she tried to open them again. Sitting up was out of the question; she wished she felt as though she could. She settled for looking at her surroundings.

She was in a room that was almost completely covered in plants. Ivy hung from the ceiling and clung to the walls, and various potted plants lined the window sill. There were two large plants in separate corners and a long table lined the wall opposite the bed she was lying on. The table held an assortment of bottles and canisters, cloth bandages and a large bowl. Zia wanted to get a better look around, but she had a terrible headache and every time she tried to sit up, she felt nauseous.

The sound of a door opening caught her attention. A young girl walked into the room. Zia was astonished by the girl's appearance. She was wearing pants and a pale green shirt. Gold earrings hung from her ears, which also happened to be slightly pointed. If that wasn't strange enough, a thick braid of dark green hair fell to her knees.

The girl turned to face Zia. A delighted look crossed a pretty face with cat-like eyes. "Oh, you're awake. How wonderful, we were starting to worry about you."

"Where am I? Who are you?" Zia began to ramble, "What am I doing here? Where are Yartu and Shadow? How did I get here? I want to see them."

The girl held up her hands. Zia noticed her nails were the same color as her hair. "Calm down. You are safe, and we have been taking care of you. Your friends brought you here, along with my brother. They are outside waiting for you to wake up."

Zia was about to ask more about where she was but she wanted to know something else first. "Shadow, he's here?"

The girl smiled, "He's the man, right, not the dragon? Completely gorgeous. I have never seen anyone like him before. He is so dedicated to you too. He carried you all the way here and stayed by your side for two whole days. I think he would have stayed until you woke up but the others told him he couldn't."

He had been in the room with her? He had stayed beside her until he had been told to leave... Zia wondered if he had to be close in order to speak to her in her mind. Her thoughts drifted back to what the girl had said about him being dedicated to her. Shadow was not dedicated to her, not like that.

The girl sat down on the bed, "He's something else. I still can't believe someone can actually look that perfect."

"I know," Zia muttered.

A smile lit up the girl's face again. "You don't sound too thrilled. Oh well, I could talk about him all day but I'll get in trouble if I do." She looked at Zia quizzically, "What's your name? Mine's Terra."

"Zia Amarra. Do you mind if I ask you what you are doing in here, Terra?"

Terra laughed. "Silly me, you have probably been wondering what I'm doing here this whole time and I just ramble. Thorn says I talk too much, though I think that if he ever listened to himself, he wouldn't be so quick to judge. Anyway, I am training to be a Healer so I get the glorious job of checking in on all the patients. You are the only one there is at the moment so it has been rather boring."

Zia was amazed at how easily the girl was able to drift between subjects. "You know Thorn? I met him, brown hair and green eyes."

Terra nodded. "Yup, that's him. He brought you and your friends here, so I already knew that you had met. He is in so much trouble for going out on his own." A mischievous laugh escaped her lips. "He deserves it, too. Always running off and leaving me, telling me I am nothing but trouble. Now he's in trouble and I'm the good one."

"You don't like him? I thought he was somewhat difficult, but not that bad." It was the truth. Zia had no reason to dislike Thorn; he was only doing what he thought he was supposed to do.

"Difficult? Well, I guess you could call it that. Almost everyone adores him, so it's nice to see him get in trouble for a change. He is always so perfect, obeys all the rules, does exactly what he is told. I'm glad that someone finally got to corrupt him." Terra noticed Zia's perplexed expression. "Thorn is my brother. If you have one you know where I am coming from."

"Brother?" Zia could not see any resemblance, except for the eyes; both were a deep emerald green.

"Twins, believe it or not." Terra smiled again. "He can be annoying sometimes, but I love him. Can't help it. How old are you?"

There was the subject change again. Zia was barely able to keep up with the energetic girl. "Eighteen, why?"

Terra wrinkled her nose. "Eighteen. I'm fifteen, well, in my years."

"Your years?" The girl was definitely odd.

She nodded. "We age differently."

Zia going to ask her what she meant but she was interrupted by Thorn as he walked into the room. "Terra, how much longer are you going to be in here? You know that you aren't supposed to stay too long."

Terra waved a hand at her brother. "Zia just woke up. I can't leave her alone without making sure she is alright. It would not be right. I am training to be a Healer, after all."

Thorn glared at his sister, "You are not training to be a Healer for *them*. You are not even supposed to be talking to her."

"I think that is absolutely ridiculous. I am not going to determine who is deserving of my help just by their race. I am a Healer." Terra returned her attention to Zia. "Ignore him, he is intolerable."

The girl went about her business as a Healer, acting as if her brother wasn't in the room at all. Zia did not feel comfortable having Thorn in the room while Terra was examining her, but he did not seem as if he was going to leave any time soon. He stood in the corner, eyes narrowed dangerously at his sister. Zia wondered if the twins' relationship was as troubled as it appeared to be.

The twins could not have been more different from each other, not just in appearance. Zia barely knew them and yet she was able to tell how different they truly were.

Terra was lively and had a cheerful personality. Zia got the impression that Thorn was trying to be more mature than he really was; he also seemed far more serious than his sister. Remembering the boy's reaction when he had seen Yartu and the way he had acted when Shadow was questioning his ability as a Guardian made her think that every so often Thorn was more like his sister than either of them knew. She doubted that the twins would have appreciated anyone finding any similarities in their personalities.

"Terra." Thorn grabbed his sister's arm. "You have to leave now. The Keeper is sending a Guardian to interrogate her. You are not supposed to be here when he arrives." There was an urgency in his voice that had not been there before.

The girl spun around to face her brother so quickly it made Zia dizzy. "Which Guardian?"

"Gryphon." Thorn grimaced.

Terra's mouth dropped in shock, "What! Is the Keeper insane? Gryphon will kill her."

"What?" Zia asked incredulously. She was growing very concerned about her safety.

"Oh. Well, um…" Terra broke off, unsure of what to say.

Thorn pulled his sister towards the door, "He won't do anything to you. He just doesn't like your kind very much, that's all. The Keeper knows what he is doing, Terra. You should trust his judgment."

Zia wanted to ask him more about this Gryphon but Thorn was already out the door, dragging Terra behind him. She leaned into the pillow beneath her head, sinking in as far as it would allow. She closed her eyes, seeking the comfort of the darkness. She opened them again. How easily it came; to call the darkness comforting felt right in so many ways. Why did she still long for the safety of the shadows' embrace? She did not understand, everything it had done, everything it would do, had caused her nothing but misery. It had led her to this strange place, a room she could not escape, and she could barely sit up. Yartu was not at her side—and Shadow, what was she supposed to do about Shadow?

The strangely beautiful young man had invaded the most private recesses of her mind. What secrets had he unearthed? What dreams had he seen? Zia knew that she should be angry; he had gone where no one was meant to be. It was proving to be more difficult than she had imagined. How was she supposed to hate him when he had saved her? Her very soul had been in jeopardy and Shadow had saved her from the darkness. No matter what she did or how hard she tried she was unable to make herself hate him for all the trouble he had caused her. Thoughts of how she was causing him all the trouble kept ruining her attempts. For the life of her she could not figure out why she seemed to be blaming herself. She was not the problem, he was.

# CHAPTER 23

Zia's thoughts were rudely interrupted by the door slamming shut. The sound sent her head spinning. She had not yet fully recovered from her headache. As she sat up, spots clouded her vision, but when it cleared, she wished that the spots would return. The sight that greeted her was not a pleasant one. A man leaning against the wall was glaring at her. His appearance shocked her even more than Terra's had. Silver hair framed his face and golden eyes gleamed at her intensely. Elegant features were distorted by anger and loathing. She was not sure what to make of this man; he seemed young but she was having difficulty determining his age. Zia wondered who he might be and what he wanted with her. She remembered what Thorn had told Terra about someone, a Guardian, coming to interrogate her. Was this the Guardian? What had they called him? There was something else. Something Terra had said about him, something that Zia had a feeling she should be worried about.

"Zia Amarra." The man's voice was dripping with disdain.

She wondered how he knew her name. Had Yartu or Shadow told him? "Yes," she said warily, unsure of how to handle the situation or the man.

Zia waited for him to speak but he said nothing. He just crossed his arms and continued to glare at her. She felt as if she had done something to offend him. She closed her eyes and wished he would go away.

"It is extremely rude to ignore a guest." The insulting tone was still there.

She opened her eyes and met his angry gaze. "What do you want? I am not feeling well and I do not feel like talking to someone who is going to make me even more miserable, which I have a feeling you want to do. So, if you could come back later I would appreciate it." Zia forced a fake smile. "Polite enough for you?"

She did not think it was possible but he seemed even angrier than before. Zia felt herself tense just looking at him. She had no idea why, but he made her feel even more scared than the Magic Council. Zia thought he was just trying to intimidate her and maybe by standing up to him he would leave her alone. She knew now had badly she had miscalculated; he was dangerous. Gryphon, the name sprung forward. That was the name of the Guardian that Thorn had mentioned. It was also the name of the Guardian Terra said would kill her. "Good gods, what have I gotten myself into this time?" she muttered.

"Something far worse than you realize. You are not supposed to be here. Humans are not welcome, even if the Fallen One brought you here."

Zia shook her head. "I don't know a Fallen One. I do not even know where I am! How was I supposed to know I was not welcome?"

"The Fallen One should have mentioned it to you. His carelessness has endangered all that we are here to protect. Humans are troublesome beings with no respect for anyone or anything. They are ignorant and understand nothing. You should have been taken care of the moment you set foot in this forest, but instead you lie there where you are not meant to be. He has risked our exposure for you." With each angry word spoken he moved a step closer to her so by the end of his tirade he was standing not more than a foot in front of her, still glowering.

She moved back instinctively. She had no idea what he was talking about but she understood enough to know that her being in the forest had caused a great deal more trouble than she had thought. "I do not understand. I don't know what it is that I have done wrong." Zia tried to remain calm, hoping that it would work better than her previous attempt. Her calm outer appearance seemed to infuriate him more than her standing up to him.

Zia could not suppress a cry as he reached out and grabbed the front of her shirt, pulling her close to him. Her face was practically touching his. She saw the anger and the hate. Hatred of her or something else, she could not tell. Struggling against his hold only made things worse. Zia was truly frightened of this man. He seemed to hate her for no apparent reason other than the fact that she existed. She was all alone in the room with him and Thorn had said that no one was supposed to be there when he interrogated her. Did that mean no one was around at all? Would crying out for help be useless, would the words even make it past her lips? She was trapped with a man who looked as if he wanted to kill her, and if Terra was to be trusted he would.

His face was so close she could feel his breath with every word. "Everything. Humans have ruined everything. They destroy that which they fear the most, and they fear whatever they do not understand. Humans understand nothing so they destroy everything. You are a disgusting and vile race who care about nothing but wealth. Your greed is never-ending; it does not stop until it consumes everything in its path. Humans are not worthy of existing; they are the worst race to ever have come into existence. Why you were ever created and for what purpose is beyond me. I despise you and everything you are. Humans should be punished for all the crimes they have committed, starting with you." As the last words were spoken a dagger came to find itself gently pressed against Zia's neck.

Zia did not move, terrified that the man would kill her. She saw death in his eyes, her death. She saw anger and hate, but she also saw pain. Pain? Did it hurt him to kill her? Zia wished her thoughts would stop spinning. She wanted to have a clear mind when he made the fatal strike. Dying would be easier if she wasn't so confused. She wanted to ask him to have mercy, although she felt that mercy was beyond him. She wanted him to draw the dagger from her throat and tell her it was all some twisted joke. It wasn't; that much she knew for sure. This Guardian hated humans with a passion and he seemed to be taking out all his anger on her. Why does this always happen to me? she thought.

Her silence did not upset him. Truth was, he actually enjoyed watching her body tremble in fear. She knew the end was near, she knew that he would kill her. Gryphon liked that. Humans needed to be taught a lesson and he took great pleasure in teaching them. He was an extremely powerful Guardian and he would have been the leader of the Guardians if it had not been for one thing; he took far too much pleasure in ridding the forest of humans. The

Keeper had told him time and again how he should respect humans as living beings; he only respected them when they were dead. This human, a strange looking one too, had violated everything he believed in. He was going to make her understand why humans were not welcome in his forest. Her death was imminent. He wanted her to know that there was no chance of her surviving. If the Keeper had wanted questions answered he should not have sent him. It was foolish of him to think that Gryphon would give up years of hate just because a girl was in trouble. There was no mercy in his heart for a miserable human.

This one was different, though. She did not scream or cry, she did not beg for mercy. There was only the sound of her ragged breathing. Gryphon pressed the dagger deeper into her pale neck. Zia gasped as she felt a stab of pain. He did not kill her and she knew why. He wanted to torment her, make her suffer for sins that were not hers. Blood trickled down her neck.

"Death is not as bad as you might think," her tormentor said softly. "I am doing you a favor. Life is far more painful than death. I am being more merciful than you will ever know."

Zia closed her eyes. "Go ahead, be merciful. You are right, my life has been full of pain and I want nothing more than for it to end." She opened her eyes and met his gaze. "End it. You will be doing me a great service."

Gryphon's blade did not move. He could not look away, the girl held him captive. She wanted to die. Her body no longer trembled and there was no fear in her eyes, only acceptance. He wondered what it was that brought the girl to this forest and what led her to this moment where she did not fear death. Gryphon knew that all humans feared death, it was a weakness they all shared, or so he had thought. This girl did not fear it; she welcomed it.

She wanted him to finish, she wanted it over and done with. It was awfully sadistic of him to make her wait. If he wanted her to scream for help or beg for mercy he was out of luck. Zia would not give him the satisfaction; he could do whatever he wanted to her but she would not beg for her life. She was no longer afraid of him, she knew that was what he really wanted, to scare her. He'll have to wait for his next victim, Zia thought morbidly.

Slowly he drew his dagger away and released his hold on her. Zia wondered what he was going to do to her now. A hand rose to gently touch her neck, and she could not help but flinch at the contact. The touch lasted only a moment before he backed away from her. He did not go far, just a few steps away, but she was grateful that he was no longer so close.

Gryphon glanced at the blood on his fingers and shook his head. "I thought humans were all stupid. I was wrong. You are insane."

Zia could not help but laugh. It eased some of the tension she felt. "I really do not understand why everyone keeps saying that. I guess it must be true."

"You are by far the strangest human I have ever met." He returned to his original position, leaning against the wall with his arms crossed.

Anger no longer distorted his face; instead it had been replaced by confusion. Zia was confused as well. She had spent so much time with Shadow she found it odd that this man did not hide his emotions. Though Gryphon seemed easy to read, Zia knew that one emotion could quickly turn into another. The man had a volatile nature, that much she had learned in the few minutes she had spent with him. Zia did not want to do anything to upset him again. She just might end up dead with his next mood swing.

"What were you doing in the forest?" Golden eyes bored into hers.

"I was running away," she said simply.

His eyes once again narrowed at her comment. Zia could not figure out who was worse, Shadow or Gryphon. Both had an intense gaze that seemed to hold her captive and look into her soul, the only difference was Shadow seemed to know all that was hidden within and Gryphon demanded to know.

"Running away? You really expect me to believe that? No one runs into this forest; it is far worse in here than it is facing whatever you think is so terrible out there. People come here when they do not care if they die. In fact, people come here if they want to die." He arched his silvery brows in anticipation. "Are you going to tell me the truth or not?"

"It is the truth," she protested. "Shadow told me to run into the forest. He is the one who said it would be alright. How was I supposed to know it was against some sort of rule for me to be here? I am not from this area. I have never even seen this forest before. You expect me to understand what it is you are trying to tell me, but you haven't told me anything. I have enough problems—I don't need this. If you want something just ask me directly and you will get an honest answer. I am sick of playing games."

A ghost of a smile appeared, "I don't care much for games either. Fine, I will ask the questions and you will answer them. What were you running from?"

"A person," was the only answer she gave him. Zia had no intention of telling him about the Magic Council or Nicolai. She told him she would answer honestly and she would, but one did not have to reveal everything in order to tell the truth.

Gryphon raised a hand to his face in exasperation. "You are not going to make this easy, are you? What kind of person?"

"One who wanted to hurt me. Shadow helped me and told me this forest would be safe because this person could not follow us in here." She shrugged. "There's not much more to tell."

"Really," he mused. "Why don't you tell me how you met the Fallen One? I am rather interested considering the only reason you are still alive is because of him. Well, that and the fact that Thorn is worthless as a Guardian."

The Fallen One, everyone kept saying that, and Zia wanted to know why. "I already told you I don't know who you are talking about. If I had met someone called the Fallen One, I think I would have remembered it. Why doesn't anyone seem to understand this?"

"It seems he neglected to inform you of what and who he truly is." Gryphon smirked; it reminded her of Nicolai. "You know who the Fallen One is, Zia. He was the one who brought you here, the one who stayed by your side in this very room."

Zia started to get that sinking feeling again. "I do not understand. Terra said Shadow was in here with me, not the Fallen One."

"Shadow is the Fallen One." Gryphon's smile was malicious. "Are you going to ask me what the Fallen One is again? Maybe you already know... I find it doubtful though. It is not something he would tell everyone he meets. The whole thing is somewhat complicated. It would prove difficult for a human to understand with their limited intellect."

She did not know what to say. What was she supposed to say? This person everyone kept talking about was Shadow. What was the Fallen One anyway? Why did everyone seem to know who and what he was except her? Once again, her mind was spinning wildly out of control.

Fallen, fallen from what? What did it all mean? Was Shadow really this Fallen One? It was true that she didn't know much about him but it just seemed that the more she learned the less she understood. Shadow was... what was he? Zia was beginning to doubt that he was human; humans did not look like him. They did not talk or act like him either, humans didn't read people's thoughts. Memories flooded her mind, memories of meeting him for the first time. She had never seen anyone or anything so beautiful in her entire life. He frightened her and made her feel strange things, he did nothing but confuse her. She had been surprised that he was able to conceal himself in the shadows, successfully hiding from her. Was that something he was normally able to do? What were the powers of the Fallen One? Did he control the darkness?

Fear began to take control. Was he working with the darkness, pretending to save her yet truthfully making her more susceptible to its control? Was everyone trying to hurt her? The Magic Council, Nicolai, and the darkness, all were trying to control her, to use her. Zia had thought that Shadow was the one person she could trust besides Yartu, and now he might be just as bad as the others. He had deceived her, betrayed her. Why? Why was this happening to her? What did they want with her? What was wrong with her?

Zia did not notice the tears falling down her face. She didn't see anything, not even Gryphon who was watching her silently, waiting to see what would happen. She had closed her eyes to the world, she had closed herself off from the world. Darkness began to creep in, shadows circled slowly. There was no one there to fight them this time, victory was assured.

CHAPTER 24

Earlier that day...

Yartu decided he was sick and tired of everything, especially the waiting. Time seemed to have slowed since they had taken Zia away from him. These blasted people that Shadow had brought him and Zia to were annoying and refused to let him stay near his beloved Zia. She was there, only a small distance from him, unconscious and in need of his comfort and care. She hadn't woken up yet and it was making him anxious. It had been two whole days since he had been able to touch her, smell her, curl up next to her and feel her warmth. The miniature dragon was tempted to bite every single one of them until they let him into the room that held his precious Zia prisoner.

Shadow had told him not to worry, but it only made the dragon angrier, especially since Shadow had been allowed to stay with her for two days. Zia was his everything; not being near her was tormenting him, and even worse was the fact that he could no longer sense her. He hadn't been able to since she had collapsed, he could not think of a better word for what had happened to her. All he was capable of sensing was that she remained alive, but other than that he felt nothing.

"Hello, little guy. How is your wing?" Yartu winced at the nickname, but he was not too angry. The speaker was the girl who had healed his wing, a cute little thing with green hair.

The dragon flew up to meet her face to face, "Much better. You are quite the healer. I want to see Zia."

Terra giggled. "You always say that, and you always get the same answer. I told you, the Keeper doesn't want anyone in there except Healers."

"I don't like this Keeper of yours," Yartu grumbled. "Wait, why can't I go in? Shadow was in there."

"I don't think the Keeper is going to keep him from doing anything he wants. I wouldn't want to upset him, and Shadow told the Keeper you would probably attack all the Healers trying to help Zia anyway," the girl said with a shrug.

Yartu was about to protest when a voice spoke for him. "I understand your concern, Yartu, but if you did not agree with what one of the Healers was doing you would attack. It is in your nature to protect Zia. If it makes you feel better, I'm not allowed back in either."

"Good," the miniature dragon snapped.

Shadow just shook his head. "Zia should be alright now. You will probably get to see her very soon."

"I had better, if they know what's good for them." Yartu glared at the door and the guard standing beside it.

"You would make a formidable foe, Yartu. They are lucky that you are not terrorizing all of them," Shadow said with a small smile.

"Why? You want me to?" Yartu asked sarcastically.

Shadow rolled his eyes. "It might make the time go by faster but I don't think it would be a good idea."

"Do they expect me to just wait?"

"I'm afraid that is all you can do," Terra said apologetically. "You will be able to see her when the Healers think it is time, until then all you can do is wait."

"Wonderful," Yartu said as he curled up on a windowsill miserably.

The waiting was the worst. The more time that passed the more Yartu felt like he was going to go crazy. It didn't help watching Shadow sitting on the floor leaning against a wall with his eyes closed. He seemed so calm it made the miniature dragon worry all the more to make up for Shadow's apparent lack of concern.

Time began to lose all meaning; for all Yartu knew, years had passed instead of minutes. Did these people know how cruel they were being by keeping him from Zia? How could they do this to him, to her? They were Bonded, and keeping them apart was the cruelest thing that anyone could possibly do to them. It did not matter if they were separated by a wall or an entire country; he needed to be near her. These horrible people did not understand the strength of his and Zia's Bond.

At some point he felt Zia; she must have woken from her strange slumber. Yartu could sense that she was alright but very confused; he wondered when the healers would let him see her. He did not know what time it was when he saw Terra go into the room, nor could he recall how much time had passed when Thorn went in as well. When the two left the room Shadow's eyes flew open.

He watched them carefully, his interest piquing Yartu's curiosity. "What is the matter with you? Do you think Zia's awake?"

"What do you think, Yartu? You are her dragon. You should be able to tell better than I." Shadow continued watching the twins.

Yartu put his face right in front of Shadow's. "I can feel her but the connection is weak. You seem to know these people, *you* find out what is going on."

"If we were allowed to see her, they would have told us by now." His words were directed at the dragon but his attention was completely on the twins.

Thorn felt Shadow's gaze. He wanted nothing more than to walk away but something compelled him to meet the dark eyes of the Fallen One. He did not like how he had suddenly been drawn into the Fallen One's plans. Thorn knew that the Fallen One would sometimes be seen wandering around the forest but Thorn, himself, had never seen or spoken to him before; now he wished he never had. All of the novice Guardians had been warned never to invoke the Fallen One's wrath. Many of the novices had tried to get close to him, believing the warnings to be a joke, only to find themselves in the care of the Healers. Thorn had always believed that it was better to avoid him altogether and he had successfully done so, up until he decided to prove his worth as a real Guardian. He had never seen the Fallen One up close, so how was he supposed to know that it was him? It wasn't as if anyone ever gave him a description. Why was he being punished? He had never done anything wrong.

"I think he wants to talk to us," Terra said.

Thorn shook his head. "You go talk to him. He seems to like you, he hates me."

"That's because you attacked his pet," she explained.

"I don't think Zia would like being called his pet."

Terra rolled her eyes. "Stop stalling, would you?" She grabbed her brother's arm and pulled him towards Shadow and Yartu. "And she is his pet, why else would he be so concerned about her? I'm not being cruel; I mean, who wouldn't want to be his pet? Look at him."

"Terra!" Thorn was shocked that his sister had said such a thing. "He is the Fallen One."

"I know. Being the Fallen One doesn't stop him from being perfection." Terra giggled.

Yartu was unable to hear the twins' conversation, but he saw them coming over. He got up off the ground in order to meet them face to face. "Is Zia awake? Can I see her?"

"Not yet. The Keeper is sending someone to question her, you should be able to see her after that," Terra told Yartu with an encouraging smile.

It did not put the dragon at ease. Instead, it made him worry all the more. "What do you mean by question? She didn't do anything wrong. If you are going to blame someone, blame your brother or him."

The *him* in question rose to his feet. "No one is to blame except for Nicolai. If it had not been for him, it would not have been necessary for Zia to enter the forest in the first place. Who did the Keeper..." Shadow did not finish for the answer to his question walked into the room where Zia was.

Shadow wanted to kill the Keeper. What was that mindless imbecile up to now? What on earth possessed him to send Gryphon? Shadow had dealt with the volatile Guardian on a few unpleasant occasions. He knew enough about him to understand that what the Keeper had just done was authorize Zia's murder.

Thorn noticed the dark eyes narrow dangerously at the door. He had a feeling that he knew exactly what Shadow was thinking. "Gryphon is under direct orders not to harm her. The Keeper understands your involvement; he merely wants to hear the girl's side of the story."

"And here I thought he would accept my word, it is good to know that I am trusted." Sarcasm was blatantly evident in Shadow's voice.

Terra shook her head and tried to resolve the situation. It would not do to insult the Fallen One. "Oh, but you are trusted. The Guardians were probably complaining to the Keeper about her presence, so in order to keep the peace he agreed to let them interrogate her."

The dark eyes met hers. Terra found she could scarcely breathe; never before had she seen eyes like his. Perfect black orbs that seemed bottomless, she would have said one could have fallen into them if it was possible. Escape was futile; one could not look away no matter how hard one tried. A part of her wondered who would want to, while the rational part of her was terrified; eyes were not meant to have such a staggering effect on someone. The Fallen One was a mystery to everyone and Terra now understood why. She also understood why the Keeper and the Guardians would be concerned about his involvement with Zia. Just what did he want with her? Terra wondered.

A ghost of a smile hovered over his lips. "The Keeper must be having a great deal of trouble with the Guardians. Gryphon will soon discover that Zia is more than a match for him."

Yartu was tired of being ignored. He began to interrogate the twins himself. Shadow ignored the miniature dragon's ramblings and the hasty assurance from the twins about Zia's well-being.

Shadow sat down again and let his mind wander. His consciousness drifted past a mind full of concern and aggression, two minds of similar quality, it came to a mind full of hate and anger, but then moved on. There was only one mind with which he intended to connect and it did not belong to a dragon, the twins or Gryphon. He was seeking a different mind, one in particular—Zia's.

He found that which he was searching for easily. He knew this mind, the foreign quality of it and the alien nature of that which dwelt there hidden in the deepest recesses of the mind. This mind had become as familiar to him as if it were his own. Shadow felt her thoughts swirling around him.

Fear, pain, death; these were the foremost thoughts in Zia's mind, they often were. Shadow was able to understand what was occurring in the room with Gryphon and Zia. He did not let her know he was in her mind, knowing that it would have made her angry. She did not like the thought of having to be protected, of being beholden to anyone. She would have gone into a rage had she known that Shadow had connected with her mind in order to make sure Gryphon did not harm her. Truth was, he would not have blamed her; he should not constantly enter her mind without permission and yet he found himself unable to avoid it. Shadow did not understand why he felt as if he had to take care of the girl, she was nothing but trouble. There was something similar about her, though, she was different like him; neither truly belonged. Whether or not that was the reason, Shadow found himself once again in Zia's mind trying to keep her out of trouble.

All seemed to be going well, Gryphon no longer appeared as if he was going to kill her. Shadow decided he should leave now that she seemed to have regained control of the situation. He began to let his consciousness drift back to his body.

Sudden panic brought him back. Zia's thoughts were whirling chaotically. Deception. Betrayal. A deep sadness filled her. Shadow was unable to find her in the chaos. He wondered what had happened to cause such a mess. He figured it had something to do with Gryphon. He would deal with him later; right now, he needed to find Zia.

It was nearly impossible—he had never seen her mind in such complete disarray before. Shadow shifted through a tangled mess of thoughts trying to find her. He was unable to make out what the thoughts were, only that they were causing Zia great pain. The darkness began to come out of its hiding place ready to take its prize. Shadow knew he had to find her, and fast, or the darkness would claim her.

Something drew him deeper into her mind. It was there he found her. She was drowning in her own thoughts, unknowingly destroying herself. Shadow tried to reach her but was forced back. The reason for her distress was revealed at that moment. Him, he was the cause of all the chaos. *Fallen.* The word drifted across her mind. Gryphon had told her about him. That was what had caused this mess. Shadow wanted to kill him, he had just kept Zia from being taken and now the darkness had an even better chance of taking her.

Shadow tried to call out to her, but his words fell upon deaf ears. Zia had turned away from everything. The darkness would consume her and she would be lost forever.

Yartu noticed that he could no longer sense Zia. He cast a glance at Shadow, who was once again ignoring everyone. Something about him made Yartu worry. He was about to make up some excuse to force him to talk, but he didn't need to. Shadow was on his feet faster than Yartu had time to think. The dragon had never seen anyone move that fast before. He didn't even have time to ask him what was wrong, Shadow practically ran into Zia's room.

Shadow pushed past the twins; he could only think of reaching Zia before it was too late. The darkness was closing in, he could feel it; he needed to get to her before it took total control of her mind. His telepathic abilities were strong but close contact was necessary for what he had to do. The connection would not be strong enough without it, even with his power.

When he got into the room Gryphon tried to stop him but he pushed him away. Shadow came to an abrupt halt in front of Zia. She sat there on the bed, tears staining her cheeks. The sight of her made him want to hold her, but the feeling made him uncomfortable so he ignored it. Shadow knelt down in front of her.

"Zia?" He wanted to try and reach her first through normal means.

He shrugged off a hand that touched his shoulder. "It won't work, I tried. The girl is out of it. She is not normal." Gryphon did not bother to try and conceal his disdain.

Shadow spun around to face the other man. "I will deal with you after I resolve this problem you have created. I suggest you leave now if you know what is good for you." His voice was threatening, he didn't care.

He returned his attention to Zia. Taking her hand in his he closed his eyes and made the connection, hoping he wasn't too late.

Yartu and the twins were just outside the door. Gryphon did not let them in. "It would be best if we let him do whatever it is he has to do."

"What are you talking about?" shouted Yartu. "What is wrong with Zia? I want to know what is going on and I want to know now."

"The girl obviously needs the unique abilities of the Fallen One. It would be wise to let him do what is necessary." Gryphon pulled the door closed behind him.

Thorn looked at him apprehensively, "Why do you think he is helping her? Should we be worried that the Fallen One has taken an interest in a human?"

"Thorn! You should be worried about Zia's well-being, not security," Terra exclaimed, appalled at her brother's insensitivity.

Gryphon nodded to Thorn and placed a reassuring hand on Terra's shoulder. "Terra, I am sure Shadow will be able to help Zia. Thorn has every reason to worry, though. The Fallen One has never associated with humans or us unless absolutely necessary. His connection to the girl is cause for concern. I will go and inform the Keeper of the current situation; he may have a better idea of what is going on."

Thorn sighed. "I hope so."

"No one enters that room or leaves it until I come back. I am leaving you to guard it, Thorn, do not disappoint me again." Gryphon did not wait for him to respond. He walked away, leaving them to wonder.

"Once again, what is going on and who is that person?" Yartu was growing tired of repeating himself.

Terra grimaced, "Gryphon is the best Guardian we have and probably the most unpleasant person you will ever meet."

"He's my instructor in the ways of the Guardian and our older brother." Thorn finished for her.

Yartu was a bit surprised; the man looked and acted nothing like the twins. He shook his head incredulously. "Who are you people?"

"Elves," the twins said in perfect unison.

CHAPTER 25

Darkness covered every part of her mind. Nowhere was safe. It pulled her and caressed her at the same time. The shadows begged her to let them help her end her misery. There was so much they could do for her if only she would let them. Whispered promises filled her ears; promises of friendship, trust and love. The darkness promised to mend what was broken.

Zia did not understand what it meant. Nothing was broken, she just wanted to disappear. It promised her that as well, a chance to get away, to leave everything behind. The shadows would care for her; she would not need anyone else. They were her friends. She could trust them. They loved her, unlike that person, the one who lied to her and betrayed her.

The darkness would give her all that she desired. It would never leave her, never hurt her, and never betray her trust. He was what she should be afraid of. Did he not make her feel things that she did not want to feel? She had trusted him, and look what happened. He betrayed her. He was working with those horrible people who wanted to lock her away. Why else would he try to keep her from the shadows, her true friends? He was not working with them; they would never hurt her like that. The darkness did not understand her angst. They thought she was perfect; it was all the others who thought there was something wrong with her. The shadows had always been there to comfort her, to wipe away the tears. They wanted to rid her of her sadness; all she had to do was give in. They could make her forget him and all the pain he caused. The darkness would protect her and love her always. What more could she want?

[Zia.]

The faint sound of her name being called made her move away from the shadows. They tried to pull her back but she wanted to know who had called her. She tried to see who was there but all she could see was darkness.

[Zia, please.]

There it was again, a little stronger than it had been before. The voice sounded sad. She wondered why. She moved towards it.

[Please. I can explain everything.]

What did it want with her? She moved slowly closer, and as she did the voice grew stronger. It did not say much, just her name, and occasionally it pleaded with her to listen to it. *What do you want?* she asked, not sure if it could hear her.

[Don't give in, Zia. I want to help you. Don't listen to them.]

The voice had grown strong enough to cause the darkness distress. It did not like this annoying person. It had grown weary of the repeated attempts made to steal her away.

The shadows began to swirl around her angrily. They would not let him take her from them this time. Their aggression frightened her. She wanted nothing more than to get away. The desire of the darkness overwhelmed her, it did not care about anything other than her, and it wanted nothing more. It would do anything to possess her, she belonged to it and no one else.

[Zia!]

The voice had grown faint once again. *Help me*, she cried. Unable to fight the shadows, she could feel herself fading, slipping away. *Shadow*, Zia whispered. She no longer cared if he had betrayed her trust or not, she just wanted him to help her. He would protect her from the darkness, he would save her.

No, the word echoed in the farthest corner of her mind. The darkness would not allow her to be taken. How could she possibly want him after all the pain he had caused? The shadows would not allow it. He was dangerous. He was bad, wrong. He would hurt her again and again and not care in the least. It would not let her suffer like that. It had promised her everything she desired. What more was there? Why did she long for him and not the comfort of the darkness?

Zia shook her head, trying to keep the words the shadows spoke from reaching her ears. She wanted them to leave her alone. What did they want with her? Why were they doing this to her? A cold sensation filled her. She tried to scream, but the sound echoed silently among the shadows. The darkness had won, she was lost.

[No!]

Warmth enveloped her, banishing the cold. Zia was no longer in the embrace of the shadows. She was in his safe embrace, protected from all that would do her harm. He had heard her call and came to save her; her Shadow.

The darkness could not reach her and the whispers of the shadows fell upon deaf ears. Nothing existed but the two of them. He filled her senses. Zia began to lose herself once again, but this time it was not the darkness that threatened to take her.

[Trust me, the last thing I want is to have you lose yourself.]

I don't understand. She spoke hesitantly, unsure if any of this was real.

[It is real. Everything you are going through is real. The darkness wants you, Zia, it wants you so much it is disturbing. The darkness cannot feel; it has no emotions. Wanting you as much as it does makes absolutely no sense whatsoever. I wish I could explain why it seems to have chosen you, but I can't. I barely understand what is going on.]

Zia's forehead and palms were resting on his chest. She gripped his shirt unconsciously, trying to make sense of it all. The darkness had almost succeeded in taking her, but he had come at the perfect time to save her. Why is it, she thought, that he always comes at the right moment? The shadows did not come near her when he was there. It almost seemed as if they were afraid of him. If the darkness was afraid of him, shouldn't she be? *Who are you?* Zia whispered softly. *What are you?*

[I wish I could tell you. It is difficult to explain. For so long I have kept too many secrets. Some secrets I keep are not mine alone; if they were I would tell you everything. Even if I were to tell you, this is not the time or place. Your mind is not where such things should transpire; it is chaotic enough without my adding to it.]

A small sigh escaped her lips. *I think you have already. I did not want this.* Zia felt a tear roll down her cheek.

[I know, I didn't want this either. I don't understand this any more than you. The connection between my mind and yours is stronger than anything I have ever experienced before. I do know one thing for certain, though…]

Zia looked at his face for the first time. So beautiful, so mysterious, and yet she knew nothing about him. Still, he was just as confused as she was by the situation they found themselves in. Sorrow was hidden within the depths of those impossibly dark eyes. A sadness so deep it was impossible to comprehend. Zia wondered what could possibly have caused such pain and sorrow. Maybe it wasn't his pain, she thought. It was most likely her own misery reflected back to her through his eyes. Something made her think that it was a combination of both. Her sadness was reflected in his eyes but his had become visible because of it, a mirror image. A reflection of each in the other's eyes, one in the same.

What is it that you know for certain? I know that I do not understand anything anymore.

[I was brought to you for a reason, Zia. I have been sent to help you. You need me, I can help with the darkness. I understand it in ways others do not. I am the only one who can help you.]

She rested her forehead on his chest once more. She did need him; he was right about that. Shadow was able to push back the darkness and, for some strange reason, it seemed afraid of him. Nothing seemed to make sense anymore. Zia was finding it difficult to determine what was real and what was a dream. Her nightmares had come to life; how was that possible? Could it be that reality was nothing but a dream? Her whole life seemed so quiet compared to the events of the past few days—it had been complicated before but not like this. Zia no longer knew what to expect. Part of her wanted to blame the Magic Council for everything; another part was placing all the blame on Shadow.

A complete mystery which was getting worse; this strangely beautiful young man did nothing but annoy and confuse her. Half the time she wanted to hit him and the rest of the time... well, she did not want to think about it. He was in her mind, the most private and secret part of her. He seemed to know things about her that she didn't know herself. It was almost as though he knew her even better than Yartu, as if that was possible. Yartu was her Bonded dragon and he wasn't able to enter her mind at will. Zia wanted, no, needed, to know what was going on. She knew Shadow would not tell her, he already said that. There must be another way.

Come back, the shadows whispered. They reached for her trying to pull her away from Shadow. Zia clutched his shirt in terror. They would take her away and she would never see Yartu again. She would be alone in the darkness, all alone.

[You are never alone, Zia, I am here. I will not let the darkness take you.]

It sounded so simple, but she knew better. The darkness would never leave her alone. It would not be satisfied until it had consumed her. Shadow could not save her. He was just a boy; compared to the darkness he was powerless. What could telepathic powers do against the full might of the endless dark? Who was he to think that he could protect her? Why did he want to?

[Don't. Your confusion will make the darkness more powerful, the shadows will find a way to reach you through it. You must trust me, Zia. It is the only way.]

Trust him? There was no reason for her to trust him, but she did. Everything she had been through; he was always there. Shadow rescued her and Yartu from Nicolai. He helped her when Thorn tried to hurt her and he protected her from the shadows. Zia trusted him more than she had ever trusted anyone before in her entire life, and she had no idea why.

The darkness was seething with rage. It would not let her go with him. It did not want to admit defeat just yet. There was still time. He had proven a stronger adversary than it originally determined, but there was still time. The darkness could still reach her but it knew that it must wait for the appropriate moment. He won this battle but he would not win the war. She belonged to the darkness; it would claim her no matter what he did. He was nothing but a nuisance—he could not change her fate, regardless of his valiant attempts to save her. The darkness would win her in the end; she could not resist the pull for much longer, even with his help. Now was not the time, though, he was strong and she was not ready. The darkness could wait, it had waited this long already, but it still had to keep up appearances.

They whispered strange things to her. The shadows once more were attempting to claim her. She could feel them closing in around her, pulling at her. She was afraid and they knew it. The shadows no longer cared if she was afraid of them, they would take her by force if necessary. Zia felt Shadow's arms tighten around her and lost herself in his embrace.

He was so warm and inviting. The whispers of the shadows could not reach her, she could only hear the softness of his breathing and his steady heartbeat. Zia felt like she was drowning and he was the only thing keeping her afloat. She was losing herself, no, she was already lost, and she did not care. Shadow would banish her nightmares, he would protect her. Zia gripped him tightly as if her life depended on it. She trusted him, she trusted him completely. He was the only one who could save her.

[I am here. You are safe now. I will never leave you alone again. You do not have to be afraid anymore. Zia.]

Her name was spoken softly in a breathless whisper. It did something to her she did not understand. That happened a lot with Shadow, she realized. It did not matter, he was going to bring her back to the real world away from the nightmarish world that was her mind. She was safe, she had nothing to fear as long as he was near.

[Let us leave this unpleasant place. It is time to return, Zia.]

Yes, she thought. Zia wanted nothing more than to have Shadow take her away from her mind. *I trust you,* she said softly.

CHAPTER 26

The forest stretched before them, vast and dark. It was impossible to see if there was anything lurking behind the wall of massive trees; he knew there was. Far too many times he had tried to enter that forest only to turn back, narrowly escaping with his life. Foul, dark creatures inhabited the dense forest, creatures most people only saw in their nightmares. There were many rumors about the forest, most of them untrue. He knew the truth; unfortunately he had found out the hard way.

Shadow had always escaped into the forest. He thought that Nicolai would not follow him, but he had. It always ended badly and Nicolai would end up having to wait for Shadow to come out again. He had never understood how Shadow was able to survive in there; it was impossible, no one survived in that forest. Nicolai had learned Shadow's secret, though, the wretch had help. He used the forest's inhabitants to stay alive. They kept him safe, giving him refuge from the horrors that traveled amongst the trees.

A race of strange beings dwelt within the forest, calling it home. An ancient race that was rumored to have never existed at all. They were a secretive race who kept an even greater secret. A secret they did everything in their power to protect. He had discovered them by accident when he was tracking that miserable, sneaky bastard.

Elves. Nicolai hated them almost as much as he hated Shadow. Very few people knew elves really existed, most thought they were nothing but myth. They existed all right, but they lived in the strangest of places. Places that most people would have avoided, places like this forest. They adapted remarkably well to wherever it was they made their home, whether it was an ancient forest or the middle of a desert. There seemed to be no logical explanation as to how elves chose their homes, but there was. If one looked closely enough there was a pattern; elves only lived in locations that were considered uninhabitable and inhospitable, places intelligent people avoided. The elven people made their cities in places of great power, places that hid ancient secrets and treasure. Elves considered themselves the guardians of these places and would do anything to keep them safe from the greed of humans.

That was how it was with the forest looming before him. The elves were keeping something hidden, a secret they didn't want anyone to uncover. The last time Nicolai had chased Shadow into the forest was the last time he had seen the boy and the first time he had seen an elf. There had been two of them; he didn't even notice them until it was too late. The first one was rather ordinary looking but the other... Nicolai thought it had been one of the strangest looking things he had ever seen. The two elves had made it perfectly clear that no one was to enter the forest if they wanted to live. Nicolai still had a scar from where the strange elf with golden eyes had sliced open his side with a sword.

His thoughts drifted to a more recent wound that was starting to scar. Zia Amarra still had not emerged from the forest with her annoying rescuer. She might not have been anywhere in sight but she was in his thoughts. His mind was filled with images of her. No longer was he willing to let her go and forget she existed. It was not about Lady Yena and the Magic Council anymore, he wanted Zia. He would do anything to get her and, when he did, he would make her suffer. She had made him Lady Yena's hound once again and she somehow had become involved with a person Nicolai hated with a passion. The hatred he felt for Shadow paled in comparison with how he was beginning to feel about Zia. Thoughts of the strange girl consumed him; an unhealthy obsession had formed.

Nicolai didn't know which was worse, the waiting, or the knowledge that Zia was so close. He did not want to go back into the forest, but he would if she did not come out soon. The danger the elven Guardians posed did not concern him as much as it should have. Nicolai's obsession with Zia was making him irrational and reckless.

Crystal, on the other hand, had become overly cautious. She was unsure of just about everything that was going on. The only thing she knew for certain was that Nicolai had officially made her life hell. Nicolai blamed Zia and Crystal blamed Nicolai. The witch wanted nothing more than to go home, but she knew that Nicolai would never let her leave. Zia was not immune to a witch's magic and as long as Crystal's magic worked Nicolai would keep her close.

The witch had just about had it with him and his brooding. He continually glared at the forest as if he was willing Zia to come forth. Crystal did not understand why it was so dangerous to go into the forest even if it was creepy. She also didn't understand how the girl managed to have survived so long in the supposedly deadly forest. Maybe it had something to do with the young man who had come to her aid. That impossibly beautiful young man named Shadow.

Now there was a mystery Crystal would have enjoyed solving if given the chance. The young man seemed to defy all reason. He had been able to ward off her attacks. No matter how hard she tried she could not figure out how he did it. Remembering what Nicolai told her about him made things even more confusing than they were before. The witch had been trying to determine the connection between Shadow and Zia. Crystal found it odd that the young man showed up at the exact moment Zia needed him most. She also wondered why he appeared again after being in hiding for so long. Everything Nicolai told her about Shadow went against all of his actions. He was not supposed to be a hero, he was supposed to be aloof, cold and uncaring.

Nicolai told her many things about Shadow when he had returned to Selia after tracking the boy for two years. Crystal was doing her best to recall all of the information, because Nicolai was of no help. He had barely spoken to her since Zia had disappeared into the forest. The witch didn't really mind, it was quiet and she needed to think.

Shadow and Zia; what was so important about them? The girl had a power unlike anything she had encountered before. Crystal had not seen the girl use her power but she had felt it lying deep inside of her, waiting. The witch remembered how things had been in the few short days she had traveled in Zia's company. During the day the girl seemed normal, but at night... at night the girl almost disappeared into the darkness. Crystal found it odd that the shadows just outside of the campfire's glow seemed to be reaching for the girl. At first Crystal thought it was her imagination but the more she thought about it the more real it seemed. The darkness appeared as if it was going to swallow Zia whole one moment and be a part of her the next. It almost looked like Zia was an extension of the shadows.

Darkness, dragons, girls with strange powers and mysterious handsome men... the witch shook her head. What had Nicolai dragged her into and, more importantly, why had she let him? She should be in her home where she only had to worry about her cats and the Magic Council. The Magic Council, that made her think.

"Nicolai, who hired you to track Shadow?"

He glared at her, angry with her for interrupting his thoughts. "It was the last job I took from Lady Yena, until now. Why?"

Lady Yena, that damn woman's name kept coming up. Crystal wondered if it was more than coincidence. "Don't you find it odd that she hired you to find Shadow and now Zia? I feel that there must be some connection between the two. Do you remember why she wanted Shadow?"

"She had heard rumors of a mysterious boy who had been found mostly dead outside the forest."

Crystal shook her head in confusion. "Why would she be interested in a boy who was almost dead? It doesn't make sense."

Nicolai smirked. "Some people had found him and brought him back to their house. Once they got him there, they went to get a healer. The healer believed the farmer about the boy being close to death, the farmer had told him about the cuts all over the boy's body and how he had been covered in his own blood. He had also mentioned two deep gashes that were on the boy's back between his shoulders. When the healer saw the boy there was not a single scratch or drop of blood on him. He thought the farmer was playing a joke on him but the farmer's daughter told him her story. She had been left behind to watch the boy until her father returned with help. Shortly after he left, the boy took a turn for the worse. She knew that her father was too late and would never make it back in time. She left the boy to get him an extra blanket for comfort; she was out of the room for only a few minutes. When she came back, he was sitting up on the bed in perfect health. The healer did not understand how the boy had fully recovered after being so close to death. It was either a miracle or magic."

"Magic? The healer assumed it was magic so he wrote to the Magic Council asking if they knew about a spell that could bring people back from the brink of death." Crystal sighed. "Healers can be so stupid sometimes, there is no such spell. Lady Yena wanted to make sure nothing strange was going on so she sent you to investigate and you found Shadow."

"The boy was Shadow."

"I see." It was so obvious and yet for some strange reason Crystal didn't want to believe it.

Nicolai became serious again. "I spoke with everyone involved, the farmer, his daughter, and the healer. None of them understood how he had recovered so completely in a matter of an hour. The farmer said it was a miracle, his daughter said the gods must have decided to be merciful and let the boy live. The healer said it was evil magic, I didn't know what to think. No one can bring someone back when they are that close to death let alone have them completely recover. Healers don't have that kind of power and even the most powerful of clerics wouldn't be able to do something like this. He must have healed himself; there was no one else in the room with him. I have seen Shadow do some interesting things but I don't even think he is capable of that, but there is no other possible explanation. Do you have any idea how many times I went over this in my head?"

Crystal placed a reassuring hand on his arm. "I can't possibly imagine. I am going crazy trying to understand how he managed to keep me from helping you fight him. Did you find him at the farmer's house? Did you ask him what happened?"

He shook his head. "He left the moment after the healer was done examining him. The daughter said he left without a single word of thanks. She said she saw him wandering around sometimes, coming from the forest. She told me that she had heard rumors that he was living in an abandoned house close to the forest's edge. I asked her if she knew or remembered anything else about him."

"And?" Crystal prompted.

"She said that they had found him lying in a pile of black feathers."

She wasn't sure what to say. Feathers? "Nicolai, that does not sound normal. Are you sure that the girl was sane? She might have just imagined it."

Nicolai rubbed his temple, "I didn't believe her either. She showed me one of the feathers, Crystal. It did not look like anything I had ever seen, it was too large to have belonged to a bird. I still can't figure it out. Everything about Shadow is strange and makes no sense whatsoever. If you have any ideas, I would love to hear them."

"No," the witch said evenly. "I just find it odd that Lady Yena sent you after Zia and you meet Shadow again."

"Why?" Nicolai was not in the mood for the witch's games. Crystal thought things through calmly and with a clear head before she did anything, which annoyed him no end. He preferred to act quickly, he did not like to wait when things could be done at that very moment. It wasn't as if he rushed headlong into things he couldn't get out of, he just moved at a faster pace, mentally speaking.

"Think about it, Nicolai. A girl with strange powers and a boy who defies logic and reason, connected not only to each other but also to you and the Magic Council. It might have been merely a coincidence that Zia met Shadow, but what led her to this unpleasant part of the country? Why does Shadow suddenly resurface and act out of character to save her? What is the connection?" Crystal wasn't really talking to Nicolai, she was just thinking out loud. The witch knew there had to be an answer; she just wished she could find it.

It had started with Zia; or had this whole thing started with Shadow? The more she thought about him the stranger he seemed. He was unnaturally beautiful; his physical appearance was almost perfect. He was like a dream, a dark dream that you never wanted to wake from. He moved things without touching them; how was that possible? Telekinesis, that had to be it. A strange power that was extremely rare, Crystal could not even recall the last time someone had claimed to have that particular kind of power. It was linked to very few people, none of them mages, with the same results every single time. Telepathy was often associated with telekinetic power, the strong psychic abilities often led to madness and premature death for the unfortunate person. She could think of no other explanation of how Shadow was able to do the things he had done.

If he was a psychic, it was surprising that he still seemed sane. He appeared to be nineteen at the most, and few psychics survived past sixteen. Once again, he was making things more confusing than they should have been. A psychic, maybe he was helping Zia because of something he had seen in her mind. Maybe Zia was a psychic as well, Crystal doubted it but that would explain Shadow's actions.

"Crystal?" The witch ignored him.

Nicolai wondered what had her so deep in thought. He assumed it was about Zia and Shadow. If it could help him get to Zia faster, he definitely wanted to know. He wanted to question her but knew that if he did she would lose her train of thought. So much needed to be explained, so little made sense. Then again, when had anything involving Shadow made sense?

Memories of a time long past surfaced and refused to be ignored. Thoughts that had been forgotten and feelings that had been suppressed once again returned to haunt him. Nicolai was not one to try and control his emotions; he learned early on in his life that they gave him power. He chose the emotions he wanted to feel—anger, hate, these emotions were his strength. Love and compassion were a weakness he would never allow, she had taught him that much. She was the one who had started it all. She taught him that the only one you could ever count on was yourself. She had never thought about him, never cared and yet she acted as if it was his fault. She made him what he was. He had grown tired of being ignored, so he had left. Now she called upon him when she needed something done and didn't want to get her hands dirty. In the beginning he refused, but now he saw it as an opportunity to make her pay for what she had done. She did not like using him but she knew he would get whatever she needed done; he knew this and took great delight in it. Nicolai hated her and her precious Selia.

It was all Shadow's fault. When he had been tracking him, Shadow had messed with his mind. Nicolai didn't know how Shadow had seemed to know some of his deepest thoughts but he did know he did not like it one bit. Shadow had brought back memories of a time Nicolai just wanted to forget. Now those memories had returned, and thoughts that Shadow had awakened long ago once more tormented Nicolai. As much as Nicolai hated Shadow, he hated Zia more for bringing the strange boy back into his life.

He could do nothing but wait for her to come out of the forest. Why hadn't the elves thrown her out yet? Even if they were willing to give Shadow sanctuary, he doubted that they would do the same for her. They certainly didn't want anyone in their forest. Nicolai knew this better than anyone. He tried to remember events that took place when he first met elves, hoping it would lead him to some sort of clue. The Fallen One; the golden-eyed elf mentioned that just before he wounded Nicolai. Why did he say that? What did it mean?

"Crystal, do you know anything about a fallen one?" he asked the witch, hoping she might have some answers.

"Fallen one? What exactly do you mean? There could be a thousand different meanings. I need more to go on here." She wondered what Nicolai was up to now.

"Someone mentioned it to me a while ago. I think it was more of a title than anything else."

The witch contemplated the various possibilities of what it could mean. "It may have something to do with someone of great power falling from grace. I think I may have heard of the term before but I'm not sure where."

Fallen from grace, what could that possibly have to do with Shadow? Nicolai thought that when the elf said it he had been speaking of Shadow. The golden-eyed elf told him that he should find something better to do than follow the Fallen One everywhere. Had Shadow fallen from grace? "Crystal, I heard someone say it about Shadow."

"Shadow," she said, stunned. There was a possibility that she had failed to consider. "Maybe he's not human."

Nicolai thought he heard Crystal wrong. "Not human?" He laughed. "Come on, Crystal. I know he's weird but he's definitely human."

"What makes you so sure?"

Nicolai was unsure how to answer. She was serious, he thought. The witch honestly believed that Shadow wasn't human.

Crystal understood Nicolai's uncertainty, she was having difficulty believing it and she was the one who had said it. "It is the only thing that seems to make sense, Nicolai. I believe that Shadow is a psychic. Psychics don't live very long and Shadow has already lived longer than most while still retaining his sanity. The only explanation for that would be that he is not human."

"Psychic? Crystal, really? You can't think of anything else?" The smirk returned to his face. She normally would have been annoyed but she was glad he seemed to be acting a little more like himself.

"Can you think of any other reason he might be able to move things with his mind? I can't, because there is none. It also explains why he might be so willing to help Zia. There is the possibility that something about her or something he discovered in her mind made him believe she was worth taking an interest in." Maybe she was reaching for an answer that wasn't really there, but the more she thought about it the more it made sense, at least to her. She hoped Nicolai would come to see things the way she did.

"Fine, maybe he is a psychic. That does not mean he isn't human." Stubborn until the very end, Nicolai refused to agree with Crystal until he received more information as to what made her think this way.

The witch closed her eyes and tried to retain her composure. "It does. He would have been dead or mad by now if he was human. What of the farmer's story, Nicolai, does that not prove he isn't human?"

"No. It only means that something almost killed him and he survived."

Crystal wanted to pull Nicolai's hair out by the roots; he was being difficult on purpose. "Psychics can't bring themselves back from death. There is no way he would have survived if he was human."

"Tell me, then, Crystal, what is he? If he's not human, what do you think he is?"

"This Fallen One, it is the clue to this whole thing. Well, that and the black feathers. Fallen from grace, he has to be of celestial origin. It would also explain why he looks almost perfect."

Nicolai could hardly believe what he was hearing. Crystal had finally taken leave of her senses. "Celestial? Crystal, you are the one who is insane. Feathers and fallen ones mean absolutely nothing at all."

"They mean everything, Nicolai. You said that the farmer told you there were two deep gashes in between his shoulders."

"So?"

Crystal shook her head as if doing so would make him understand. "Feathers, wounds on his back, and psychic powers; Nicolai, there is only one thing that Shadow could be. I can't think of anything else, it is the only thing that makes sense. It is how he miraculously recovered after he was only moments from death and it also explains his connection to Zia."

"Tell me, Crystal, what is he? I would love to know," Nicolai said sarcastically. He had a feeling he knew what she was going to say, for he had just started to think it as well. He just couldn't admit it. It would be the only reason he was able to survive the cursed forest and have the elves protect him. They would protect that which was of importance. If they considered him something of great value, they would guard him as well as they guarded their forest.

The witch met Nicolai's eyes and knew he was thinking the same exact thing she was. She understood his hesitancy; if it was true then they were in deeper than either wanted to be. Zia had gained herself a powerful protector. "He's an angel."

That was all she needed to say. They did not need to know anymore. Angels rarely walked among mortals, preferring to watch over them from the heavens. It meant only one thing; he had most likely gone rogue. That would have been disturbing enough by itself, but the fact that he was so young made it worse. There were few things in the world as dangerous as a rogue angel; few were ever heard of, for the angels punished their rebellious kind harshly. They were cast out of the heavens, their wings taken from them forever. Two scars upon their back were the only reminder of what magnificent beings they had once been. Disgraced, most took their own lives instead of living as something else, something less exalted. He was one of these beings. Shadow was a fallen angel.

CHAPTER 27

Zia had yet another headache. In the past week she felt as if she had had more headaches than she had in her entire life. She wondered if they would ever go away and, if so, when. Shadow said the headaches had something to do with the darkness trying to take over her mind. The darkness had not tried anything in the past two days. Zia wondered when it would come back. Not that she wanted it to, it just seemed inevitable. She no longer knew what was going on; in a matter of days her life had been turned completely upside down. It wasn't all that long ago she was in Selia with a relatively normal life and now... she didn't even want to think about it. How could everything go so wrong so quickly? Thinking about it made her head hurt even more.

Shadow, the elves, the Magic Council, and the darkness; it was impossible to figure out how they were all tied together. She decided that Shadow was definitely at fault for everything, the Magic Council received only a small portion of the blame. It had all gone awry after she had met him. The darkness never tried to completely take over her mind until he came into her life. A part of her said that it was all a coincidence and that if she had never met him she would have been consumed by the darkness anyway. She told that part of herself to shut up. No matter how many times he rescued her from the darkness she was still mad at him. For what reason, she really didn't know, it was just easier to blame him. The alternative to anger was something she was unable to comprehend and it scared her.

If Shadow remained her only problem, she might have been a little easier on him. Now she had to deal with Gryphon. The elf was rude, mean, and enjoyed telling her how pathetic she was for being a human. It wasn't as though she didn't already know. His hatred for humans ran deep, that much was obvious. Yartu had told her everything about where she was and what the twins and Gryphon were. It just made things worse. If humans were not allowed in the forest why would Shadow bring her here? How did things get so complicated?

"Would you please stop? You are going to give me a headache." Shadow ran a hand lazily through his hair as he spoke from where he stood at the end of her bed. For some reason just seeing him made her mad. He had been spending far too much time in her room, more than Yartu even did. It had gotten to the point where he almost never left her side. Closing her eyes and willing him away hadn't worked, not that she was about to stop trying.

"Get out of my mind." Zia wanted to hit him. Give him a headache, ha, she would give him one. All she had to do was find a very large and heavy item.

His eyes met hers, emotionless as always. "This is why I had the elves remove any dangerous objects from the room. You are exceedingly violent when you are not feeling well."

Zia threw her pillow at him, but unfortunately he caught it. "I want you out of my mind now!"

A smile crossed that impossibly beautiful face. "You didn't seem to mind too much before."

She sat up and punched him in the arm, she did not appreciate his teasing. "Well, I mind now. I minded before too."

"A little late for that. Besides I can't get out of your mind, I've told you that before; not fully, anyway." He rubbed the place where she had hit him absently. "Was it really necessary to hit me?"

"Yes," she grumbled. Zia knew all of this. She knew it was wrong to be mad at him but she couldn't help it, especially now that he didn't hide the fact that he knew her thoughts, even if they were only the top layer, whatever that meant.

Shadow sat down on the bed beside her, causing her to become tense. "I know this is not the most desirable of situations. It is a very complicated situation we have found ourselves in, isn't it?"

Zia was unsure what to say. Complicated was an understatement. She had no idea what one was supposed to call the situation they were in or the weird relationship that had developed. He could read her mind and she needed him to pull her away from the darkness. Zia wished that she didn't need to be rescued from her own mind, but she did, and he was the only one who could do it.

"I'm sorry."

She glanced up at him, surprised by the tone of his voice. Shadow seemed to be genuinely apologetic. Zia wondered why. "What for?"

"For everything. I suppose I could have handled things better than I did. I should have told you about my abilities right from the beginning. The moment our minds formed this connection I should have told you."

"Why didn't you?" She was somewhat unsure if she really wanted to know. Shadow's strange abilities scared her and him not knowing how he had connected to her mind made things worse.

"Would you have believed me?" His voice was soft as his dark eyes met hers.

Zia couldn't look away, she never could. His eyes held her captive, she was a prisoner in their dark depths. How many times had she almost lost herself in them? She wondered what was more terrifying; the darkness or his eyes. "I don't know. I'm not sure I believe you now," she whispered softly.

"It is all insane, right?" He laughed. "That seems to be a reoccurring theme, doesn't it? You, me and insanity."

She began to laugh as well. Saying that reminded her of the way he sounded when he was just the voice. Zia realized that even though it was Shadow in her mind, he spoke differently there than he did when he was talking to her face to face. In the real world he was serious and aloof, sometimes sarcastic. In her mind he was annoying, even more sarcastic than usual, and insulting. It was almost as if there were two different versions of him. Which one was the real Shadow? Maybe they both are, she thought. Was he like her, silent and indifferent on the outside while screaming on the inside?

So many secrets, so much that still needed to be said. She trusted him, she had meant it when she had told him that, but she was still afraid. There had never been anyone in her life that she had been able to trust completely except for Yartu. Zia did not know how she was supposed to act around him. Shadow knew every thought that came into her mind. Did she even need to talk to him at all? How was she supposed to keep certain things to herself, things she did not want him to know? He seemed to know everything about her. He knew what she was going to say and do before she did. Normal people couldn't do that; friends were not supposed to read your mind. He was her friend, wasn't he?

"Yes. I want to be your friend, Zia."

Shadow covered her hand with his. She could feel the warmth spread through her, that safe feeling she had whenever he touched her. "I never had a friend before."

"I have never really been close to anyone in my entire life. I want to be close to you, Zia." He spoke softly but his words were filled with so much sadness it surprised her.

She remembered all the times he told her that she was not alone. Had he told her that hoping she would stay with him and end his loneliness? Her whole life she thought she had been alone but she knew now she was wrong. Yartu had always been there for her. Had anyone ever been there for Shadow? What could have caused this strange and beautiful young man such sorrow? She wanted to know but was afraid to ask. Shadow was all alone in the world, just like her. He lifted his hand from hers, the warmth fading all too quickly. She didn't want it to.

Zia reached out and took his hand in her own, their fingers intertwining. "As long as you stay out of my mind." Her smile took the harshness from her words.

The look in Shadow's eyes made her blush. It was a look of such profound longing it almost made her want to cry. He suddenly smiled. "I'll do my best."

"I don't think it will work very well. Do you?"

Shadow continued to smile. "Might as well try."

"It had better work." She muttered as she rested her head on his shoulder. After a few minutes a tired Zia closed her eyes and fell asleep.

Shadow did not move or say a word. He didn't want to wake her. She needed to take advantage of any moment when she could rest undisturbed by the darkness. He glanced down at her hand still in his; he was amazed that she felt so comfortable near him, regardless of what she claimed. Would you still care if you knew the truth? he wondered.

He wanted to tell her everything. It was only a matter of time before she told him her secrets. He wanted to reveal his when that time came as well. If he told her, nothing would be the same. There was so much more to him than telepathy, she would turn away in fear. He wouldn't blame her either; if he was her, he would. The girl's world had been turned upside down; she had Nicolai hunting her, the Magic Council afraid of her, and elves ready to kill her. The darkness trying to take her soul was the worst of it all, and the last thing she needed were his problems making things worse.

Come to think of it, he didn't need a girl making life more difficult for him either. That was all Zia seemed to do. He hadn't asked to find her that night, and he still wasn't sure why he did. The last thing he wanted was to get attached. He had not expected or desired the girl to affect him so, but she did. Now he was involved more than he wanted to be. It would have been different if she was just another stupid mortal, but she had to be an annoying mortal who had almost as many issues as he did. He couldn't turn away now; if he left her the darkness would most definitely consume her. It wasn't kindness that kept him from leaving; it was a bond that had been created while he had been preoccupied with saving her from the darkness.

She thought she was alone and she had been right. People always were talking about falling into the darkness and straying from the light, but they didn't know. Sin and darkness were two completely different things. She knew the darkness, she had felt it, heard it. Yartu couldn't relate to Zia no matter how hard he tried or how much she wanted him to, he would never understand the darkness. She was alone surrounded by the darkness. No one else knew what it was like; the darkness had remained silent for so many years. She was the first mortal in over a thousand years to have the darkness take a personal interest in them. She was alone, all alone in this knowledge; at least she was among mortals. He wanted to tell her. Tell her that she didn't have to be afraid anymore. She wasn't alone. She had him, the only other one who knew what it was like.

Two souls lost in a place where no light dared shine, a world of everlasting darkness. It was his fate to walk in this world alone. He would not condemn her to the same cruel fate. He would save her; the darkness had taken him, he wasn't about to let it take her. He would fight until he was lost completely if it meant saving her. When it had come for him, he had not fought, even though he had known how. It would be different this time, he had promised her that he would protect her, never leave her alone. He was not about to break that promise. He had already lost everything. What more could the darkness, or anyone for that matter, do to him? She was the only one who could possibly understand what he had gone through. He would save her no matter what the cost. This was his destiny, he was meant to save her. It was just as she had said before, he thought.

He let his head come to gently rest on hers. "Your Shadow."

CHAPTER 28

Gryphon glared at the closed door. A human was behind that door. One who did not belong in his forest. He did not understand why the Keeper would let the wretched being stay just because the Fallen One was involved with it. As much as he hated humans, he would admit to himself if no one else that this particular one was different. She had stood up to him, a stupid thing to do, but it had gained the girl a small portion of his respect. Humans lived such fleeting lives; because of this most were afraid of death. She had invited it, an odd thing for a human to do. It didn't matter, if the girl had a death wish he would be all too happy to grant it for her.

Unfortunately, she had the Fallen One protecting her. He wanted to know why. Shadow did not associate with anyone unless it was absolutely necessary. Why would a mere human rate higher in importance than the Keeper? Everything that involved the Fallen One seemed to have no logical explanation behind it at all. Gryphon did not like anything that was not what it appeared to be. He preferred things to be plain and simple, much like he thought himself to be. Nothing hidden, no secrets, the complete opposite of Shadow.

"Gryphon, I thought that they assigned someone else to guard her room."

He barely glanced at the speaker to acknowledge their presence. There was no reason to. He already knew who it was and had no desire to speak to her either.

Terra poked her older brother in the arm, "Hey, are you ignoring me?"

Gryphon rolled his eyes in response.

"Fine, it's not like I care anyway." The elven girl waited for a reaction. There was none. "You know you're a horrible brother, right? I mean you are really bad. You are not supposed to ignore your little sister."

That got her the attention she wanted. "It is not my fault that the only siblings I have are annoying and incompetent beyond belief. I never asked for a brother or sister, and the last thing I wanted was two of you. If you value your life, I suggest you leave me alone."

Threats did not bother Terra; she was used to them, especially from him. She and Thorn were threatened at least three times a day. Gryphon was just plain mean, but Terra believed that somewhere deep, very deep, down he actually cared for them. She had not found proof of this but she thought that he did care for them in his own way. Terra wrapped her arms around her older brother. "I love you too."

"Get off of me, you little parasite." Gryphon roughly pushed his sister away. She always did this to him. He had no desire for affection of any kind, it disgusted him. Not once in his life had Gryphon shown affection towards anyone or anything, especially his brother and sister.

Terra smiled and kissed his cheek. "You don't mean that. You're a lot nicer than you let people think."

He glared at her as he wiped at the spot where she had kissed him. "I am not nice. I'm warning you, for the last time, to stop hugging and kissing me."

"Never," she said, and stuck her tongue out at him.

Gryphon didn't respond, and it wasn't as though she really expected him to. One day he would tell her that he liked it when she hugged him and that he really did love her. Terra honestly believed that. She had always adored her older brother. No one seemed to understand why, least of all Gryphon.

The moment he was told that he was going to have a brother or sister he just shut down. When he found out that twins had been born it was worse than he had imagined. His parents told him to look after the twins, take care of them. He wanted to know why his parents actually thought that he would care about their well-being. Nothing mattered more to him at that time than becoming a Guardian. Not much had changed over the years either. The forest and its secret were the only things he cared about protecting. That was why he was the best Guardian.

Behind the door he found himself staring at was something that kept him from doing his job. The other Guardians all seemed to have forgotten about the human in their midst, but he couldn't. He wondered how they were so easily able to ignore her existence. She was everything they were supposed to keep away. The Keeper and the Fallen One said that it was fine to have her in the forest, so everyone just believed them. What was wrong with everyone? Did they not realize that their enemy was among them? Their blind faith in the Keeper was infuriating. Gryphon wanted to strangle them all, but unfortunately he couldn't. He was just going to have make up for their stupidity and get rid of the girl himself.

The door opened before him. As Shadow walked out, Terra greeted him in her usual friendly manner. He ignored her just like everyone else did. The dark eyes were focused on her brother. Terra felt bad for Gryphon, the Fallen One really didn't like him. It wasn't as if Shadow liked everyone. In fact, he basically stayed away from everyone, but he tolerated them all with a cold and distant air. Everyone but Gryphon, Terra did not understand why. Gryphon was difficult, but he was only doing his job as a Guardian. She thought that was admirable, then again everyone seemed to disagree with her when it came to her older brother.

"How long do you intend to stand there?" Shadow asked.

Gryphon's eyes narrowed, "For as long as that human is in my forest."

"Your forest?" The corner of Shadow's mouth turned up. "My, how arrogant of you."

"At least I don't consort with humans. Considering who and what you are I am surprised you didn't kill the girl the moment you saw her." Anger and malice filled Gryphon's voice and soul. He wanted the Fallen One to cringe; it might make up for the human that was out of his reach.

The reaction he wanted was not the one he got. There was no reaction at all. Shadow's face was even more impassive than usual. "Why kill her? That is your job, is it not?"

It took every bit of self-control Gryphon had to keep from driving his dagger into Shadow's black heart. "I would if I could, but it seems the Keeper feels that she should remain unharmed. I wonder who is pulling his strings. I had thought the Keeper above cheap manipulation."

A smile lit up that impossibly beautiful face, leaving poor Terra breathless. "I did not think you were one to follow orders so faithfully. After all, Thorn would never have disobeyed in the manner he did if he had not learned it from his mentor."

Terra couldn't help but giggle. This unfortunately drew attention to her. She would have preferred to remain invisible; it was safer. Her brother looked as if he wanted to kill her, not all that unusual, but still uncomfortable. Shadow's face once again was unreadable. The beautiful smile was only a memory now, though she wished it had remained. Terra wished for a lot of things that never came true. For instance, at the moment, she was desperately wishing she could be invisible.

"If you do not get out of my sight right now, I swear I will..." Gryphon was practically growling.

"You'll what? Kill your younger sister? That's not very brotherly of you, now, is it?" He spoke in a voice untainted by emotion.

Gryphon's attention returned to Shadow. "Protecting her now? How disgustingly sweet. First a human and now Terra. Tell me something, now that you have decided that people are not a waste of your celestial time are you going to do what you were originally meant to do? Protect the innocent and all that?" A disturbing smile appeared on Gryphon's face. "Oh, wait, you kill the innocent. That's why you fell, isn't it? Does your precious human know how you really came to walk among mortals? You have blinded her to your true nature. Just when do you intend to tell her what you really are? Maybe you are afraid? It might make her see you in a different light. She might even begin to hate you, considering how much she seems to trust you."

Terra stared at her older brother in amazement. All the elves knew what Shadow was but no one ever mentioned it. Even if he had fallen, he was still a being who should be respected. True, most of the respect came from fear, but the elves believed that Shadow truly regretted the act that had caused him to fall. That was why they never spoke of what he used to be. He was simply the Fallen One. A being to be pitied. Gryphon had just broken the unspoken rule.

Shadow did not move. Gryphon felt triumphant; the Fallen One had lost this round. If he had known how easy it would be, he would have used the human girl as bait before. It seemed the Fallen One did have a weakness after all. Words could not possibly have expressed how Gryphon felt at that moment. The face he saw in the open door behind Shadow made it even better.

He had sensed her the moment she had woken from her slumber. He knew she was behind him. She had seen and heard everything. The triumphant look on Gryphon's face made him angry. Anger was bad, very, very bad.

CHAPTER 29

The sunlight that streamed through the windows turned to darkness. The shadows began to move with a will of their own.

Terra was terrified. She had never seen anything like this before in her life. Darkness had completely enveloped them. The only things that were visible were her and her brother—Shadow had disappeared completely. She knew this was the work of the Fallen One. Her brother's words had been harsh, but was it necessary to go this far? He would destroy them all. This was the power of the Fallen One, she thought bitterly.

She screamed when the shadows shoved Gryphon forcefully against the wall. Shadowy tendrils moved across his body, holding him tightly in their grasp. They moved slowly upwards, working their way towards his neck. They twisted and coiled, all the while wrapping themselves tighter.

Gryphon was not afraid. Death meant nothing to him. If he died now, at least he had broken Shadow. Unfortunately, death had to wait. He wanted to do one more thing before he died and that was to kill the wretched human girl. If he couldn't do it himself he would have Shadow do it unknowingly.

She was so close, but it was difficult for him to move. He had to, though; if Shadow killed him he was going to kill his little pet too, Gryphon would make sure of it. It took all of his fading strength to move his arm. Pain shot through every part of his body, his lungs were screaming for air. Yet none of this mattered to him, she was foremost in his thoughts. He channeled all of his hate and rage into one simple act.

Terra had tried to break away from the darkness and find help, but was unable to. Being trapped in a world with no light and a homicidal fallen angel was not good. She knew she had to get help somehow. Thorn. She could reach him. The twins had long been able to sense each other's pain and right now she was hoping it would save her and the others. The elven girl frantically attempted to send her brother her feelings of fear and helplessness. She wondered if they would reach him through the darkness. Thorn had to come, and soon, or else Gryphon would die. Terra looked at her older brother to see how close he was to death. He seemed to be in great pain, and she wanted nothing more than to help him.

She gasped as his arm twitched. Terra wanted to go to him but was frozen in fear. There was nothing she could do for her brother, she was helpless. It did not seem as if he needed her help, though, for he moved again. This time it was not just his arm twitching. Gryphon's whole body moved as he pushed himself away from the wall. The shadows angrily reached for him as he left their deadly embrace.

He did not have time; he had to reach her before they once again had him in their grasp. Gryphon pushed all thoughts of the darkness from his mind, she was more important. There was not that much distance between the two, but the space seemed to go on for miles. Each step was a struggle and it felt as if it was taking forever for him to move an inch. Finally, he reached his goal.

Terra watched as Gryphon rushed past her. She wondered what he was doing and then she remembered. Zia was in the room behind her. Gryphon was after Zia. Terra assumed that her brother thought that getting to Zia would protect him from Shadow. After all, why would the Fallen One kill his pet human?

Zia had no idea what was going on. Her nightmares had become reality. The darkness was swirling around her, but this time it did not seem to be after her. This time its focus was on Gryphon. She just watched as he was pressed against the wall, the shadows acting as shackles. There appeared to be no escape for him as the shadows twisted around his neck, effectively cutting off his air. It surprised her when he broke free of the darkness. It surprised her even more when she noticed that he seemed to be heading towards her.

Gryphon swept Zia into his arms. The darkness encased them in a dark shell. Zia suppressed a scream and tried to keep from crying. She clung to Gryphon because there was nothing else to do. He held her so tightly she could barely breathe. This was it, he had finally won; Gryphon wanted to laugh. Both hearts beat fast, one in fear, the other in anticipation. Each waited for the end to come. In the darkness one heart whispered a single word. *Shadow.*

The darkness retreated as the sun's rays broke through. Light flooded the hallway. Terra blinked frantically to clear her vision as she sought to see whether or not she still had an older brother. The elven girl saw her brother safe with his arms around Zia. She was unsure which shocked her more, the fact that Gryphon had survived the Fallen One's wrath or that he was holding a human.

Gryphon dropped Zia to the ground as he turned around to face his enemy. "Can't kill your pet? I'm disappointed in you." He laughed mockingly. "So much for the power of the Fallen One, eh?"

Zia followed Gryphon's gaze to where Shadow was standing. He stood with his back to the wall. The sunlight coming through the window behind him served as a stark contrast to his dark hair and clothing; a single shadow amidst the light. If she thought it was possible she would have said that it appeared as if the light was rejecting him, refusing to touch something so perfectly dark. Strange too, were the shadows on the wall behind him, the only shadows that had remained from before.

"One day I am going to kill you. I promise you that." Shadow spoke in a voice that was eerily calm and devoid of emotion.

The elf laughed again. "And I promise that your pet will die that very same day. I think I might let her live a while longer, she has proven to be useful."

Gryphon did not turn away from the dark gaze of the Fallen One. He had no reason to fear him, he had learned his secret. The human girl was Shadow's one and only weakness.

"What, no witty comment?" Gryphon could not have explained how much he was enjoying this. "I expected more from you. The fallen angel and the human girl; how predictable."

Zia thought she was dreaming. "Shadow?" Her voice trembled as she spoke his name. The truth was all she wanted.

She saw it then, the image that the shadows had created on the wall behind him. Stretching out to each side were shadowy wings. Angel. Shadow was an angel. No, he couldn't be. Were angels even real? she thought. Dark eyes met her pleading ones. The truth was hidden in the dark depths of his eyes. They drew her in. She was captivated by the promise of forever. All the secrets she longed to know, a way to end all her pain, they were there waiting for her.

Tears began to fall from her eyes. She could see it now, the true beauty that was Shadow. Did the others see? Did they know? The darkness to banish the cruel light. There was no more fear, he would save her. He had promised her this. Yet, what was it he had to protect her from? If he belonged to the darkness, was it truly as bad as she had originally thought? There was nothing to fear, nothing could hurt her anymore. She had an angel by her side.

[Fallen. I have fallen.]

The words echoed in her mind. The Fallen One, that was what the elves called him. Gryphon had called him a fallen angel. What did that mean?

[I turned away from the light. I killed innocent people. I am not kind and merciful. I do not save the lost. I destroy them.]

No, she thought. He had helped her. He was not cruel or evil, why did it seem as if he wanted her to believe he was? Zia had to believe that he was good. She had to.

[Why? What is good, what is evil? Do you know? I questioned this. Good can be just as unforgiving as evil. Good is not light and evil is not necessarily darkness.]

Zia buried her face in her hands and shook her head in confusion. She understood nothing, she had thought that she had just begun to. What was happening to her? Was she going insane? Elves were a myth and impossibly beautiful young men were not angels. They were a figment of her obviously twisted imagination.

Laughter echoed inside her mind. [Ah, there you are. That is the Zia I know. Brooding is not really your style.]

Shut up, she thought. The annoying voice was back. It didn't matter if the voice belonged to a mysterious Shadow or an angel. It was the voice that brought her comfort when she was frightened, regardless of how annoying it was. It was the voice that brought her back from the edge of madness more then once. Zia couldn't help but smile.

[You are mad, but then again so am I. Right?]

Gryphon couldn't stand the silence. The girl's odd smile made it even worse. She should have been screaming in outrage, not smiling. A fallen angel was standing before her; didn't she know what that meant? Why wasn't she begging for answers that he would never give? Why wasn't she afraid?

"Ah, it seems your plan failed. What will you do now, Gryphon?"

The elf glared at the fallen angel. He wanted nothing more than to cut that mocking smile right off his perfect face. A hand touched his shoulder, a human hand. Gryphon turned and found himself face to face with Zia.

"Thank you. It seems your hatred saved me from that which I truly fear."

He glared at her this time. The last thing Gryphon wanted was this wretched human thinking he was heroic.

"Don't get me wrong; it's not like I think it was a friendly gesture, but still... I guess it's better than nothing. It seems your hatred saved the day, huh?" She said all of this with an odd smile while trying to suppress a giggle.

Gryphon really wanted to strangle her. Laughter interrupted his exceedingly violent daydream. The beautiful sound startled him and the two girls. Terra stared at the source of the sound mesmerized; Zia erupted into laughter as well. Gryphon did not understand what the hell was going on.

Terra was hypnotized by Shadow; she could not have thought that anyone could sound so perfect when laughing. Then again, everything Shadow did seemed perfect, including trying to kill her brother. The elven girl was surprised that Zia was handling the situation as well as she was. After all, she had almost died. The human girl was doubled over from laughing so hard.

"Gryphon, heroic? Gods, that's even more insane than me being a hero." Shadow could barely speak, he was laughing so hard.

Zia shook her head, trying to regain control. It was like before when she hit Shadow and saw that strange scene. Now that she thought about it, had that been something that came from his angelic powers? The hysterical fits of laughter, neither was sure what to do, so all they could do was laugh. She knew that the one controlling the darkness had been him but he had not been trying to hurt her. He was after Gryphon, and the elf knew this, so he used her as a shield. Both were at fault for what had happened but she was not angry. In a weird way she was relieved; for the first time in days she had not been the darkness' target.

The elf wanted to hurt someone. He was so damn frustrated it was insane. That seemed to be going around though. Shadow and the human girl were both completely crazy. It made sense that the fallen angel had chosen this particular human for a pet. He had won, or so he had thought, but the Fallen One had gotten the best of him yet again. Now he was in a really bad mood. Gryphon found himself muttering various colorful curses under his breath.

His poor sister had no idea what she should do. Zia and Shadow were hysterical and her brother was seething with rage. There was only so much the good-natured girl could handle. Her older brother was impossible, but that was no reason for Shadow to try and kill him. Terra heard the sound of footsteps rushing down the hall. She turned to see Thorn coming, with Yartu flying close behind.

# CHAPTER 30

Both came to an abrupt halt when they saw the scene before them. Thorn could not believe what he was seeing. The eerily unemotional Shadow was laughing and the human was doing the same. His sister looked confused and his older brother seemed to be really mad, dangerously so. Thorn wondered what had happened. He had felt Terra's panic but it seemed as if whatever happened was over now and the danger too had disappeared. It still concerned him, though. Terra had been really scared, she was not exactly the bravest person alive but he had felt true fear; the kind of fear that most likely indicated something deadly.

The miniature dragon was just as confused as the young elven boy. They had been waiting patiently together until someone gave them permission to let Yartu see Zia. That was, they had been until Thorn stated that something was very wrong. The boy claimed that his twin sister was in danger. Yartu believed him, too, for he had felt panic from Zia as well. The two had rushed to her room hoping that everything was alright and the two girls were safe. There seemed to be no immediate danger but everything was definitely not alright. Both the elven boy and dragon could see that.

"I demand to know what is going on right now. Someone explain. Now." Yartu spoke with all the authority he could muster from his small frame. Intimidation only made things worse.

Zia grabbed him and spun around. "Everything's fine. You don't have to worry. Gryphon saved the day."

Both she and Shadow had managed to regain some control, but that made them both start laughing all over again. Well, that and the expressions on everyone else's face. A strange mix of shock and horror; after all what could possibly have caused Gryphon to save the day?

"I did not!" Gryphon shouted. He pointed at Shadow accusingly. "He was trying to kill me."

Thorn gave his brother an unsympathetic look. "Is that all? Hasn't everyone who knows you tried that at least once?" He cast a glance at his twin. "Is that what you were so freaked out about? Come on, Terra, everyone hates Gryphon, we both know that. You are the only one who even seems to like anything about him. I know I don't and I'm his brother. He probably deserved whatever it was that Shadow was going to do to him."

Terra felt tears prickling her eyes. "Thorn, how can you say such a thing? He is not that bad. True, he is not the most amiable of people, but he still does not deserve to be treated in such a way. Gryphon is still your brother no matter what."

"Yeah, and he's practically killed me countless times," Thorn responded angrily. He looked at his sister like she was the one who was crazy. "I don't get why you are always defending him. He's even crueler to you than he is to me, and he treats me worse than he does anyone else, so that's saying something."

The elven girl stared at her twin brother, anguish clearly evident in her clear green eyes. She could not believe what she was hearing. Thorn was the one who was being cruel. There was a reason Gryphon was constantly being mean, he was trying to push people away. Terra believed that this was because he was afraid of getting close to people. Deep down he loved her just as she loved him, she had to believe that. No matter what, she had to believe that her older brother loved her. There was goodness in him; no one ever saw it because no one ever looked hard enough for it. She did and she was going to find it, then she would show everyone. Show them that they were the ones who were cruel and judgmental.

Zia wanted to put her arm around the younger girl and comfort her. Terra really cared about Gryphon, Zia had no idea why or how it was even possible, but it was. Thorn had truly hurt his sister with his words. She could understand why he said them, Gryphon was horrible, but he was their brother.

[Which means nothing to him; Gryphon cares about no one. He loathes everyone and everything; himself, most of all.]

She thought that she heard sympathy in Shadow's mental voice. Zia wondered if it was because he felt the same as Gryphon. Maybe they despised each other so much because each hated what they were or what they had become.

[An interesting notion; I won't say I agree but it is still interesting nonetheless.]

"If you are done arguing about me, I would like to state once again that I did not save anyone." Gryphon said, glowering at his younger siblings. Thorn rolled his eyes and Terra attempted a smile.

Zia chuckled. "I thought Yartu was bad. He pales in comparison with you. He at least wants people to acknowledge when he does something good or helpful."

Gryphon glowered at the girl while Yartu started protesting her hurtful remark. She met the elf's golden gaze just as she had when he had held his dagger at her throat. There was no fear; she was different, this human. Once again, he was surprised by this girl. She was gaining more of his respect and his grudging admiration. He hated it but it was true. This of course made him angrier and amplified his desire to kill her. He could not respect a human. It was something he would never allow.

"I suppose we should call a truce for the time being, Gryphon. Don't you agree?" Shadow spoke in his usual detached tone.

The Guardian growled something unintelligible and walked away. They watched him leave, Shadow shaking his head in disbelief.

"He's never going to change. I feel bad for anyone who has to deal with him today. After this he is going to be worse than usual."

Thorn groaned. "You don't have to deal with him every single day, I do. Training with him makes it even worse for me."

Terra was about to say something but was beaten to it by Zia. "Complain all you want; you are not human. He probably has envisioned killing me a hundred different ways by now."

"More, actually. Gryphon has quite the vivid imagination." Shadow smiled.

Zia hit him. "I don't want to know. He's scary enough as it is."

[He is not as scary as you can get.]

She hit him again, harder this time. The smile stayed in place and she was comforted by its presence. Yartu was still grumbling from her arms, muttering about how insensitive she was being, ignoring him. She pulled him in tighter, holding him close. When she looked up she noticed that the twins were staring at her open-mouthed.

"What?" she asked, puzzled by their behavior.

"You hit him." Thorn spoke as if she should have understood what she did was a crime.

She really didn't understand what he was talking about. "Who?"

He looked at her incredulously. The boy pointed at Shadow. "Him."

"So?" She laughed. She had no idea why the twins were acting like it was such a big deal.

The twins glanced at each other. Both wondered if she was truly that dense. "So? Zia, you just hit the Fallen One." Thorn said it like it explained everything. It didn't.

"I know. It's not like I haven't done it before."

Terra looked as if she was about to faint from shock. "You've done it before? Zia, you don't hit the Fallen One. He's... he's the Fallen One."

"It's Shadow. You elves really over dramatize." Zia shook her head, it was just Shadow. What was the big deal?

"No, we don't," Thorn protested. "You just don't understand. He is the Fallen One. You are to show him the proper respect, and that includes not hitting."

[Even if I have fallen they still have to respect me. It is unacceptable for anyone to hit the Fallen One. Well, that is what the elves believe. I may have fallen but I am still an angel. If that even means anything.]

Zia really didn't get it. Why should he be treated specially just because he had been born an angel? He wasn't special, he was Shadow, he was just irritating.

[Thanks. It is always nice to feel appreciated.]

If that didn't prove her point, she didn't know what would. If only the twins could have heard. "He may be the Fallen One but he's still a person, and an annoying one too."

Terra gasped. "Zia. He is not just another person. He is..."

"The Fallen One; I know. You really have to get over that. So what if he was born an angel? He may look perfect but he's not. He makes mistakes just like everyone else. He's annoying, cynical and extremely sarcastic." She was mad at them for behaving like they were. He was a person, just like they were. True, they were not of the same race, but that did not mean he should be treated differently.

"Angel?" Yartu squawked. "Since when did he become an angel? What did I miss? Is someone going to explain or not?"

Zia rolled her eyes at her dragon's behavior, overreacting as usual. She had forgotten for a moment that Yartu had not been allowed to stay with her so he was unaware of just about everything that had happened. A part of her wished that he had, it would have saved her a lot of explaining, but she was glad that he wasn't there. She didn't think she could have had the conversation she did with Shadow if Yartu were there. Shadow only seemed to open up when he was alone with her or in her mind.

Luckily for her she didn't have to explain. Thorn was doing that for her. "Shadow is the Fallen One. An angel who fell from the heavens to earth. To fall is the greatest punishment an angel can receive. He is here to atone for his sins. We must respect him and the effort he is making."

Yartu was speechless. How was he supposed to respond to something like that? A fallen angel? The miniature dragon was not happy. He didn't trust normal people with Zia—he was definitely not going to entrust her to a fallen angel. There was nothing worse, he didn't care if the elves thought that he was atoning for his sins. Depending on how long ago he had fallen it would affect how dangerous he was. Considering the fact he had not yet committed suicide made Yartu worry even more. Fallen angels did not live long without their wings, so if Shadow had been in this world for a long time it was really bad. It meant he didn't care about atoning for his sins, it meant he was even more of a danger to Zia than the human-hating Gryphon. Yartu wondered what Shadow had done to have fallen and why he didn't seem to care.

Yartu's gleaming red eyes fixated on Shadow. He had not spoken a word since this particular discussion started, which made Yartu even more nervous. The dragon met the fallen angel's gaze. Those impossibly dark eyes reflected the darkness in the soul. A dark figure with a dark soul; one who would steal Zia from the light. It was not the Magic Council, Nicolai or Gryphon that Zia had to be afraid of. It stood before her now, a fallen angel who would lead her into true darkness, steal her soul. Yartu would never allow that to happen. Zia was his.

[No,] the word whispered in the miniature dragon's mind. [I am hers.]

Yartu did not understand where the odd voice inside his head had come from or what it meant, which made the dragon's small form quiver with suppressed anger.

Zia felt Yartu's trembling but did not let it bother her; he was often mad and displayed it in such a manner. "Yes, Shadow is a fallen angel. So what? It just means that he is more like the rest of us than you would think."

Yartu wanted to scold her. Did she not know what it meant to have fallen? How could she brush it aside so casually? He knew she said that she trusted Shadow, but how could she after finding out what he really was? Had he blinded her from seeing the truth?

"Terra, I don't feel very well. I think I should go lie down." Zia was unsure of where the sudden fatigue had come from. All she knew was that she was exhausted and beginning to feel lightheaded.

Terra gasped when Zia started to fall. Yartu flapped furiously in an attempt to remain airborne after her arms released their hold. Thorn tried to catch her, for he was the closest, but he was beaten to it. Shadow moved at an impossible speed and caught her in his arms. The twins and the small dragon just watched in silence as the fallen angel cradled her in his arms. He walked into her room and placed her on the bed.

Terra was the only one who followed him. She watched silently as he gently brushed the human girl's hair out of her face. The intimate gesture surprised her. Zia was Shadow's pet, everyone knew that, but had the fallen angel started to develop actual feelings for the girl? It couldn't be, she thought. The Fallen One never displayed any sort of emotion, ever. The more Terra thought about it, though... in the past few days had he not shown emotion? It was only when it concerned Zia, but he had shown emotion. Terra wondered if that was a good thing. What did it mean if a fallen angel developed feelings for a human? Was Zia more than just Shadow's human pet? What was she to him and what was he to her?

"Her Shadow." The words were spoken in a hushed whisper. Shadow stood up and was now facing Terra.

"W-what do y-you mean?" she stuttered.

He did not respond. Shadow walked past the elven girl into the hallway. "Let me know immediately when she wakes up," he said as the door closed behind him.

Terra was left alone to contemplate his strange words. She shook her head, trying to rid her mind of all the strange thoughts, and focused on the unconscious girl on the bed. It would be much easier to help her than to muse over cryptic messages said by a fallen angel.

CHAPTER 31

Gryphon was perched high in the trees. He found a place that gave him the perfect view of the human's room. It was safer here than right in front of her door. It wasn't as though he was afraid of Shadow; he just didn't feel like getting involved at the moment. Gryphon was not a fool. He knew when to pick his battles. It was easier to watch from a distance. The window was open so he could hear everything as well; elves had excellent hearing. Not that there was much to hear at the moment.

It was all rather boring; the human had fallen unconscious, again. He wondered if she was ever awake for more than a few minutes. He had seen the strange interaction between his sister and Shadow. If it mattered to him he might have wondered, like Terra, what Shadow had meant. It didn't. The only thing that mattered at the moment was *her.*

So innocent and vulnerable lying there on the bed; how easy it would be. All he had to do was climb through the window. It would be over before anyone knew what was happening; Shadow wouldn't be able to get there in time. He smiled an evil hate-filled smile. Such a pleasant thought, though unfortunately that was all it could be for now. Terra was in the room and it was unlikely that she would leave anytime soon. Or so he thought.

Gryphon almost laughed at how things were playing out. Everything was working in his favor. He watched as Thorn came into the room with the human's dragon on his shoulder.

"Terra, they need you. They said that the human could wait."

She rolled her eyes, "Zia. Don't they realize she has a name? Why does she always have to be the *human?*"

"Don't ask me. I don't think she is all that bad." Thorn smiled when Yartu rubbed his head on the boy's cheek.

"That is why I like you two. You are not like the other elves. I understand that you want to protect this forest, but Zia is just an innocent girl. You are the only ones who seem to understand this." The dragon spoke with genuine affection. He had come to appreciate the elven twins a great deal in the short amount of time he had known them. Most of all the boy; the two thought alike.

Terra grinned. "Thanks, Yartu. It means a lot to hear you say that."

"Of course. It's not like I approve of everyone."

She giggled, "Well, I guess Thorn and I are special. If only the other Healers and Guardians thought the same thing."

"Not going to happen anytime soon. Especially since Gryphon is our brother." It was true the other elves were all afraid of Gryphon and didn't want anything to do with him. This included his siblings.

"Oh, well, I guess I should go see what they want now." Terra sighed. "Thorn, you can't stay in here. Same goes for you too, Yartu; sorry."

Thorn nodded, "I know. Do you think she'll be alright?"

"Yes. I don't think she is going to wake up anytime soon. I still can't figure out what is wrong with her. Maybe that's what they want to talk to me about." She shrugged and held the door open for her brother.

Gryphon waited until he could no longer hear their voices. It was all too easy. Fate was on his side for the first time in his life. This time he did laugh. He would win. Shadow could kill him afterward; he didn't care. He still would have taken his pet from him. He could die peacefully with that knowledge.

He moved nimbly from tree limb to tree limb, reaching his destination in a matter of seconds. Perched on the window sill he listened for any sounds coming from the other side of the door. Nothing; they had foolishly left her all alone, and in such a condition. How could they call themselves Healers? he thought with an impish smile. He swung into the room and landed softly on the balls of his feet.

Right in front of him slept the human. It was as though she was waiting for him to come. How sweet of her to make this easy for him. He silently moved to the bedside. Her breathing was slow and steady, she was deeply asleep. Gently, with a tenderness that surprised even him, he moved her long black hair away from her neck. The smooth, pale skin that lay beneath taunted him. Slowly his dagger came to rest upon the exposed skin. All he needed to do was press a little harder and blood would flow. It would be all too easy to take her life. Gryphon watched with morbid fascination as blood began to trickle down her neck.

This was it, this was everything he wanted; this girl, this kill. No one ever understood just what went on in his dark mind, and he doubted this would help. He didn't care. He had sacrificed so much of his life, now he only wanted to do what he wanted. No one else mattered. It did not concern him that his family would be disgraced by his actions. In his mind they deserved it. Humans were miserable beings that needed to be eliminated. This girl was the worst. She had done something unforgivable. She unnerved him and because of that she needed to die. Before her eyes had only showed a calm acceptance, and he wanted fear. For that he needed her to wake up. The dagger pressed deeper into her soft flesh.

Zia's eyes flew open with a gasp of pain. The warmth of the blood flowing from her neck sickened her. She did not know what was going on. The last thing she remembered was fainting. Now she was bleeding, and she wanted to know how that happened. A soft chuckle caught her attention. She would have moved to see who it was, but it was unnecessary. Her tormentor had returned. Gryphon was once again trying to kill her. From the amount of blood she was losing she assumed he intended to accomplish his task this time. It had been easier to remain calm before when she had not been injured already. It was different now. She had no idea what he was going to do to her. The insanity was plainly visible in his golden eyes.

"How do you feel?" he asked.

She grimaced. "Been better."

Gryphon traced his dagger along her skin. The blade was cool against her warm skin. She shivered in spite of herself. He smiled, this was it. He would get everything he wanted.

"Why are you doing this? What could have possibly made you hate humans so much that you want to kill every one you meet? I know that it is not just part of you being a Guardian. There is something more to it." She was trying to stall him. Hopefully if she managed to keep him from doing any more damage someone would eventually come to her aid.

"Stalling for time are we?" A quick cut came with a merciless smile. "Too bad no one is around but me. They won't hear your screams."

"I don't intend to scream."

Blood began to flow from yet another new location. It amazed her at how sharp the dagger was. She didn't feel pain until after blood was already flowing. Gryphon wielded it with great skill and precision. Each cut was expertly placed, meant only to cause pain. He was playing with her and she knew it. He was the cat toying with the mouse before it pounced. Unfortunately for her, she was the mouse.

"Fine, I don't really care."

Zia was not going to let him know how truly afraid she was. Before Shadow, Yartu and the twins had been close by; now she was all alone. She closed her eyes.

Get a hold of yourself, she thought. You can get out of this, you've done it before. Remember when you didn't have Shadow to rely on? This is no different.

She could get out of this, but how? Think, Zia, think, she thought. Yes, that was it. "You didn't answer my question."

"I really don't have time for this." Another cut, and she winced in pain.

Zia took a deep breath. "The least you could do is tell me why you so desperately want me dead."

"Why?" The dagger performed its grisly task once again.

Damn, he was intolerable. Say one little thing he didn't like and blood poured out of your neck. "Consider it my last wish."

"Hmph." The dagger moved slowly across her skin, although this time it did not draw blood. "Very well. How can I say no to a person's dying wish?"

Zia felt him remove the dagger from her neck. She might have been relieved if Gryphon had not moved closer to her. He was far too close for comfort. It was a dangerous game she was playing, made even more so considering her opponent was completely insane.

"I hate you." She felt his lips brush against her ear with each word spoken. The warmth of his breath made her cringe. He was too close, and she fought the instinct to scream.

"You don't even know me." Zia tried to sound calm but she knew she failed.

Gryphon ran a gentle finger along her neck; the contact forcing her to keep from gagging. "True. I would say I care, but I don't. I don't care about anything, you see."

He moved away giving her back her space. He held his hand up examining the blood that stained his finger.

"You seem to want to kill me badly enough. I would consider that caring." Each word passed through gritted teeth.

He smiled at that, an evil malicious smile that sent a shiver running down her spine. "Didn't anyone tell you? I can't care. I have no compassion, no ability to love. You have to have a heart in order to do those things. Unfortunately for you, I don't have one. I am heartless."

Heartless? How easy it would be to believe that. Gryphon had no respect for life of any kind. He was as cruel to his siblings as he was to people he despised. No compassion, no mercy, no love. Zia really did want to know what had made him that way. Something had to have pushed him to this. Thinking about his problems was not going to help her, though. She had to think fast, the dagger was once again finding its way back to her neck. He wasn't just trying to scare her, this time he was going to kill her.

Gryphon watched her squirm, immensely pleased with himself. The human's time was running out, her fate was in his hands. He had grown tired of playing; it was time to finish this.

Zia met his golden gaze, no fear in her eyes. She was sick of it, sick of being scared. "If you are going to kill me just do it. Stop fooling around and end this now."

It was just like it had been before, when they had first met. No fear, only acceptance, she wanted to die. His dagger was pressed against her flesh, digging in, drawing blood. The final strike would come. One quick slash and it would all be over.

He couldn't do it. Gryphon wanted nothing more than to grant her wish, but he couldn't. It was impossible. What he wanted more than anything, he couldn't do. Her death was supposed to be by his hand. Why couldn't he kill her?

His internal struggle was visible to Zia. She could see it in his eyes. He had intended to kill her, but something was holding him back. She watched him battle himself for a few moments. It surprised her, the amount of pain he seemed to be in.

Gryphon cried out in frustration as he threw his dagger to the floor. He moved away from her, drawing his knees up to his chest and burying his face in his arms. Zia was shocked by the childish action. She sat up slowly, pain shooting through every part of her body. Blood flowing freely from the various wounds on her neck, she ignored the pain. She didn't know why she should be concerned about Gryphon, he had just tried to kill her.

The elf was rocking back and forth. When Zia placed a hand on his shoulder, he flinched but did not look up. She called his name softly, hoping to get his attention. He still didn't respond. She had no idea what she was supposed to do. A sane person would have run out the door screaming for help; unfortunately Zia was not quite sane.

Hitting him was an option but not one she wanted to use. It would not be the same as Shadow, Gryphon would hit back. Kindness might work, but she doubted it. There was only one way she knew how to deal with Gryphon.

"You can try again later if you want. It's not like I'm going anywhere."

That got his attention. He looked at her, disbelief in his eyes. She was kneeling next to him, hand on his arm, blood dripping from her neck. It was a gruesome sight but oddly comforting.

"You really are crazy," he muttered.

Her smile turned into a grimace. "Well, so are you. Can you do something about this? Not to complain but it hurts. A lot." She gestured to her neck, the movement causing her to wince in pain.

He nodded. Zia watched him get up, and at first she thought that he was going to go get a healer, but he did not go near the door. Good thing too, if he went for help he probably would have been in more trouble than he already was. He grabbed some bandages and salve. She couldn't help but flinch as he began to clean the wounds he had inflicted. He worked quickly but not painlessly. Every touch was agony, but she suffered in silence. It was just another way for him to hurt her; he had said he would help, but he never said that he would be gentle.

"I'm not a Healer. If you want one get one yourself." Gryphon had noticed he was causing her more pain. The girl was biting her lip and fighting back tears. The harsh words were the closest he would allow himself to get to sympathy.

"Sure, I'll just walk out the door with blood pouring out of my neck and ask the first elf I see if they would kindly fetch a healer for me. That will definitely work." Sarcasm came naturally to her at times like this.

Gryphon snorted in response. The girl was getting more and more irritating by the minute. He gave her credit, though. She remained in the room with him. Once again, he found himself beginning to respect her. He hated it but he could not seem to stop. As much as he fought it, he was starting to like her. This was not something he wanted. Humans were miserable beings that should all be destroyed. That was what he had always believed until this girl came into his life. Now she was turning everything upside down. This girl, a mere human, was completely messing up his life. She was making him *feel*, and he hated that.

Zia waited for the pain to subside. It was going to be a long wait—Gryphon had done some damage, nothing too serious but bad enough. He literally wrapped the bandage around her entire neck; it was the only way to cover all the lacerations. It was extremely uncomfortable and made moving her head awkward. Then again, he did tell her to find a healer if she wanted proper care. It was her own fault, why did she feel like she needed to help him?

"If you don't like it, fix it yourself," he grumbled, having seen her rubbing the bandage.

"No, it's fine," she lied. For some reason she felt it necessary, he looked so pathetic. Not killing her seemed to be killing him.

The two lapsed into silence. Both were uncomfortable with the situation, neither knowing what to do or say. Finally, Gryphon stood up. Zia gasped when he launched himself out the window. Her momentary concern for his well-being disappeared when he caught a hold of a tree branch and pulled himself up. She ran to the window, stretching out as far as she dared. He was sitting on a branch higher up.

"What are you doing?" she called up to him.

He rolled his eyes. "You don't have to shout, I can hear you. Elves have excellent hearing."

"So what? Even if you had the best hearing in the world you still would ignore me."

"Do you think you could stop being so annoying?"

Zia grinned. "Not a chance."

"You should get back inside. I don't feel like having to explain to people why you fell out of a window."

"Thanks for the concern. It is nice to know that you are trying to be helpful instead of trying to kill me."

Gryphon bit back a nasty retort. A loud crash interrupted the somewhat pleasant moment they were having. Shouting could be heard from the hallway. Zia ran to the door to see what was causing such a commotion. Elves were running up and down the hallway in a panic. Screams echoed in the distance. Something was very wrong. She tried to get someone's attention but everyone just ran by.

She grabbed a man by the arm. "Please. What is going on?"

The man pulled away. "It is your fault. We never should have allowed a human in the forest. We are all going to die because of you." He shouted a curse at her as he ran off.

"My fault?" she whispered. What was going on?

A foul stench drifted down the hallway. The smell of smoke had her nostrils flaring. Smoke? Something was burning. "Oh no," she said breathlessly.

"Gryphon!" she called as she ran back to the window. "Something is burning."

He was leaning as far out as possible without falling out of the tree. He held out his hand. "There is no time. Come on."

"No. Something's wrong. We have to help," she said defiantly.

He shook his head. "You can't help. The city is burning. We have to get out of here now."

"What!" How could the city be burning? Who would do such a thing? The elves seemed as though they were extremely careful with fire. How did this happen, and why wasn't Gryphon panicking?

"Come on," he said again, hand outstretched. He had just tried to kill her and now he was trying to save her. She wished he would make up his mind about what he was going to do.

"We have to help."

"You can't, you stupid girl. It's burning because of you. Humans are in the city. They would only be here for one reason, and that is you. Now take my hand, damn it."

Her? Humans in the city? Crystal and Nicolai, they must have followed her. Now they were destroying the city of the people who had helped her. It was all her fault. People were going to die because of her.

Gryphon shouted Zia's name but she did not respond. She stood still, frozen in place. "Great," he muttered. What a perfect time to freeze up. Threaten to kill her and she laughs but scream fire and she's worthless. "Why must I do everything myself?"

He climbed back into the room and picked her up, hoisting her over his shoulder. This she noticed, having come out of shock, just his luck. She fought him, kicking and even biting. He shook her once, hard, for good measure and went back to the window.

"It will be a lot easier if I don't have to carry you all the way. Think you could do as you are told for once?"

She glared at him. An interesting feat considering he couldn't see her face. "Fine. Just put me down."

Gryphon did as he was told. Zia fell to the floor hard as he threw her to the ground. As she struggled to rise she kicked him in the shins. The blow didn't faze him in the slightest.

"We don't have time for this." Once again, he was in the tree outside the window. He held out his hand.

Wonderful, she thought. She was going on the run with a homicidal elf. She felt like she would be safer with Nicolai; he wasn't allowed to kill her. More shouting in the hall drew her attention. A faint voice could be heard in the distance. She heard enough to recognize the speaker. She looked at Gryphon's outstretched hand. As dangerous as he was, she was more afraid of Nicolai and the Magic Council. With a silent apology to Shadow, she grasped the elf's hand and he swung her onto the branch.

She swayed, unable to maintain her balance, but Gryphon steadied her. Zia could see it now, flames spreading over the city, but they seemed to be somewhat contained, stuck in the city. She might have wondered why, but then she saw elven mages using their spells to keep the fire from spreading into the surrounding forest. Some trees had already caught fire. She could see more mages attempting to put the flames out. Their efforts seemed to have no effect, the flames only grew. Magic, she thought, remembering the witch, Crystal. She was most likely responsible for the fire.

Zia would have stayed frozen where she was if Gryphon did not pull her arm, indicating which way to go. She had thought that it was impossible to follow Shadow, but following Gryphon was worse. He stayed in the trees, moving swiftly from branch to branch. It would have been better if he had dropped to the ground. Zia could barely move; with each step he had to pull her back up after nearly falling. Their escape from the city was a great deal slower than he had anticipated.

Finally, he just gave up the through the trees approach and let her fall to the ground with her next misstep. The fall hurt, and she lay where she had fallen, stunned. Gryphon landed nimbly next to her. He pulled her to her feet without a word and ran off. She did her best to follow him. Once again, her best wasn't good enough for him. He had to stop every few feet to make sure that she was still behind him. She was doing better on the ground than in the trees, he gave her that much credit.

Every time she tripped or stumbled she could feel his golden eyes boring into her. She knew what he was thinking too. Stupid human can't even stand on her own two feet, helpless without Shadow to protect her. It made her mad. Yes, she wanted Shadow but she was stuck with Gryphon. Shadow would have waited silently, encouraging her along. That was not the elf's style. In a way Gryphon's disdain was more effective than kind encouraging words. It made her mad, her anger fueling her to keep going. She would not give him the satisfaction of watching her fall to the ground and give up. No matter how much she wanted to, she would never allow that. Those hate-filled eyes pushed her to do what her body told her she could not. She would go on simply because she didn't want him to be right.

Gryphon watched her silently. Every misstep, every fall, and still she kept going. He didn't offer her help. Shadow had done enough of that. The girl needed to toughen up. Every so often he would see her glaring at him, muttering curses under her breath. He couldn't help but smile as he continued deeper into the forest. She was a pain but she didn't give up. He knew how difficult it was following him, he purposely made it that way. She did a remarkable job keeping up, for a human anyway.

They continued on, going deeper into the forest with every step. Zia was amazed at the sheer size of the forest. She couldn't remember how long it took to get to the elven city from where she had fainted but she knew it was deep in the forest. As they had left the city behind Zia had noticed that it was really a ruin that the elves had adapted to suit their needs. She had wondered who would build a city that large and why the elves would move in after it was nothing but ruins. The forest was a mystery and a maze that made her dizzy. Far too much was happening for her to figure out anything. So she just focused on the task at hand, keeping up with Gryphon. If she let her thoughts stray she would think about Yartu and Shadow. She dearly longed for her dragon to be at her side. He would tell her everything was going to be alright; even if it wasn't, she still wanted to hear it. Yartu would yell at Gryphon for being so difficult and causing her pain. He would tell him to stop and let her rest. Yartu wasn't there, though, so she had to deal with things on her own. She wondered about him for a moment and hoped he was safe. Him and all the elves; even if they had treated her like she was carrying a contagious disease, she didn't want them to come to any harm. Most of all she felt guilty and she hated it. Their city was burning and people were going to die, all because of her. Why did the Magic Council want her so badly? What was so special about her?

She ran into Gryphon's back and fell to the ground, again. "Why did you stop?" she asked angrily, as she rubbed her side, trying to alleviate the pain.

He pointed. Following the path his finger indicated she saw an entrance to a cave. The mouth of the cave was so large she bet a whole house could fit in it and still have space overhead. It was not the most pleasant or inviting of places. In fact it gave her a sinking feeling in the pit of her stomach. It was the kind of place your parents told you not to go near as a child, the kind of place they said monsters lived in. Zia would not have questioned it if someone said monsters lived in that cave. It looked as if it would eat whoever went in alive. She didn't even want to know what it looked like inside.

"What are we doing here?" It was all she could do to keep from running in the opposite direction.

Gryphon walked to the cave entrance and stopped. He turned around when he noticed that Zia had not followed him. "Come on."

"You want to go in there? Fine, go alone. I am not going into a creepy cave with you. I draw the line at that." She crossed her arms and stayed in place.

Golden eyes narrowed. "If you want to remain in one piece, I suggest you get over here now."

She didn't move. "Not a chance. I would rather take my chances out here than in there."

"Would you come if I told you the answers to all your questions are in there?"

Zia thought it over; it was most likely a trap. There was a chance he was telling the truth but she doubted it. How did he know she had questions and, more importantly, why would the answers be inside a cave. "Really? I would love to know how that is possible. Oh, and while you are at it, try explaining why you think I have questions."

"Are you always this impossible?" Gryphon sighed while she just continued staring at him expectantly. "Fine. Inside the cave is that which we Guardians are sworn to protect. I won't tell you what it is; you will see soon enough. All I can say is that it might help you better understand what is going on and why you attract so much unwanted attention."

She contemplated his words. The chance that he was telling the truth seemed more likely, but she wasn't certain. Why would he bring her here, what purpose did it serve?

What did he get out of it? These were all things she wanted to know, but she knew that he would not tell her. She had to find out for herself. Gryphon had planted the bait; now all she could do was take it.

Slowly she entered the cave. It was extremely dark inside, and going further in was not a pleasant thought. She had to find out, though, if there were answers in there she wanted them. What was the worst that could happen, Gryphon would kill her? It wasn't like he hadn't already tried a few times.

Zia took a deep breath and nodded to Gryphon. "Let's go."

He stepped inside and a faint light appeared around him. Zia saw that the source of the light was coming from one of three rings he wore. A useful little trinket, she thought. She wished she had one. As she came to stand beside him, she suppressed the urge to shudder. It was cold and the light coming from Gryphon's ring barely lit up the cave. It actually made it worse, shadows seemed to be jumping out at them. She felt as if something was watching them from the surrounding shadows. It made her uneasy and rather jumpy. The fact that the cave was completely silent except for her and Gryphon's footsteps made things even more unnerving. Gryphon, of course, appeared unfazed by everything, while she was biting her lip to keep from screaming.

It wasn't as if she was afraid of caves; she wasn't. However, what with everything that had happened to her in the past few days, taking a walk in a dark cave was not something she wanted to do. It was just plain stupid. The darkness was after her and she was walking right into it. It might not have been so bad if Shadow was with her. Unfortunately, she was stuck with Gryphon, who was more likely to hold her still to make it easier for the darkness to capture her as opposed to rescuing her from it. Still, she had to do this; she had to trust him even though she knew she shouldn't. Her life was in his hands and she could do nothing about it. So into the darkness she went, following a man she knew she couldn't trust. It wasn't as if she had any other options.

CHAPTER 32

Shadow stood in the empty room. There was no sign of Zia. The only thing in there was a bloody dagger. He knew whose blood it was and he knew who the dagger belonged to. He hadn't made it in time. The gods only knew what had happened to Zia—well, them and Gryphon. Shadow reminded himself to kill the troublesome elf the next chance he got.

"They finally managed to put the fire out," Thorn said as he came into the room.

Yartu was perched on the elven boy's shoulder. He had been screaming about Zia being in pain but the elves had ignored him. Shadow had believed him but it was too late. He tried to hurry to Zia's aid but fire had erupted all over the city. The fire prevented him from going the direct route to her room. He was too late. Zia was gone and the only thing left behind was a blood-stained dagger. Shadow knew she was with Gryphon; she had to be, why else would she be gone when Yartu was still here? The only thing he didn't know was where or, more importantly, why.

He also knew that the fire had been started by the witch, Crystal. A fire that grew the more one tried to put it out was definitely the work of a witch. Three flames placed in three different locations, all growing to insane strength and power. The idea for the separate flames was something Nicolai had probably come up with, it felt like something he would plan.

With no respect for the sanctity of life, Nicolai would have no problem destroying an entire city to obtain that which he desired. Zia had been his objective and, since she was no longer there, he had most likely gone after his prey. The elves had not found any sign of him or the witch; it wasn't as if they were looking too hard. The fire had almost completely destroyed the city, and they blamed Zia. Shadow blamed himself. He had not thought that Nicolai would be crazed enough to follow Zia into the forest. Shadow now knew that he had underestimated Nicolai's obsession. A miscalculation he would not make again.

"Shadow?"

He turned to face the boy. Thorn looked positively depressed, and making it worse was the depressed miniature dragon on his shoulder. "Do you think Zia is alright? I know Gryphon doesn't like her but you don't think he killed her, do you?"

"If she was dead Yartu would know. Their Bond is stronger than you think." His words seemed to cheer the boy up a bit, not much though.

"Where do you think she is?" An innocent enough question, but one Shadow didn't know the answer to. This made him less likely to respond. He didn't.

Thorn hated the silence. He hated the thought that his home was in danger, the forest that had kept the elves hidden for so long was no longer safe. He hated that his new friend was all alone with his psychotic brother. Gryphon would kill her without a second thought; he hated humans with a passion. Thorn hoped Zia was safe and that Gryphon was more concerned with the safety of the forest than he was with killing her.

"Thorn," Shadow spoke his name softly. "Do you have any idea where Gryphon might have gone?"

"What makes you think I would know?"

"You are his student and his brother. You spend more time with him than anyone else. That makes you more likely to know what he would do." A reasonable enough explanation, although not the one Thorn wanted to hear.

He laughed nervously. "It's not like I had any choice. Seriously, Gryphon has practically killed me a few times. He doesn't care that I'm his brother. I don't know what he would do. I can barely understand him or his motives for doing anything when I am with him."

Shadow knew the boy spoke the truth. Even with his psychic powers he had a difficult time understanding what went on in Gryphon's mind. The elf was more trouble than he was worth. The worst was that he had Zia and Shadow couldn't do anything about it. The longer she was away from him the more susceptible she would be to the darkness. It would only be a matter of time before it tried to take her again. He had to find her, and fast.

For the time being she was safest with Gryphon, although it killed Shadow to admit it. As dangerous and erratic as the elf was, he would keep her safe if Nicolai caught up with them. He would most definitely kill the mage hunter and the witch before he took Zia's life. From a few memories he had seen in Gryphon's mind he knew that the elf had dealt with Nicolai before. Hopefully

Gryphon's preexisting hatred for Nicolai would prove beneficial.

Terra entered the room. Her mind was full of death and sorrow. She had been forced to watch helplessly as her friends died and her home burnt to the ground. There was nothing but emptiness. As a Healer, not being able to help made her feel worthless. She longed to go back to when everything had been alright.

"How many are dead?" Thorn inquired.

"Too many," she sniffled. Her brother placed a comforting arm around her shoulder.

Shadow heard the twins discussing the tragedy that had befallen their home. He remained silent, listening, trying to find any psychic remnants of Gryphon or Zia in the room. The elven forest was odd in that some areas of the forest suppressed his psychic abilities, and as such he needed to find a mental trail to follow in order to find Zia. The fires had also made it difficult to connect to her mind since he was being overwhelmed by the panic and fear of the other elves. Depending on how difficult it was to pick up Zia's or Gryphon's trail, Shadow would have settled for a trace of Nicolai since the man would inevitably lead him to the other two. The man was trained in finding that which no one could find. He was an expert tracker and knew how to locate things and people that wished to remain lost; he was a magical bloodhound that didn't give up the chase until its quarry was found and preferably dead.

Unfortunately, the twins and Yartu's worrying made it difficult for Shadow to find anything. The harder he concentrated the more he could sense their thoughts; why was it so difficult for him to focus? The first contact he made was with the residual remnants of Zia, the only problem was that all traces of her were of pain and anger, and this made trying to track her more difficult since there was no real clear mental remnant of her. The pain he assumed to be because of the wounds that Gryphon had inflicted. The anger was also because of the elf; Zia was more likely to get mad with every cut instead of becoming afraid. The more someone tried to hurt her, the angrier she became, unlike Yartu, who panicked if she was in danger.

The only traces he could find of Gryphon were not pleasant. They were much like the elf whose mind they had come from, dark and disturbing. They consisted mainly of death and the various ways to inflict pain. Gryphon was a sadist with a history of destructive and antisocial behavior. Shadow hated going near the elf, his mind always felt tainted whenever it came in contact with Gryphon's. That was part of the reason he got into so much trouble whenever the elf was around, Shadow had a habit of picking up his aggressive tendencies. This was because of Shadow's strong psychic power and Gryphon's out-of-control mind.

Nicolai was nothing but a faint memory. He had barely been in the room for more than a few moments. In one way this was a good thing, it meant that he had picked up Zia's trail. The downside was that it made things complicated for Shadow. The fainter the memory the harder it was to read. He paced back and forth; anyone watching might have thought that it was odd, but it helped. The more he moved around the easier it was to find the stronger traces. He was focusing on the one left behind by Nicolai. The closer he got to the window the more his mind became assaulted with various psychic remnants. Zia, Gryphon and Nicolai were all there; each one strong, each one with the same outcome. They had all gone out the window.

Shadow smiled. Of course, why hadn't he seen it before? Gryphon literally lived in the trees, moving stealthily among the treetops, watching and waiting for some unsuspecting human to pass underneath. Many Guardians hid in the trees but none seemed to do it as well as Gryphon. He knew the forest better than anyone and he would most likely escape using a route that anyone else would never be able to follow. Having Zia with him probably slowed him down but Shadow knew it wouldn't have much effect. Gryphon would probably drag her along. Even with his unusual talents, Nicolai would have difficulty following them, since the treetops were a veritable maze and even other Guardians would have been hesitant to follow Gryphon up there. That gave Zia and Gryphon some time, as well as Shadow. He could follow the psychic trail left behind far better than Nicolai could track them from the ground. There was only one problem, and it was small and very loud.

"My poor Zia is all alone with your crazy brother. If he does anything to her I swear I will rip him to pieces." Yartu had meant the words to sound menacing, but they came out miserable. Just like the poor little dragon. He didn't know what to do. The elves had kept him away from her for three days and now she was gone. He had no idea where she was or if she was in any trouble. Yartu wanted to fly to her side; he wanted to sit in his usual spot on her shoulder. Thorn was not enough, he wanted her.

Thorn seemed to understand Yartu's misery. "I don't think Gryphon will do anything, and even if he does, I get the feeling Zia can take care of herself." Thorn did not believe a single word of what he said, he was trying to comfort Yartu, not scare him to death.

"Shadow, do you have any idea as to their whereabouts?" Terra asked him. She wondered why he had been silent for so long. She desperately hoped he could help. If a fallen angel couldn't find her older brother and Zia there was no hope to be had.

He nodded. "They went out the window. I assume that Gryphon figured out that the person who set the fires was after Zia. I think that he took her to keep anyone else from claiming his kill. Not the most desirable of situations but it is preferable to the other choice."

"That sounds like Gryphon." Thorn agreed with Shadow's conclusion of what had transpired. "He most likely took a route through the trees. It would be difficult to follow and nearly impossible for Zia to keep up, but he wouldn't care."

"Wait, so you know where they went? Let's go. What are you waiting for?" Yartu said anxiously. If they knew where she was, he wanted to get there as soon as possible.

Thorn ran a hand through his hair. It helped him think. "It shouldn't be too hard to pick up his trail. I have a lot of experience following Gryphon around. Sometimes he would leave me all alone just to see if I could track him. He called it learning by doing, but I know he was just being mean. I have gotten better at following him through the treetops, though."

Shadow knew what was going to come next and he didn't like it. Thorn was going to suggest that they go after Zia and Gryphon. Yartu would hastily agree and Terra would insist on coming too. After all, they would probably need a Healer. Shadow worked better alone, that was how it had always been. He didn't like having to keep an eye on companions, which was why he remained alone. It was out of choice, unlike Gryphon, who was alone because no one wanted to deal with him. This time, though, Shadow had no choice. If he wanted to find Zia, he had to bring them; a pair of troublesome elven twins and an extremely irritating miniature dragon with an inferiority complex. Shadow wished he had not found Zia lying unconscious that fateful night; he wouldn't be in this position now. Then again he had been led to her for a reason. He had to help her. In order to do that he had to find her, and that meant taking her dragon and the twins with him.

It was relatively easy for him to pick up the trail once they were in the trees. Thorn proved helpful too. He found broken branches and traces of torn clothing from where Zia had fallen or stumbled. It seemed that this had happened a lot. No one said it but they all thought it. Gryphon must have been furious at her, slowing him down and destroying his precious forest all at once. They all hoped that they located the two of them soon; before Gryphon completely lost all control.

Shadow went first, Thorn was right behind him and Terra brought up the rear. She kept up well too. She stayed close on their tail. Shadow was pleasantly surprised at the progress they were making. Yartu flew ahead every so often scouting the way. They made their way through the trees for about an hour and stopped when they saw no more signs of anyone passing by. Thorn was the one who noticed that there were a few broken branches below them. They all knew what that meant. Zia had fallen and Gryphon had probably decided that traveling on the ground would be the safest route.

It was much easier to track them from the ground. They made excellent timing. Thorn had taken the lead now, being much better at tracking on the ground. It wasn't that Shadow couldn't follow their trail, it was just easier for Thorn to be the one concerned with where they were going. Shadow concerned himself with one thing and one thing only at this point, making sure Nicolai was nowhere close by.

Every so often he felt the man's mind. It was in the distance but closing rapidly. It must have taken him a while to follow the treetop path the two had taken from the ground. He had reached the spot where they had continued on the ground. This was bad. He would pick up speed now that he was tracking them from the ground. Shadow could feel him closing in on his small group. They had to find Zia, and fast.

Thorn stopped suddenly, causing Shadow to become agitated. "Why are you stopping? We don't have time for this. Move. Now."

The elven boy shook his head. "You don't understand."

"What don't I understand?" he snapped. His patience was wearing thin.

Thorn looked at him a grave expression on his face. "I know where Gryphon is taking her."

"And that would be..." Shadow prompted.

"The Dragon's Den." He spoke softly as if he was praying he was wrong.

Yartu growled with impatience. He was curious, though. "What is the Dragon's Den?"

Terra shot a worried glance at her brother. "Are you sure? Maybe you are just confused. This forest looks similar in a lot of places. You might be wrong."

The look she got in return told her he wasn't. Terra started to get a feeling of dread.

"I ask again, what is the Dragon's Den?" Yartu wondered what made the twins so worried.

Shadow answered his question. "The Dragon's Den is exactly what it sounds like."

"Are you telling me there is a dragon in this forest?" Yartu squeaked.

Thorn smiled a little. "You mean another one besides you, then yes."

Yartu's wings faltered for a moment. Terra caught him before he fell. A dragon, one of his larger cousins. This was really bad. They were rare and most were not very pleasant. Unlike miniatures, who were very friendly, well, for dragons. If there was one here it would most likely not take kindly to people invading its territory. It would be even worse if it found them in its cave.

"The dragon is part of what we elves are guarding," Terra explained. "Very few actually have seen the dragon. Only a handful of Guardians."

Thorn made a face. "Everyone who did, died. All but one."

"Do I even want to know?" Shadow asked wearily. He felt he already knew the answer.

Terra's expression told him he was right. "Gryphon is the only Guardian to have seen the dragon and lived to tell about it. If you think about it is quite an amazing thing. To have seen a dragon, and survived."

"Sure, it is." Thorn said, each word dripping with disdain. "Everyone thinks it is because the dragon did not want anything to do with him. If anyone could best a dragon at being mean and intimidating it is Gryphon."

"Y-you don't t-think he will take Zia there, d-do y-you?" Yartu couldn't help stammering. The thought of his precious Zia in a dragon's cave terrified him. The elf was leading her to her death. A cruel and brutal death it would be too.

Shadow sighed. Things were spiraling out of control. Gryphon must have thought having a dragon kill her would be more fun than doing it himself. The elf would assume Zia would follow him, trusting him. Shadow prayed that she knew better than that. He had faith in her but he knew that she was in a delicate state of mind. She was likely to do something stupid if she thought it would help her fight the darkness. Shadow knew that Gryphon would use this to his advantage.

Gryphon or Nicolai, Shadow could not figure out who was worse. Both wanted Zia, one wanted her dead now, the other wanted her to suffer. A long slow, painful existence; life in a cage, that was what Nicolai would condemn her to if he took her back to the Magic Council in Selia. One was catching up to her and the other already had her. Shadow silently cursed his fate and the current predicament. He had to act fast. Time was running out.

"I am going after them. If you think it is too dangerous, stay behind." Shadow continued down the path they were on; it led him to a cave. He stared at it, knowing she was in there.

The twins stopped beside him. Terra had Yartu resting on her shoulders. Both had grim expressions on their faces. They were scared but they wanted to help their new friend. They were trying so hard to be brave. Shadow felt sorry for them.

"We can't let the Fallen One take on a dragon all by himself, now can we?" Terra said with a friendly smile.

Thorn snorted. "It is not the dragon we have to worry about. No one should go up against Gryphon all alone. He is by far much scarier than a dragon."

"I don't care about him or some musty old dragon. If either one hurts my Zia, I will tear them apart," Yartu snarled.

Shadow smiled at them. The twins and even Yartu were comforted by the beautiful smile. It did not matter to them that he was a fallen angel. He was in this mess with them and he was most likely the only one who would get them out of it alive.

He faced the cave. There was a strong presence dwelling deep within, he could feel it. It was almost overpowering. Shadow had only seen a dragon once before; it had tried to kill him but he had survived. The only problem was he had been an angel at the time. He had retained many of his powers when he had fallen, but he was still weaker than he was as a full angel. One thing was for certain, this was going to be interesting.

CHAPTER 33

Zia tripped, again. She was barely able to stand. After fleeing the elven city through the trees and stumbling over every root in existence when they had taken a path on the ground, she was ready to collapse. What had it been, four days with Shadow, three with Nicolai and Crystal, two in the forest before she passed out and four in the elven city? Approximately two weeks, and only four of those days spent in a decent bed. Not that she had gotten much rest; the elven city had proven to be quite hazardous. It would have been easier to rest if the darkness had not tried to steal her mind every time she closed her eyes. Between the darkness, Nicolai, Gryphon and last but not least Shadow, the past 13 days had been painful. She wanted nothing more than a comfortable bed and ten days of undisturbed sleep. Her life had become one big, painful, chaotic mess and it didn't look like it was going to get better anytime soon.

Gryphon was no help. If she stumbled he pulled her back to her feet and continued walking. She wondered if he ever got tired. He didn't even suggest stopping to rest. He probably figured she would not get up again if she sat down, and she didn't think she would. It was probably best that she kept going, although it was painful.

Five seconds wouldn't have killed him, would it? Zia knew he was doing this on purpose. Let the weak human go until she fell down dead. She was going to show him. Her stubbornness came in handy at times like this; it was also the reason she hurt so much. She would rather have died than ask the *superior* elf to stop so she could catch her breath.

Gryphon saw that she was struggling. She needed to stop and rest; he wondered why she didn't say something. If she kept going on the way she was she would collapse. What good would she be to him if that happened? He hated the fact that she was making him be the one to suggest stopping. Was it stubbornness or stupidity that kept her from asking? He could not decide.

She hit the ground with a thud when he pushed her down. "What do you think you are doing?" she demanded.

"I don't feel like carrying your dead body back to the entrance," he retorted.

Zia was so relieved it was ridiculous. Finally she was able to rest. That is, she would have been able to if she wasn't angry at Gryphon for shoving her to the ground. If he thought that she was just going to let him bully her he had another thing coming.

"I was not ready to stop yet. We could have gone on further."

"Right." Gryphon rolled his eyes. "And then you would have collapsed. You are not as tough as you try to be."

"Like you are?" she snapped. "Forgive me for not being born a perfect elf. What a magnificent race you are. Superb hearing, grace and beauty; I am so jealous of you."

Gryphon wanted to choke her. How was it that she could be so annoying and at the same time sound so spirited; he had to respect her. She didn't just sit still and take the blows that came, she fought back. He was unused to such a reaction. No one fought him, they knew they couldn't win. Yet here was this human girl who matched him blow for blow.

"What, nothing to say?" she said mockingly. "I would think that you would leap at the chance to defend your amazing race. After all, arrogance and egotism seem to be elven traits too. I guess I was wrong. What could a pitiful human like me know? Oh, well."

Did she have any idea how close she was coming to pushing him over the edge? One look at her face told him that she knew; she just didn't care. "I would defend the elven race but I think very little of them. Much like you, it seems." There, he thought, that should shut her up.

It did, but only for a moment. "So you hate your own race too. I guess the honor doesn't just go to humans. Tell me, how many other people do you look down upon? Who meets your impossibly high standards?" Her words were dripping with disdain.

He laughed; he had to. She sounded so much like him at that moment it was strange. He either had to laugh or bury his face in his hands. He chose the former. "No one. Not even me."

Zia could tell he spoke the truth. His reaction when he had been unable to kill her proved it. He held himself to the highest standards. It was only natural that he did the same for everyone else. It was unfair, though. "How do you survive? I would go mad trying to reach that level of perfection. It does not exist. Why try? We can only do our best. And, most of the time, our best is not perfect. Why try to reach for such an unobtainable goal?"

The criticism and sarcasm were gone. She spoke what she felt; it sounded almost like pity to him. He did not know why but this angered him immensely. "I do not want your pity. I am the best Guardian there is. This is not arrogance, it is truth. Ask any elf. I have worked hard for everything that I have. I am not to be pitied."

His tone was harsh but she knew the anger was just misdirected. He hated himself and this was how he dealt with it. "What have you accomplished? What good is being the best Guardian if you are not happy? It is not pity I feel for you, Gryphon. It was contempt, maybe even hate, but now it is sorrow. How can you live the way you do?"

How was someone supposed to respond to that? He didn't know. What was she trying to do to him? He was happy, wasn't he? Damn that insufferable girl. Why couldn't she be satisfied with making him miserable? Now she had to make him wonder why he was miserable, too. She was supposed to hate him; that was his intention. It made things easier for him. If people hated him, they would purposely try to avoid him, and he wanted that. He *liked* being alone. He would be again soon, she wouldn't be bothering him for much longer.

Zia saw that he was deep in thought. He's probably thinking of a new way to torment me. She was glad; it gave her time to rest and to think about what she was going to do. First of all, she was stuck in a massive cave that was basically a labyrinth.

She had no idea which way they had been going from the moment they set foot in the cave. From the entrance it had been fairly simple, a long tunnel leading down. From there it began to get complicated. Farther in, the main tunnel branched out. Not two separate paths, but four. The tunnel they had taken was the second one from the right.

There was barely room to stand; it was definitely a tunnel that made you claustrophobic. There had been more twists and turns somewhere but she couldn't for the life of her remember where they had come from or which direction they were actually going. The last path fortunately was a straight shot down and it was slightly bigger than the previous tunnel.

The path led to a massive cavern with an underground river. There was also a huge waterfall. At this point they no longer needed the light of Gryphon's ring. The cavern was full of strange crystals that glowed. Each one was a different color, and all were beautiful. The light of the crystals illuminated the whole cavern. It gave a strange glow to the water as well. The light lent the whole cavern an ethereal quality. There were crystals on the ceiling of the cavern as well, making it look like the night sky—if the stars were a hundred different colors, that is. It was one of the most beautiful places she had ever seen.

This was where they stopped to rest. Now all she needed to do was figure out how to find her way back to the entrance. She had entered the cave knowing that she was most likely not going to get out alive, although she fully intended to do so. Gryphon had lured her in here for some reason. Whatever it was she wanted to get out alive. Survival was all she was thinking about at the moment. It was all that mattered ever since the Magic Council had tried to capture her for experimentation. Now she was running for her life and freedom. It might have been better if she was not lost in this cave. She could complain all she wanted but she needed to do this on her own. There was no one else around. Gryphon did not count. He was one of the variables she had to be careful of.

What was he planning? That was what she wanted to know. Why lead her into this cave? Was it as he had said, was there something in here that would help her? He had mentioned that it would answer her questions, of which she had so many. There was one she wanted answered most of all. Could this thing tell her what she wanted to know? A fallen angel didn't know the answer, so how would this thing? Zia sighed deeply.

"This is what I live for; to protect this." Gryphon spoke softly more to himself than to her.

Zia glanced at him. He looked just as miserable as she did. "This cave?" she asked, hoping to understand him a little better. It might help in the future.

He nodded. "This is what we Guardians are sworn to protect. Most believe that we just protect the forest but we actually protect what the forest hides."

"What would that be? This godforsaken cave?" She couldn't help but sound bitter. The only nice thing in this case was the cavern they were in now.

Gryphon arched his eyebrow. "This godforsaken cave as you so eloquently put it is in fact quite special."

"I know that." His quizzical look made her laugh. "You get lost before you barely even set foot in it; very special."

He snorted in dismay. "This cavern is unique." He pointed to the crystals above them. "Each crystal holds raw magical energy. The smallest one has more power than most human mages dream of. The larger ones can destroy a whole country with the amount of magic they contain."

"You can't be serious! Those crystals have magic in them?" Of course, why not? It made sense, how else would they be able to glow like that?

"Long ago there was a kingdom here where this forest now stands. The king was a foolish man. He had built his empire upon sacred ground. The spirits of the land grew angry and rose up to destroy him and all that he had created. A great storm appeared over the kingdom for eight days. By the end of the eighth day the only things that remained were ruins of the once magnificent city.

This forest also appeared, it had grown during the time of the storm. A haunted forest filled with Wraiths, the lost souls of the people who had once made their home where the forest now stood. It was created to protect the land from those who would cause it harm." He spoke solemnly as if to respect the power that controlled this land.

Zia found she was fascinated by the story and wanted to hear more. "The ruins, that is the elven city now, right?"

"Yes, the elves moved here after they had heard what had happened. Elves are the sworn guardians of places like this. Places that should be left alone. Sacred places with immense power. We protect that which needs to remain untouched. It is the duty of a Guardian to keep those who would use this power from doing so."

She nodded in agreement. "I can see why. If this forest was created to conceal this cave, then it is only natural to protect the forest. If these crystals are as powerful as you say then you are right. No one should have this power, even if they intended to use it for good, that kind of power can corrupt the soul. That's what happened to the king, isn't it? He used the power of the crystals to build his kingdom, but the power corrupted his soul. He probably thought he was invincible. I guess he learned the hard way that he wasn't."

Gryphon chuckled. "You heard the story before?" He was surprised by her reasoning. He thought that she would have felt sorry for the people who died. She seemed to think they were just as stupid as he did.

"No, but I like it. It explains a lot about this forest... and you."

"Me?" He wanted to know how.

Zia smiled. "You take your duty as a Guardian way too seriously. This is because you're scared, isn't it?"

His eyes narrowed dangerously. The effect was lost on her. He had threatened her life too many times, and she was not afraid of him anymore. "I am scared? I would love to know what makes you think that."

"Your greatest fear is that someone will use the crystals' power again. If someone does that then you have failed in your duty as a Guardian. That is why you hate humans so much. We are easily corrupted by power. When we have it we tend to destroy everything. Unlike elves, humans don't try to live with nature, we try to control it. If a human, no matter how good or bad they might be, got their hands on one of these crystals it would prove disastrous. Someone with good intentions would use the power hoping to help, but it would only cause harm, even though it would be unintentional. A bad person would use the power to wreak havoc; this of course would be intentional. Who knows what would happen, how much damage there would be?"

Gryphon did not respond. He could only stare at her. She was unlike any other person he had ever met, it didn't matter whether she was human or elf. The girl kept surprising him. Every time he thought he figured her out she did something to prove that he knew nothing at all.

Zia felt his eyes on her. It made her uncomfortable because it was different this time. He did not look upon her with scorn and loathing. Early on she had learned that Gryphon did not bother concealing his emotions. She doubted he would be able to, he was a passionate person. He seemed to feel everything a hundred times more than a normal person. Most of the emotions he showed were not good ones but they proved that his feelings were almost always intense. Right now, she would have preferred the intense hate to what she saw in his eyes, a look she was unable to describe. Her words seemed to have had a profound effect on him.

She wanted him to stop looking at her like that. Zia stood up and brushed herself off for no reason, it was just something to do. "We should probably get going. I have rested enough. There is no point in staying here anymore, we should continue on."

It never occurred to her that this is what he had intended to show her, to tell her the story of the crystals.

Gryphon got up and moved towards the river. She followed him; the closer they got to the river the more the roar of the waterfall intensified. "Where does the waterfall come from?" she asked. It was probably the stupidest question in the world but she wanted to know.

"I don't really know. I believe that the river runs through this entire cave. The cave itself is a series of tunnels connecting to each other; many are dead ends or just circle back to where we started. We are fairly deep inside the earth at the moment. The river could come from anywhere. It is unusual for a waterfall to be underground. Maybe it comes from the crystals' power."

His explanation didn't help very much but it did seem to distract him. They continued to walk until he stopped when they had reached the riverside.

Zia knew what was going to come next in a flash. "Oh, no. I am not going in there," she protested. He was not going to force her to cross the river, not in this lifetime. It was most likely freezing and deep. He didn't even ask if she knew how to swim. She did, but that was beside the point.

"Fine, suit yourself. You can wait here until I get back." Gryphon walked right into the river, leaving Zia to stare at him incredulously.

She watched helplessly as he disappeared beneath the surface. Panic began to set in, not out of fear for Gryphon's life but because he was the only one who could get her out of the cave. She ran to the edge and leaned over as far as possible without falling in.

Where the hell was he? It was difficult to see how deep the water was or if anything was in it. She felt so stupid, she had just let him go and leave her. He was probably in a different cavern; after all he had said that the river ran through most of the cave. Was this what he had been planning? Bring her to this cave, take her in so far that she got lost and then leave her to die. That was what was going to happen. She was going to die, alone, trapped in a cavern that was filled with super-powered crystals. It was so much better than having him slit her throat.

CHAPTER 34

A dark shape moved just below the water's surface. Zia could not tell what it was but she knew that she didn't want to know. Maybe Gryphon had not abandoned her; this thing could have gotten him. Wraiths haunted the forest, who knew what lived in this cave? As she scrambled backwards to get away the figure burst to the surface. It grabbed her and dragged her into the water.

She struggled to break free of its hold. The thing grasped her ankle and pulled her down deeper. It was so dark in the water she couldn't see what the creature was. She kicked and squirmed trying to get away.

The hold it had on her was nearly impossible to break free of. She twisted and kicked hard with her free leg. The creature fell back, momentarily stunned. Zia swam for the surface as quickly as she could. She made it, but only for a moment. A slippery hand wrapped itself around her ankle once again and dragged her back down. Luckily, she had been able to get some air, not much though. Her lungs felt like they were on fire, and it was all she could do to remain conscious.

Claws scraped her leg above her boots. She knew what the creature was doing. It was pulling itself on top of her as it dragged her to the bottom of the river. She felt something bite her hand. She suppressed the urge to scream even though it was painful beyond belief. If she did she would only swallow water and lose precious air. She tried everything she could think of to get away from the creature but it didn't let go. No matter what she did it still held on. It was going to drown her.

The only thing she could do was kill it before it killed her. She curled up in a ball forcing the creature to find a new place to hold on. It wrapped its arms around her, and she held perfectly still, letting the thing think that she was dead. As its claws tore at her flesh she unfurled, kicking out with both legs and pushing with her arms. She came into contact with slimy skin. The creature fell away, surprised by the movement.

Her lungs screamed for air, and Zia knew she would not make it back to the surface. The water swirled around her; the creature was coming back for her. Normally she would have used her own dagger but the elves had taken it away from her. The creature had every advantage. It was faster, stronger and it could breathe underwater. She was at the end and she knew it. She had survived everything up to this point only to die now. Where was the justice in that?

Sharp claws ripped tender flesh from her body. She could taste her blood in the water. The creature worked furiously, wanting her dead. Zia felt the last of her air leave her body. She was losing consciousness. The darkness was creeping up on her. Promising to end her pain; whispering that it was going to grant her peace.

Something grabbed her arm, pulling her to the surface. Air filled her lungs, and she gulped it in. She rolled onto her side and spit up the water that she had swallowed. It was difficult to breathe, but at least she was. Trying to focus proved more difficult than she thought. The strangely lit cavern did not help, she could barely see anything. Blood was flowing from various parts of her body; the bandages around her neck had fallen away as well. Pain was all she could feel. Well, pain and something touching her, moving her body.

She tried to sit up but was shoved back down. Moving her body hurt; she wanted to tell whatever it was that was touching her to stop. A cloth brushed her face, wiping away blood. Someone was helping her. Her eyes began to focus a little better. She tilted her head to the side to get a better look at her rescuer.

Gryphon was kneeling beside her, water dripping from his silver hair and clothes, no shirt though. That he was holding in his hands, tearing it into shreds. She now understood why she had felt she had been moving. He had been lifting her arms and legs, bandaging her wounds with the torn pieces of his shirt.

"You saved me?" Her voice was weak when she spoke.

He continued what he was doing. "I didn't save you to be merciful. I am the only one who is going to kill you."

Zia would have laughed if it didn't hurt just to breathe. "I do not want to die by anyone else's hand."

Golden eyes met hers. They were like Shadow's, they drew her in. Instead of darkness they trapped her in a golden light, blinding her.

"Did you kill that thing?"

He nodded. "Yes. It wasn't that hard. It was so preoccupied with trying to eat you I was able to kill it quickly."

"Eat me!?" she squeaked. The creature had been trying to eat her. She felt dizzy. So that was why it bit her hand.

His lips curved into a small smile. "What do you think it was trying to do? Invite you to dinner?"

She hit him. It was pointless, she could only hit his leg, but it made her feel better. "Where were you? I thought you had left me. You never came back to the surface."

"I was waiting for that thing to come out of hiding. I had intended to get rid of it before you got in the water but it got to you first. I did tell you to wait." He was talking like it was her fault that thing had almost eaten her.

"I don't believe you. No one can hold their breath for that long. Not even super elves like you." Bitterness stained every word.

Gryphon held up his hand for her to see; his three rings glistened on his fingers. "This ring is enchanted. It allows me to breathe underwater as if it were air."

She made a face at him. "A ring that has an illumination spell, a ring to breathe underwater. Anything else I should know? No other little trinkets that give you super powers? I don't suppose you have one that heals wounds? No, didn't think so."

"Are you always like this?" He shook his head in disbelief. The girl was crazy. She had almost been eaten and yet she was mad at him for having a magical ring. He wanted to know what her priorities were.

"Do I have to answer?" she asked hesitantly.

Gryphon laughed at this. "I wish I did have something that would heal wounds. The Healers wouldn't give me anything. They said I had to learn on my own in order to learn caution."

"Not really something you would do. What do healers know? They think that a smile makes the pain go away. Like that really works."

"I know. It makes me angrier. I don't want a smile; I want the blood to stay in my body."

Zia giggled, even though it hurt. "Kind of like now. Are you almost done?"

He helped her sit up. She swayed as dizziness overcame her. If he had not been holding her up she would have fallen over. She felt faint again; how many times did this make it now?

"If you don't mind, I would appreciate it if you got off me." She wondered why he sounded so amused.

Zia realized that she was holding onto Gryphon, it was more like she was leaning on him. She could feel his muscles underneath her palm. It surprised her that his skin was so smooth. His body was still wet from the water. It gave his skin an odd feel. When it should have been warm it was cool, and droplets of water slid onto her hands. She noticed a strange mark on his chest. It reminded her of the tattoo that Thorn had encircling his upper right arm. This was slightly different, though. It consisted of interlacing lines, she was unsure if there were more than one; a continuous line that wove in and out. There was no beginning and no end. An unbroken, unending line that formed a crescent moon. She found herself tracing the tattoo with her finger, fascinated.

Gryphon held himself absolutely still. The girl had taken leave of her senses. What did she think she was doing? He really wanted to know. Her touch made him shiver. This was not good, he had to stop her. The contact was making him tense. Gryphon did not like physical contact of any kind. He wanted her to stop, he wanted...

"Find something interesting?" he asked gruffly.

His voice brought her back. She pulled away from him so quickly she lost her balance. He steadied her. When he let go Zia felt relief flood her. How was it that she hadn't noticed that she was touching his bare chest? She must have hit her head. That was the only possible explanation. It was also the only one she would accept.

Finding it rather difficult to stand, she wobbled as she stood. Biting her lip to fight back a wave of nausea it came to her attention that they were on the opposite bank of the river. This was it, there was no going back. The cave entrance was across the river, which she had no intention of crossing again anytime soon. She would be surprised if she ever swam again after her run-in with that creature.

Throwing her hands up in the air she sighed. "All right, what next? A cave-in might work, or is that too easy?"

"Who are you talking to?" He followed her gaze upwards. There was nothing there but crystals sparkling back at them. It was almost as if they were laughing.

"Whoever is listening." She shrugged. "I don't know whether to blame the gods or fate. Probably fate, even the gods can't control fate. It seems to enjoy making my life hell. I was just seeing if it was going to give me a hint about what it is planning next for me."

Gryphon rubbed his temple; she was enough to give him a headache. One minute she was lying helpless and the next she was daring fate to make things more interesting. He wondered what fate did have in store for her. It did not seem as if it was just going to let her fade away. Somehow Shadow was connected to this as well. What could a fallen angel and an elven Guardian possibly have to do with a human girl? What *did* fate have in store for them? Whatever it was Gryphon was going to fight it. Fate did not control him. He created his own destiny.

He motioned for her to start walking to the tunnel opening a short ways away. She had some minor difficulty walking, but she managed. They walked together in silence. Zia tried to avoid looking at him. The fact that he was shirtless made her very uncomfortable. Making things worse was the way she had acted when she had first noticed. What had she been doing? She had to have lost her mind for a few seconds. What else could it be? No, don't even think that, she told herself silently.

This tunnel was different from the previous ones. There were small crystals lighting the way. There were no tunnels branching off of this one either. It was large and the ground and tunnel walls were smooth, as though somebody used this passage often. As they traveled farther, she saw scratches on the walls. Zia did not want to know what was capable of scratching a wall of stone. Upon closer inspection she observed that the scratches were in fact claw marks. She knew of no animal that could create such deep gashes into solid stone. Claw marks were only the beginning; after a short time she saw scorch marks. Something was playing with fire down here. Giant claw marks and scorched stone, what the hell was in this cave?

A bright light was before them, leading them to the end of the tunnel. It opened up into a cavern that was even larger than the previous one. This one had no crystals, there were torches lining the walls. Stone pillars were placed throughout the cavern in a circular formation. Magical flames hung in the air, illuminating the entire cavern. Zia could barely breathe; the sight that lay before her shocked her.

Gold and jewels covered the floor. There were mounds of them; some that reached higher than she was tall. Solid gold, Zia had only seen this on the rich people who frequented the Crystal Dragon. Never had she seen it up close or so much of it. Amongst the gold were some pieces of silver, but it seemed all the silver was jewelry of some kind. Jewels that lay scattered throughout the piles of gold sparkled in the magical light tormenting those who encountered their beauty. There were rubies, sapphires, emeralds, diamonds and every other kind of precious stone she could think of. There weren't just gold coins, fancy silver jewelry, and gems. There were golden chalices, silver platters, jewel-encrusted crowns, strings of pearls, and fine garments made of silk. Magnificent tapestries hung from the stone pillars. A few large chests were placed in various locations around the cavern, each one filled with treasure the likes of which Zia could only dream about.

There was one thing that had escaped her notice as she gazed in wonder at the treasure stretching before her. In the middle of the cavern, situated comfortably amongst the piles of gold, lay a massive form. This had to be the creature that had made the claw marks and scorched the walls of the tunnel. Large dark red scales covered the body of the sleeping creature. Spiny ridges protruded along its neck and back. In an instant she knew what lay before her. She had spent her entire life living with such a creature. The large reptilian form meant only one thing.

Zia was looking at a dragon, one of the rarest of creatures in existence. She might have been thrilled at her luck if she didn't remember all the stories Yartu had told her about his larger cousins. They were extremely territorial and vicious when woken from their slumber. The worst thing you could do when you were near a dragon was take its treasure. They did not care if you were going to steal it or had accidentally found their hoard, you would still end up dead. Once again fate was toying with her. It was just her luck to stumble upon a dragon's cave.

Gryphon walked into the cavern. Zia tried to grab his arm and pull him back but he moved out of the way. She was going to warn him about the dragon, tell him what it would do to them, but the words did not come. It was not necessary, for when he stopped inside the cavern and turned to her expectantly, the expression on his face told her everything.

The elf had known all along what was in here. He had brought her to the cave with the sole purpose of leading her to the dragon. For a moment she had thought that he was actually trying to help her but now she saw how wrong she was. If he brought her here to die then why had he saved her from that creature in the water? What purpose did it serve? This was all to get her to trust him. It would make the kill that much sweeter. She had been such a fool. Gryphon had led her to certain death and she had followed him blindly. Zia knew that she should not trust the elf but she was unable to stop herself from doing so. Now she was going to pay for that error.

There was no remorse within those golden eyes. All had worked according to his plan. She wondered if he was pleased with himself. The dragon began to stir...

CHAPTER 35

The twins stared in wonder at the crystal cavern. Yartu flew around, going as high as he could and flying through the mist of the waterfall. Terra did not think that she'd ever seen anything more beautiful in her life. As the elven girl looked around, she saw Shadow standing surrounded by a bunch of little crystals. Their light made him look even more striking, as if that were possible. The light seemed attracted to him. Terra wondered if she was imagining things. Thorn was chasing Yartu around as the dragon searched for signs of his Bonded partner.

Terra walked over to where Shadow was standing. "Do you think we are close to finding them?"

Shadow closed his eyes, tilting his head back. He remained silent, she did not mind. That was the way he was, Shadow kept to himself. The light around him grew brighter until it was almost painful to look at. She knew that she should look away but she didn't. The unbearable light soon began to grow fainter.

As it faded Terra saw shadowy wings within the light. They came from Shadow. He was a perfect dark being surrounded by the glorious multi-colored light of the crystals. The girl felt her heart skip a beat. He was too perfect to be real. Angels were all supposed to be beautiful, but Terra thought that Shadow must have been the most beautiful. She knew it was wrong to think such thoughts about the Fallen One but she couldn't help herself. All else paled in comparison with his beauty.

The light returned to normal, the shadowy wings nothing but a memory. Nonetheless he still looked exalted. Dark eyes opened, all the light reflected within. "I can feel the power."

"What power?" Terra asked, barely able to speak.

Shadow tilted his head to the side, gazing into the distance. "The power in the crystals. This place is full of power. It is calling to me."

"Calling to you?" She was becoming concerned. It was bad if someone heard something that was not there. She might not know that much about angels but she assumed the same rule applied to them as well.

"Can't you hear it?" Shadow's eyes became unfocused.

Terra knew this was a bad sign. She called his name, shook him but nothing woke him from the strange daze he seemed to be in. Just a moment ago he was fine, he had been speaking; what was happening? What had changed in the matter of a second? She needed to do something, someone needed to do something. "Thorn, help." She didn't know what to do. This was bad.

Thorn saw his sister near Shadow. She was trying to get his attention, not that unusual. Yartu heard the girl shout for her brother's help. Where Thorn saw nothing,

Yartu saw trouble. Shadow looked as he had the day when Zia first had the dream during the day. Standing perfectly still, eyes open but not seeing anything.

"Thorn, you have to help her."

"Why?"

"I have seen him like this once before. This is not a good thing, Thorn. We have to snap him out of it." The urgency in the miniature dragon's voice made Thorn run over to his sister.

She shook her head, tears in her eyes. "I can't get him to respond. I don't know what to do."

"Don't touch him. Zia did and she saw what he did. It was really bad too, she was scared." Yartu said as he circled Shadow.

Terra looked confused. "I already did. Nothing happened, though. I didn't see anything."

Yartu was the one to be confused now. "But Zia, she saw something. I don't understand."

Thorn pushed Shadow. This time he fell into a sitting position. Shadow looked up at them, and his eyes returned to normal. He blinked and buried his head in his hands. Yartu remembered Shadow had told Zia that the pain was excruciating. Terra asked politely if she could examine him but he said nothing.

"Care to explain what happened?" Yartu asked. He didn't bother to sound concerned, he wasn't.

Shadow wished the little dragon would just shut up. His head felt like it had been split in two. Visions normally hurt, but this time had been one of the worst. He thought that it was because of the power in the crystals. He had absorbed some of it, intensifying his vision. Now all he needed to do was get rid of the headache and stop the vision from coming true.

Terra placed a gentle hand on his back. He felt a cooling sensation envelop him. Her healing magic spread throughout his entire body. The elven Healers were all idiots, he thought, this girl had more power than all of them combined. The headache disappeared. He had known all along about the girl's power, but to be able to cure his vision headaches was impressive. Nothing had previously worked. He was glad that she was able to help. He would be able to do what was necessary now.

He stood and nodded his thanks to Terra. She blushed, quickly turning away to hide her face. "We have to hurry. Zia is in great danger."

The dragon was even bigger when it was standing. Zia felt queasy. Did dragons really eat people or was that a myth? She didn't want to find out. She jumped when the dragon let out an angry roar. The entire cavern shook and a crack appeared in the ceiling. The dragon lifted its head, sniffing the air. It was trying to find her—or had it seen Gryphon?

The elf was crouching behind a stone pillar. She wondered what he was going to do. Setting her up had put him in a dangerous position as well. The dragon spun around, digging through the treasure. The magical flames in the air began to flicker as they grew brighter.

She knew she had to find a place to hide. Staying in the open was just stupid. There was an overhang nearby. If she could get to it, she would be shielded from the dragon's sight. There was a large pile of gold in front of it, which would keep the dragon from seeing her on ground level. The height of the dragon gave it a better view of the entire cavern, but the overhang would block its view of her. The best thing about it was that between the pile of treasure and the overhang the area was cast in shadow. The magical flames did not reach that spot; no one could find her when she hid in the shadows.

Zia ran as fast as she could. The dragon spun around having heard her move. She tripped a few times in her mad dash to her hiding spot, but she didn't stop. Sliding into the safety of the shadows, she hugged her knees to her chest and prayed.

The dragon charged the area where it saw gold falling off one of the piles. It was one of the piles Zia had fallen on in her rush. Gold coins clinked together as they fell to the floor. The dragon roared again in anger. It knew that someone was there and that someone might steal its treasure.

She heard it moving around, scales scraping against stone. She didn't dare look to see how close it was to her, it was too risky. If she moved it would sense her. It mattered not whether or not she looked, she could hear it. It was close. All that separated her and the dragon was a pile of treasure that was the height of three men.

Gryphon watched as Zia made her mad dash for the apparent safety of the overhang. What a fool. The dragon would still find her. He stayed near one of the pillars waiting to see what the dragon would do next. He was not concerned about it coming after him, it had a definite advantage but he was faster. That he learned the first time he had encountered the dragon. He was faster and meaner. This dragon was not a fully mature dragon so it was less dangerous, although not by much. As it spun around to see where its treasure was falling from, the tail swung in his direction. He rolled out of the way.

Zia was not faring too well. The dragon was very close to her hiding place. She had maybe a few minutes at the most left before it found her. Zia was holding her knees to her chest and rocking back and forth. Stupid girl, he thought. Then he noticed that she seemed to be fading in and out. Her image was flickering. The magical light barely touched her in the shadows. The light was being rejected.

Zia herself appeared to become part of the shadows. He had no idea how she had managed that but it made things more difficult for him. If the dragon could not find her it would seek him.

A single sweep of the dragon's massive paw sent the treasure flying. Gryphon had to duck in order to avoid the treasure flying at his head. Zia's hiding spot had been revealed but it was almost impossible to see her. She faded so well into the shadows.

The dragon may not have been able to see her but it could smell her. It reached out with its sharp talons, trying to hit something it knew was there but could not see. Gryphon watched as a claw almost scraped Zia's back. She didn't move; he assumed that if she did she would become completely visible. The dragon kept lashing out, gold flying everywhere. It knew she was there and it would not stop until it located her.

He had fully intended to let the dragon kill the girl but he could not. Just like when he himself tried to take her life something was keeping him from doing so. She scrambled out of the way as a claw nearly tore her head off. Gryphon swore under his breath. He twisted the third ring on his hand.

The dragon was way too close for comfort. Every sweep of its paw practically hit her. It was all she could do to avoid its attacks. She knew it could not see her but it still seemed to be able to sense her general location. The beast just kept lashing out, hoping it would hit her, knowing that eventually it would. She hastily fell backward as it almost decapitated her.

She was on her own and there was nothing she could do but try to last as long as possible. Rolling out of the way, she came up in a crouch, prepared to dodge yet another attack. They came faster and more frequently; the dragon didn't care what it hit. It only wanted to get her. Her body was crying out in pain, she was pushing it to its limits. It did not help that she was already injured. Her reactions were much slower because of it. Every time she moved she felt like she was going to die. She needed a plan and she needed to think of it quickly.

The spiked tail swung past her, slamming down hard on the ground, causing it to shake the floor. Pieces of stone fell from the ceiling. She covered her head with her arms. A strange pain-filled shriek echoed throughout the cavern. As she unfurled her body, she saw a large gash in the dragon's tail. Gryphon stood nearby with a blood-stained sword in his hands.

He grabbed Zia roughly, dragging her to her feet. "Run!" he shouted as he shoved her back to the entrance of the tunnel.

There was no need to tell her twice, she ran. The dragon whirled around and leapt to the tunnel opening. Zia skidded to a halt. The dragon loomed before her, its bulk cutting off the only escape route. Gryphon came to stand beside her. The sight of its own blood seemed to infuriate the dragon. They were trapped in a cave with a horrifically enraged dragon.

"You ready to die?" Gryphon asked, a strange smile on his face. He was awfully calm despite the situation they were in.

Zia nodded solemnly. "Are you?"

With a strange grin he twirled the sword in his hand. "Always."

She felt the same. It was better to be prepared to die. There was no point in crying about it. Zia bent down and grabbed a sword that lay at her feet. Her hand gripped the hilt tightly. Never before had she used a sword, but it did not matter. Its sole purpose was to bring pain to the dragon before it killed her. She may have been ready to die but that did not mean she would go down without a fight.

The dragon roared a challenge. The crack in the ceiling grew and a large chunk fell to the ground. The tail thumped the ground, creating a slight tremor. The elf and girl fought to keep their balance. The dragon lunged. Gryphon pushed her out of the way. As he dodged the dragon's leg he spun around, sword piercing the soft underbelly.

Another scream. As the tail swung around Zia drove her sword into the already open wound. The head came around to snap at her; she fell back just in time. Giant teeth snapped at her. Very sharp, she thought in a panic, avoid teeth at all costs. Gryphon rolled under the dragon, slashing as he came up.

He could not damage it where there were scales. Dragon scales were the most impenetrable armor there was in existence. He wasn't trying to hurt it, though, he just wanted to distract it so Zia could get away. The dragon was preoccupied with Gryphon for the moment. It had forgotten Zia, so she attacked the tail again. It was the easiest place for her to reach and she did not know what a dragon's weaknesses in battle were. He had already damaged it; why shouldn't she make it hurt just a little bit more?

They did not let up on their attack, Gryphon hitting the dragon's weak points and Zia going after the deep gash on its tail. It was working well. Every time Gryphon hit its belly the tail would swing around allowing Zia to drive her sword into it.

She had taken up a defensive position with her back to a stone pillar. She waited for the tail to come near her while Gryphon danced around the dragon. They were doing fairly well considering they were up against a dragon. It wasn't going to last long. Zia could barely stand and Gryphon had narrowly missed getting a talon in his chest. There were a few cuts and scrapes on his body, and she could see blood. The dragon seemed to have noticed that they were weakening. It still had strength to spare. The attacks came faster and with more power. Gryphon spent more time dodging than attacking and Zia was leaning against the pillar for support. The battle was almost over.

CHAPTER 36

An arrow flew past her straight into the wound on the tail. Zia turned to see where it had come from. Thorn stood at the opening of the tunnel, bow in hand, Shadow beside him. The dragon spun around and saw the reinforcements. It roared once again. Thorn answered with another arrow. Shadow held his right arm out to his side; shadows swirled down the length of the arm forming a sword. In his left hand a dark ball of energy appeared, sparks flying from his fingertips. Lifting his arm up, fingers pointed at the dragon, dark rays shot forth. Never had anything looked so beautiful or seemed so deadly.

The distraction their arrival caused had proven to be enough time for Gryphon to regain some of his strength. Well, either it was that, or seeing his little brother and the person he hated most coming to his rescue. The battlefield was even now. The dragon faced two elves, a fallen angel and a human girl who didn't know when to give up.

The dragon lifted its head high. Zia was unsure of what it was going to do but she had a feeling it was going to be bad. She heard Thorn scream at her to run behind the pillar. Gryphon had taken cover, as had Thorn and Shadow. She knew she should follow their lead. Zia started to do as Thorn instructed when a blast of hot air hit her. Glancing over her shoulder she saw the dragon open its mouth. Fear and self-preservation had her moving as fast as she could. She needed to get behind the pillar, and fast. Scrambling over gold coins and jewels, she barely made it. Flames shot past her on both sides. The heat of the fire was unbearable. The flames singed her hair and what was left of her clothes. The fire seemed never-ending. Flames filled the cavern, making it hard to breathe. She had no idea how long it lasted, time had no meaning in the fiery inferno.

A shrill cry cut through the roar of the flames. The fire disappeared in a flash. All that remained were some seriously burnt tapestries. Zia moved so she could see what was going on behind her. Yartu had flown into the cavern and was attacking the larger dragon's eyes. He flew up high and dove down, talons scraping the full-sized dragon's head. Arrows acted as cover for the miniature dragon as he dodged snapping jaws full of sharp teeth.

Dark bolts of energy hit the dragon on all sides. Gryphon weaved in and out of the dragon's legs, slashing as he went. Shadow had entered the cavern as well. His dark sword pierced the dragon's scales wherever it hit.

The dragon was in a bad position. It was growing weaker and it was now fighting three people. The attacks came slower now. Zia saw that her friends were gaining the upper hand. A hand on her arm made her jump. Terra knelt beside her.

"You look awful," the elven girl said with a smile.

Zia felt Terra's healing magic envelop her. She felt all the injuries that she had received in the past few hours start to heal. Her strength was slowly returning, although not fast enough for her. She wanted to help her friends fight the dragon. Shadow could take care of himself, but Thorn and Yartu were out there.

Terra understood Zia's expression. "It will only make things worse if you go out there. They will worry about you and not focus on fighting the dragon."

The girl was right, but that did not mean Zia had to like it. She took the time to rest as Terra continued treating her wounds. The sounds of the battle filled her ears, the ringing of steel against scales and the screeching of Yartu's battle cries. They would be alright, she knew they would be. The dragon was losing. A dark figure on a ledge high on the cavern wall caught her attention. There were a few ledges that she had seen in this cavern but they were all very high up. The figure moved closer to the edge and she could see it clearly. The smirk that had haunted her ever since she had first seen it had come back to taunt her. Her heart skipped a beat.

She wondered how long he had been up there. What was he waiting for? She watched apprehensively as he waved to her, a crystal glowing faintly in his hand. Fear overtook her; a scream of warning was frozen in her throat. She had to tell them, tell them that he was here. Tell them that the dragon was no longer their biggest threat.

The smirk tormented her. Hazel eyes gleamed with madness. He clenched his hand. As the crystal broke into pieces Zia was finally able to scream. The battle ceased momentarily as the magical flames all went out. A faint blue light took their place. It covered everything it touched with its soft glow.

Gryphon looked at his arm and the cut on it slowly disappearing. The blue light was healing whatever it touched. He knew now that Zia's scream had been a warning. The light could only have come from one source. Someone had a crystal and was using its power. Who was it? Thorn looked confused, as did Yartu; he knew that Terra had not done it. That left Shadow, but why would he need the crystal's power? Gryphon saw him then, the figure high on the ledge.

"Nicolai," Shadow hissed.

Thorn had no idea what was going on. He was not paying attention to Gryphon or Shadow. All he could see was the dragon before him and its fatal wounds disappearing.

It had not escaped Yartu's notice. "Shadow, the dragon!"

Shadow spun around and found the dragon fully healed. This is what Nicolai had planned, to heal the dragon. He would not have to worry about having any problems taking Zia if everyone who could stop him was dead.

He held up his hand ready to shoot Nicolai when he saw another form in the blue light. The witch was here as well.

"Let's see how you do now, shall we? I wonder if you can defeat a witch, a dragon and me? I owe you, Shadow, and I will take her from you." Nicolai's words echoed in the cavern. He dropped to the ground.

Thorn was shocked. No one should have been able to jump from that height and land on their feet. It was not natural, Gryphon couldn't even do it. Shadow might have, but he was an angel.

"Shadow," Gryphon growled. He wanted to know what the fallen angel had planned. The elf had not anticipated a human to show up or use the crystals. A witch made things complicated too; their magic was very effective when used offensively.

Dark eyes met golden ones. "Take them and get out. Whatever you do don't let Nicolai get Zia."

Gryphon nodded. Thorn grabbed his sister and Zia; they ran to the tunnel. All of them tripped at the same time. Crystal laughed at them. Zia glared at the witch and she grew silent.

Shadow was preoccupied with the dragon. He needed to keep it away from the others until they were safe. Thorn and Yartu could handle the witch. Gryphon had almost reached them too. The only problem was Nicolai.

Gryphon dodged a bolt of lightning. The witch seemed to know that he was her biggest threat. Thorn was busy shooting arrows at the dragon and the witch, helping both his brother and Shadow. Gryphon advanced slowly; the witch was busy firing spells at him and deflecting Thorn's arrows. A bright light flashed as he swept his sword down in an arc. The witch had some impressive defensive spells as well. He wondered how long she would last. Golden eyes flashed with murderous intent.

Zia and Terra did their best to get to the tunnel. Crystal kept knocking them over with spells, even though she was fighting Gryphon. Her attention was divided and, while that might be a problem for most people, the witch seemed unfazed by it. She knew what she was doing.

Shadow had his hands full with the dragon. He alternated between striking it with his sword and shooting dark energy. The dragon was at full strength now and Shadow's attacks had less effect than they did before.

Two different battles waged at once, and all Zia could think of was Nicolai. Where he was and what he was going to do. She saw him leaning against one of the stone pillars, trademark smirk in place. He was watching everything, waiting for his turn. She knew she should have run but she couldn't leave everyone behind. They were there and in danger because of her. There had to be some way she could help. Everyone was risking their lives for her.

The dragon hit Shadow with its tail. He fell to the ground hard. Laughter filled the air. Nicolai advanced on him, sword unsheathed. A ringing sound echoed as sword hit sword. Gryphon had run to Shadow's aid. His sword keeping Nicolai's from striking Shadow. The fallen angel understood what Gryphon was doing. The elf may have hated him, but no one could kill Shadow but Gryphon. That was the elf's strange way of thinking and right now it proved beneficial.

Nicolai faced the elf. Memory swamped him; golden eyes. Before him stood the same elf who had almost killed him three years ago. The scar from that day stretched along his entire left side. This was revenge.

The human attacked furiously. Gryphon blocked every blow with ease. He would not be able to for long, he was already pushing himself to his limit. All the previous battles of the day were taking their toll; even the healing light of the crystal could not prevent it.

The dragon was tired of all the fighting. It wanted the trespassers out of its cave. They had disturbed its rest and injured it. It was tired, hurt and angry. The mean dark one would not leave it alone.

Zia watched as Nicolai and Gryphon fought. Shadow was once again fighting the dragon and Crystal was busy with Thorn, who had drawn his sword, and Yartu. Terra was already in the tunnel, shouting for her to hurry. She didn't move. Anger overcame fear. Nicolai was not going to kill her new friends and he was most definitely not going to take her to the Magic Council. She would not allow this.

Gryphon looked at the blood flowing freely down his arm in a detached way. Nicolai watched him smugly. The elf recognized the human whom he thought he had killed three years ago. The wound he had inflicted had been fatal, no one could have survived. There was something wrong with this human, something unnatural.

"I think I will leave you to die this time. Tell me, elf, do you like pain?" The threat had no effect on Gryphon.

He had trained himself to withstand the most excruciating of pain. All of it self-inflicted, he did not trust anyone else to do it right. He had prepared himself for this sort of situation. That was how he was able to go on when he'd reached his physical limits. He knew exactly how much longer until he collapsed. Gryphon was not going to let some mere human get the better of him. Zia was the only one allowed to do that, she had earned the right.

A loud thud and tremor shook the ground; the dragon had fallen hard to the ground, sound asleep. Shadow had cast a sleep spell on the poor beast. He had never intended to kill it. Dragons were rare and this one had done nothing to deserve death. The Guardians were supposed to protect the dragon, for it protected the crystal cave. Shadow knew that Gryphon was not going to kill it. He took his duty as a Guardian seriously. With the dragon out of the way he could now help the others fight Crystal and Nicolai.

Crystal had her hands full with Yartu and Thorn. Shadow thought the two made a surprisingly good team. Terra was safe in the tunnel and Zia stood in the middle of the cavern. He followed her gaze to where Nicolai was taunting Gryphon, who just stood there glaring at him.

Shadow shot off three dark bolts, all aimed at Nicolai. The man spun so fast that it was a miracle he didn't fall over from dizziness. He held up a hand and the dark energy pooled in front of his palm.

"You've gotten stronger, Shadow." That god-awful smirk appeared again.

Nicolai flicked his hand and the dark energy returned to Shadow. The fallen angel sent more shooting towards the man as he dodged the counter-attack. Gryphon leapt at him from behind. The fallen angel and elf attacked at the same time. Nicolai did a flip and landed behind Gryphon. His sword slashed across the elf's back before he could turn.

Pain shot through his body, but he ignored it. Anger was in control now, and he wanted nothing more than to kill this man. Shadow saw the change in Gryphon, felt it in his mind. The elf had gone berserk. This was very bad; he would destroy everything in his attempt to kill Nicolai, even his allies. It would also be easier for Nicolai to manipulate him.

"Gryphon, no! This is what he wants." Shadow tried to warn the elf but his plea was not heard.

Gryphon was impressive in battle, even more so when he lost control. He fought with wild abandon. His sword whirled in a deadly dance, it was almost hypnotic. It was all Nicolai could do to avoid the attacks. Each one was closer than the last, each one bringing him closer to death. The man was impressed; the elf was just as good as he had remembered. Too bad he would not live to fight another day.

Nicolai dropped his sword to the ground. Eight knives, four in each hand, appeared like claws. As Gryphon came at him, he crouched low and spun. The knives scratched the elf's body. He stopped his attack for a moment, assessing the situation, choosing how to best advance. A second later Gryphon was attacking again. Nicolai sidestepped and lashed out, the knives acting like claws.

It made sense that Nicolai fought better in a more animal-like state—he was one. Shadow knew he needed to help Gryphon. The elf did not understand what he had gotten himself into. Blood flew everywhere as Nicolai ripped Gryphon to pieces. The elf's chest was riddled with cuts. His blood flowed freely and still he kept coming.

Thorn and Terra watched their brother in horror. They had heard rumors of things that Gryphon had done. Hushed whispers of self-mutilation were heard often. Terra had once overheard her superiors talking about him, how he was unable to feel pain. How detached he had forced himself to become from any emotion involving pain. They claimed that he was a monster. Guardians always worked in pairs, but never Gryphon. No one would go near him, they were all afraid. The twins were beginning to see why. The others had seen what he could do. The twins had never witnessed it until now, and now they were glad they hadn't.

Nicolai was wondering when the elf was going to fall. He didn't die; Nicolai wanted him dead. It would take a little longer than expected. He could have some fun while he waited.

Zia felt her heart pounding. Her breaths were coming in short and ragged. Every time Nicolai cut through Gryphon's flesh, she felt it. It was supposed to be her. Gryphon would die because of her. He was right, humans destroyed everything. She was destroying him. Tears welled up in her eyes. Her vision began to blur. All she saw was the elf. He couldn't die, she needed him. Her need came as a surprise, much as it had with Shadow. She needed the fallen angel to save her from the darkness and she needed the elf to keep her from giving up. His hatred and disgust of humans made her want to prove him wrong. It pushed her to do better. She could not bear to lose either of them. As insane as Gryphon was he had helped her just like her Shadow. Zia was not going to let him die.

Shadow felt the change in her mind. It was as if she had opened a floodgate, the darkness poured in. He was about to enter her mind fully and rid it of the darkness when he realized something. Zia had invited it in.

CHAPTER 37

Anger and hate filled her entire being. There was nothing else. Rage in its purest form. Fear turned to anger and anger turned to hate. Pain was nothing but a faint memory. Sorrow was fuel for the fire. It built up until it was unbearable. It needed a way out. It had to break free of its small confines. It was like that day with the Magic Council. Rage consumed her. The desire to hurt the one who was hurting her was overwhelming. Revenge was all that she wanted. She did not need to control it. It knew who the target was. Zia released her rage. *Suffer as I have suffered.*

Darkness flooded the cavern. A darkness so pure no light could shine. Crystal could not cast her spells. The words were frozen upon her lips. Thorn could not feel his sister for the first time in his life. Terra no longer felt her brother; there was only a sense of dread. She could feel anger and pure hatred. It was within the darkness. Gryphon fell to his knees; the rage within the darkness mirrored his own. He wondered how it knew what he felt. Nicolai knew what was happening. Lady Yena had told him about Zia's power. So this was it; he had never felt such power before. What was she?

Shadow knew. He was the only one who could save her. The darkness whirled around her in a frenzy. What a horrible mistake he had made. How could he have been so blind? The darkness did not want Zia. She was part of it, a vessel for its use. Zia was the embodiment of the darkness.

They could see nothing in the darkness except for each other. None of them save Shadow could see Zia. They all stood still; no one knew what was going on. Each face was a reflection of another, fear was the main emotion that all felt.

Light began to filter through the darkness. They all wondered what was going to happen next. Shadow observed that the light only came in from certain points. The darkness surged and twisted. It was taking on a form. Terra screamed. Shadow did not blame her.

The darkness had taken on the shape of a dragon, one born of nothing but shadows. Shadow was able to manipulate the darkness but he was unable to give it form, no one could. Most shadow creatures were born from out-of-control magic. A shadow dragon was the hardest creature to create using the darkness; it was also the most powerful. Glowing sapphire eyes were the only light that emanated from the creature.

Shadow could sense Zia's thoughts in the thing. She was controlling it and he knew who the shadow dragon was going to attack. The shadow dragon lashed out at Nicolai, who made it out of the way just in time.

The man did everything he could to evade the shadow dragon's attacks, but he could not. There was nowhere for him to hide; how could he when the creature itself was born of the shadows? He could not run, for he was unable to see that which surrounded him. Nicolai felt the creature bearing down on him. Sapphire eyes appeared directly above him. They promised pain and agony.

Suffer as I have suffered.

The words echoed in their minds as well as the cavern. They could feel the pain and the sorrow, Nicolai most of all. It wanted him to suffer most of all, for he was the one who had caused the pain. He screamed as the concentrated mental and emotional attack overwhelmed him. The pain was excruciating.

Shadow knew he had to stop her. Zia did not know what she was doing. As much as she hated Nicolai and was afraid of him, she never would have wanted to kill him, Zia wasn't a killer. She was doing just that. Her emotions were providing the power for the creature; the stronger the emotion, the stronger the shadow dragon. If she was not careful it would kill all of them. He needed to reach her before it was too late.

"Stop." A calm, clear voice rang through the cavern.

Gryphon was standing before the shadow dragon. His body was covered in blood but he stood straight and still managed to glower at the creature. It was about to strike Nicolai with its talons but stopped. The head lowered to get a better look at Gryphon.

He must die.

The elf raised his sword and pointed it at the creature. Normal weapons had no effect on a shadow creature but Shadow knew that the elf did not wield a normal weapon. Gryphon held a magical sword, the blade glowed with a brilliant golden light. Magical weapons could harm a shadow creature, but this one was linked to Zia. Shadow had to stop him.

"Gryphon, don't hurt it," he shouted.

"Why not?" the elf growled.

"It's Zia. If you hurt it, you hurt her. She doesn't know what she's doing. If you kill the thing it is the same as killing her." Shadow desperately hoped that what he said would not make the elf want to kill the creature even more.

Gryphon stared at the thing. Zia? She had disappeared when the creature had formed. In a way what Shadow said made sense. Gryphon remembered the emotions he felt contained within the darkness before it took form. The anger and the hate; emotions as intense as his own. The sorrow and the pain, had they been her too? Zia was in the shadow dragon. The voice that had spoken from within the darkness had been hers. He looked at the thing and saw only the sapphire eyes that gleamed in the darkness. The only light in the darkness. He smiled.

The elf took his sword and cut open his palm. The shadow dragon shrieked in rage. Nicolai screamed again as another wave of powerful emotions crashed into his mind.

"Calm down. I was just checking something." Gryphon held up his hand for the shadow dragon to see. The shadow dragon had reacted to his wound, his pain. Pain was what connected them. "I'm fine, see."

A shadowy snout gently touched his hand. It felt weird, like standing in front of a waterfall and feeling the spray of the water. That and the gentle touch of a breeze as it brushed your face. It was cool and comforting. He felt the pain in his hand subside. As the creature drew away he glanced at his hand; it was fully healed. The damn shadow dragon was better than a Healer and a crystal combined. The creature pushed against his chest, knocking him to the ground.

He laughed when he sensed the creature's anguish. It thought it had hurt him. It peered down at him, inspecting him for further damage. He playfully swatted the creature. It recoiled, taken aback by his action.

The others were just as surprised as the shadow dragon was. The twins had never seen their older brother act so normal. Shadow understood what he was trying to do. Gryphon had sensed how distressed Zia was and he was trying to calm her down. Shadow would have tried to calm her but he knew Zia would not listen to him, not in that form. In that form she needed someone who understood the intense emotions she was feeling, and Gryphon was the only one who could. All Shadow and the others could do was watch. They could not escape the darkness until Zia let them.

The shadow dragon sniffed him, and he swatted at it again. This time it blew in his face. It was her alright. No one else would treat him like that. The creature touched his chest again. Gryphon felt the shadows surround him. A strange sensation washed over him. He saw that all his wounds had fully healed. The only sign that they had existed was the blood that stained his body. His tattoo was visible and the dragon touched it. It began to glow with a strange dark light. The light reminded Gryphon of her eyes, a dark blue like the sky before a storm.

Pain shot through him the likes of which he had never felt before. It felt as if someone was ripping his heart right out of his body. That actually would have been less painful. There was nothing but pain. He couldn't think, he could not breathe. The room began to spin around him. His vision faded in and out.

"No!" Shadow shouted at the same time as Yartu. Both knew what was happening, and neither wanted it to happen.

Yartu cried out in pain and dropped to the ground. Two pain-filled screams pierced the darkness. A bolt of electricity appeared between the shadow dragon and Gryphon. It looked like lightning connecting the two bodies. Within the shadow dragon Zia's form could be seen suspended in the air. Her head was thrown back and her arms and legs hung limply. Gryphon was in a similar position, hovering a few inches off the ground. The form of the shadow dragon began to flicker around Zia. She was losing her ability to sustain that form. A faint aura appeared around both the human girl and the elf.

Nicolai watched the scene unfold with great interest. The girl's dragon had fallen to the ground unconscious and Shadow looked downright horrified. Nicolai understood why, he had not thought it possible for the Bond to occur between anyone other than human and dragon. It was an ancient magic that remained a mystery even now. When a human Bonded a dragon their souls became fused together; the process was painful beyond all belief. The Bond only ever occurred between human and dragon. Yet here he was watching a human girl Bond an elf. He wondered what would happen if the Bond was interrupted before it was completed. It would only be fitting to find out.

Shadow sensed Nicolai's thoughts. If the man interrupted the Bond both Zia and Gryphon would die. He generated another dark energy ball. Just as he fired off a couple of bolts a blast of wind knocked him to the ground. Crystal had regained her ability to use her spells. That meant that the darkness's power was fading.

Nicolai held a crystal that glowed white in his hand. He pointed it at Gryphon. A bolt of pure energy was released. It hit Gryphon on the arm; the elf did not feel it. He didn't feel anything. He had no idea what was going on. Shadow had to help him. He got to his feet only to fall again. The witch was getting on his nerves. He wondered why Thorn did not help him. The boy was frozen in place, unable to move thanks to the witch's spell of binding. Shadow was on his own.

Another bolt hit Gryphon. Two hit Nicolai. The witch fired three spells off at once, forcing Shadow to block her attack. It gave Nicolai the time he needed. One bolt shot forth from the crystal. It hit its mark—well, almost.

It would have if darkness did not surround her. Darkness had been swirling around her as she hung in the air. As the energy bolt shot towards her the shadows covered her. There was a flash of blinding light.

When everyone could see again the darkness was gone, and so was Zia. The elf was nowhere to be seen as well. Shadow knew that the darkness had protected its own. He assumed that was how she had ended up in the middle of nowhere, unconscious, waiting for him. This time Gryphon was going along with her. He had been saved by association only. The darkness was protecting Zia and Gryphon was now a part of her.

Nicolai cursed. The girl was gone. She had escaped from him the same way she had escaped the Magic Council. There was no reason for him to be there anymore. He had to get out of the cave. He motioned to the witch. Crystal came to his side and threw a potion bottle to the floor. Both vanished in a puff of smoke.

CHAPTER 38

Thorn was able to move once she was gone. Terra held Yartu in her arms. The miniature dragon was still unconscious. Shadow knew that he should have stopped Nicolai from leaving, but he had more important things to deal with at the moment. He walked over to the twins. Both were extremely shaken.

"We have to go. It will not be good if the dragon wakes up and we are still here."

They nodded in unison. They all had forgotten about the real dragon. It was still under the effects of Shadow's sleep spell. The small group walked back in silence. They stopped to rest when they reached the crystal cave.

"Do you think he will be alright?" Terra asked Shadow. She meant Yartu; she had tried to heal him but could not. She was sitting with him cradled in her lap.

Shadow ran a hand through his hair. "I don't know. He is going to be really mad when he wakes up, though."

"Why? What happened in there?" Thorn could barely keep his voice from trembling. He was sitting as close to his sister as possible.

"Before or after the shadow dragon?"

"Both," the twins said.

Shadow sighed. "Zia has the power to control the darkness. When her emotions became uncontrollable, she unleashed her full power. She turned into a shadow dragon to hurt the person who was trying to hurt her, Nicolai."

"She can control the darkness. Like you?" Thorn wanted to understand as much as possible.

Shadow shook his head. "No, not like me. It would be difficult to explain to you, when I barely understand it myself, how she does it."

Terra bit her bottom lip, deep in thought. "What about what happened with Gryphon? That I really don't get. Why did she listen to him when she was the shadow dragon and not you?"

"He better understood the extreme emotions she was experiencing. You know your brother, intense emotions are the only kind he feels."

This made the twins laugh and Shadow smiled. He was glad he could lighten the mood, if only for a moment.

"That explains the first part." Thorn sighed. "I'm afraid to ask, but what about after, when... I don't know how to explain it."

He didn't have to, both Terra and Shadow knew what he meant. "That was the Bond."

"The Bond? Wait, I thought that the Bond only occurred between humans and dragons. Not human to human, well, you know what I mean." The elven girl waved her hand in exasperation. Dragons could Bond elves as well; it was just easier to say humans. More humans had Bonded dragons than elves.

"I did too." Shadow shook his head in an attempt to sort out his thoughts. "Maybe because she was in the form of a shadow dragon, they were able to Bond."

Thorn glanced at the unconscious miniature dragon. "What about Yartu? Is he still Bonded to Zia?"

"It seems like it. There have been instances in the past where a single person was Bonded to both a full-size dragon and a miniature one. I assume that this is the same sort of thing. Well, just replace the full-size dragon with an elf."

The twins sighed. It was all so complicated. "Where do you think they are now?" Terra asked softly.

"I have no idea. I intend to find them, though. Nicolai is going to hunt down Zia. I want to find her first."

"We'll go too." They spoke at the same time, both voices daring him to stop them.

The radiant smile lit up his face. "I could use a good Healer and master archer." He spoke the truth. He was glad they said they wanted to come.

Shadow knew the journey would be long and difficult, but at least they would have each other. After all these years he had finally found friends. Fallen angel or not, they would stand by him; this they had proven in the Dragon's Den.

When they reached the cave's mouth, Shadow let the twins go on ahead. The fallen angel looked up at the sky and made a vow. "Zia, I will find you. I promised to protect you and I will. This bond we share is stronger than the one you share with him. I will let him keep you safe for now."

✳✳✳✳✳

Rain pounded the ground. The cool rain felt good upon her feverish skin. Pain filled her entire body. She ached all over, and her eyes felt heavy. It took all of her strength to pry them open. She was lying on her back; above her she could see the sky. The rain was coming down hard and she had to blink as water ran into her eyes.

She reached a feeble hand toward the sky. On the inside of her wrist she saw a strange mark, a tattoo of a crescent moon. Where had it come from? she wondered. Now that she thought about it, where had she come from? *Where* was she? *Who* was she? Why couldn't she remember?

Her head was pounding in time with the rain. She could not collect her thoughts. Had she ever felt this much pain before? Yes, a faint memory came to her. She had felt pain like this before, but where, when? There were so many questions. How was she supposed to find all the answers?

A flash of a memory came, and she did her best to interpret it. Darkness. Light. Fallen. What did it all mean? Slowly the memory grew stronger. Angel, there had been an angel. No, he had fallen. A fallen angel. He was beautiful and had helped her. Her Shadow. A comforting presence that had hidden her away from the one who wanted to hurt her.

There was something else, something important that she had to remember. Gold? No, golden. A golden light that had saved her. Unlike her Shadow the light was cold and cruel. It had hurt her, not intentionally, not completely at least. It had protected her from that unscrupulous man just as her Shadow had.

The man who had tried to hurt her, who was he? Why did he want her? Why was he trying to hurt her? She needed to know. *Who* was she?

"Zia."

Yes, that was her name. She was Zia Amarra. Memories came back now that she knew who she was. Shadow. Where was he? Who had called her name? Where was she?

"Zia." The voice called again. It was rather persistent. Why wouldn't it leave her alone?

"Zia." Louder this time and sounding annoyed. She recognized the speaker at once.

She sat up, every part of her body crying out in pain. He sat next to her. The rain had washed away most of the blood. He still didn't have a shirt on, then again when had there been time to find one? Golden eyes watched her every movement, silver hair hung in his face. Her gaze focused on the tattoo on his chest. A crescent moon, just like the one she now had on her wrist.

"What happened?" he asked impatiently.

Zia closed her eyes, she couldn't look at him. She had remembered where she had felt the pain before. The only other time she had ever felt that much pain in her life. "We Bonded. I don't know how, so don't even ask."

Gryphon rubbed his temples, "Bonded, huh? I guess I can't kill you now."

She looked at him and saw that he thought she was lying. She held out her wrist for him to examine. His eyes narrowed at the sight of the tattoo; it was identical to his.

"Believe me now?" She arched her brows waiting for the protesting and denial to start.

A finger lightly traced the tattoo. He said nothing, just stared at the mark. She wondered what he was thinking. She wanted to ask him, wanted to know if he was scared too. The Bond was only supposed to happen with a dragon.

"Why me?" The question surprised her, as did the way he asked. Softly, barely audible, as if he was afraid of what the answer might be. It was as though he was asking her why she had chosen him, he didn't deserve it.

She was unsure of how to respond. He didn't even look her in the eyes, his were glued to the moon tattoo. "I wish I knew. I have no idea how or why this happened. I am sorry."

This time he did meet her eyes. The look in them made her want to run away, it made her want to stay with him. It did something strange to her. Her stomach twisted into knots and her head began to spin. She had to look away from those golden eyes.

"Why?" Once again, he spoke softly. It was strange to hear.

She shrugged. "You seem to hate me and you have tried to kill me multiple times. I guess I just thought that you would be angry."

He tilted her chin so she was forced to look into his eyes. "I do not hate you."

Gryphon released her and stood up. She watched him, unsure what to do. He didn't hate her? He hated humans and she was human. The way he had said it did funny things to her. He had placed the emphasis on *you*. Was she different? Did she want to be? She shook her head, trying to rid herself of thoughts that would only lead to trouble.

Zia got to her feet slowly. Coming to stand beside him she asked a very important question. "Where the hell are we?"

"I have no idea."

Can you feel it? Can you feel the power? The power that is mine to control. The power that all fear. This power is the ultimate power. The power of the night. A never-ending night where no light can shine, not even the moon. This is the power I command, in a place you have only dreamt of. A place of everlasting night. The source of my power and your nightmares. The place where all fear to tread. A place of naught but shadows and darkness.

Come to me.

AUTHOR'S NOTE

The beginnings of this book can be directly traced back to a high school science class. It was close to the end of the year, it being the last class of the day both teacher and students wanted nothing more than for it to be over. I do not recall what the teacher was saying nor do I remember what we were even doing in that particular class. What I do remember was wondering about a very specific scenario, what if there was a voice within the darkness speaking to someone. I wrote the beginning of that conversation in that class. I continued to write it on my way home that day.

That conversation, that voice within the darkness, became this book. It took on a life that even I was surprised by. So much has happened in my life since that hot summer day, that boring science class. So much pain and sorrow. I could never have even imagined what transpired or how it would affect my life as well as the life of my mother and sister. We survived so much and we endured many hardships. Zia's journey is perhaps a reflection of our own.

In order to process everything that was happening, I wrote. This book became a way for me to understand and make sense of the chaos that had taken over our lives. My frustration with humanity and our destruction of the world we live in became Gryphon. Shadow was the hope, the promise of someone being able to help, to guide you and protect you. He was also the uncertainty that something which seemed too good to be true might not be real. Nicolai was the fear, the lies, and betrayal hidden behind smiling faces. The confusion, the inability to trust oneself, and the feeling like nothing was within your ability to control, that was Zia.

Zia, Yartu, Shadow, Gryphon, even Nicolai, they helped me through those terrible years. It is my hope that they can help others now. Maybe through their struggles you might find your own strength. I hope you will continue this journey with them.

ACKNOWLEDGEMENTS

There are many people I need to thank. The making of this book was a long journey for me, one I learned a great deal from. I should start with the professionals who assisted me in bringing this book to you the reader., I would like to thank Deborah Murrell for her amazing editorial work. She helped make this book what it is. My brilliant cover designer Thea for bringing Zia, Yartu, and Shadow to life in a way I had not thought possible. The cover is so beautiful and I love it so much.

Over the years there have been many who were willing to read this book before I was able to properly refine it. I appreciate all of you. I may not be able to list all of your names but you were a part of this journey as well. Thank you.

L and J, I wanted to thank you for always standing by us and supporting us. Lastly, I would like to thank my family. My mother and sister put up with a lot from me over the years, but they always believed in me and this book. Without them standing by me this book would exist only in the secret confines of my computer.

Author Bio

Lindsey Blake grew up with a love of both books and fantasy. Her overactive imagination is what led to the creation of her debut novel. She lives in New England with her family and cats.